WHEELS OF STEEL
BOOK 1

Pepper Pace

Wheels of Steel book 1

PRAISE FOR WHEELS OF STEEL BOOK 1

Every time I read a Pepper Pace novel, I think it is my absolute favorite until I read the next novel. That was true with "Beast" and "Juicy", but now my favorite is Wheels of Steel.
-Karen Green-Berry, Building Relations Around Books Online book club

The best IR New Adult book by far, Loved this book series!
-Andrea's Book Blog

I am a proud *Wheels of Steel* series fan! Romance novel series like *Wheels of Steel* "validates" the experiences and need for love and companionship of those with disabilities...
-Vilissa Thompson, Ramp Your Voice with Vilissa

Pepper Pace is one of the Young Turks in the multicultural niche. She deliberately chooses unconventional characters, and it usually works.
-Karen Knows Best, online blog

Wheels of Steel book 1

Editor, Andrea Watts
awattsedit@aol.com

Cover design,
Ho-Z Design
http://hozdesign.com/

ISBN-13: 978-0991174928
Wheels of Steel book 1 first published and distributed in the United States of America in 2012.

Wheels of Steel book 1

Contents

DEDICATION

I would like to thank the many people who have fallen in love with this story. One such person would be an awesome individual by the name of Andrea Watts. She contacted me after reading the published and badly edited version of this book. She offered to do the editing for the series and I was dubious until she informed me that she was an English major and that this was a journey of love. I definitely get that. Due to her interest, you are now holding the edited and improved version of Wheels of Steel.

This book is also dedicated to my friend Ho-Z and for his tireless involvement with WOS beyond just the storyline; but the music and products and art. Thanks Ho-Z and than you fans and readers.

-Pepper Pace

ABOUT WHEELS OF STEEL

Most who are familiar with my writings know the origins of Wheels of Steel. A young man by the name of Ho-Z sent me a letter about creating a romantic story that includes a man in a wheelchair. Afterwards, Ho-Z became a dear friend of mine, as well as my musical 'twin'. We could talk music for hours upon hours and the fact that this 21 year old Caucasian Norwegian kid knows more about hiphop than I do was mind-blowing. The fact that he is also stricken with cerebral palsy is a stumbling block but not a blockade. A digital artist, musician, as well as an entrepreneur, Ho-Z taught me that you don't have to 'ignore' your perceived disabilities — but be proud of your accomplishments despite them.

As I used him as an inspiration for the hero in the story I decided that the character of Top would have cerebral palsy as well. Top and Ho-Z are not one in the same but his musical knowledge was an aspect of the story that I had to incorporate. How could I not?

But what many people don't know is that there are very many elements of WOS that have been pulled from my own personal life. At the time that I wrote this story I was going through the same stomach problems that Robin was experiencing. Robin was coming to terms with the loss of her father — as was I, and the scene where she remembers her last days with him was pulled straight from my own life. My dear friend had the same unfortunate history as Belinda and perhaps that is why this story touches so many people — because pain recognizes pain.

As mentioned before, this story has appeared in separate books but it is still truly only one story. It is not my intent to leave you with cliff-hangers, however that will probably be the case. Some may ask how long this series will be and for that I have no answer. I do not want this story to die and so as long as I have the power to do so, I will continue to breath life into it. Thank you.

WOS

Girl, you amaze me! Music has no color.
-Ho-Z

Wheels of Steel book 1

CHAPTER 1

"That's why people go to college. Do you think people *like* sitting in class studying and paying good money to do it? They do it so that they can get good paying jobs," mama said.

Robin bit back her response. She was twenty-one years old and her mother still spoke to her like she was three. She knew exactly why people went to college, because her mother reminded her at every possible opportunity. If she asked to borrow money to float her until payday, mama would remind her that she would be making three times as much if she had gone to college.

Robin fingered the wire to the telephone, trying to think of a polite way to discontinue the phone call, but deep down she wanted to snap at Betty. She wanted to say, *'You ask a loaded question about how work is going, knowing that if I work drive-thru at a fast food restaurant, then it's very likely that my life pretty much sucks!'*

"Mama, I need to start getting ready for work," she lied.

"Hmmph," was the response she got. Her mother was a successful certified public accountant. She made six figures a year and she had been pushing her profession down Robin's throat since she was fifteen years old. It was a great career, if you could stomach math. If you hated math, then it was about the worse job in the universe.

"Well, I don't want to make you late for work Robin. And I know that I keep talking about college, but it's never too late. That college fund is still sitting here whenever you want to use it." Robin's foot began to tap in annoyance. Her mother always managed to bring up the fund that she and daddy had sacrificed for. Whenever her parent's told her that she couldn't have something because it was too expensive, she would be reminded that at least they were able to make a deposit into her college fund.

She would love to be able to dip into that fund right now, when her car payment was due, because she'd just paid rent, and really didn't have any money left over. Working at a fast food restaurant thirty hours a week meant that you never had enough money to pay all of your bills at once. But she had received a rude awakening long ago when mama had coldly told her that the money was for college and *not* for anything else. It had been worse when daddy died and money that should have come to her from his insurance policy had gone directly into that fund.

Going to college was the inevitable answer, except her mother was a dictator and Robin was through being a slave to her whims. She loved her mother; a strong black woman that never took shit off anyone. But her mother couldn't understand that loving someone and controlling their actions weren't synonymous.

And there were other reasons that college was out of the question, things that her mother had no idea about; like her crippling shyness, the twisting and knotting in the pit of her stomach, and worse — the fact that things just did not come to her as easily as it did to the other kids. Mama just refused to see that her bad grades had nothing to do with lack of motivation. Robin truly felt that there were things that smart and outgoing people did; like go to college, and that description just did not fit her.

"Well, I'll see you Sunday." Robin said after exhaling a long, but quiet breath.

"Uh-hmm. Bye Robin." Mama had no right to seem annoyed but she did. She hung up and Robin held onto the receiver until the recorded message demanded someone to hang up or make a call.

She scooped up the newspaper and checked the want ads. Over the years she had tried it all; telemarketing, janitorial and restaurants, but she still had a hard time making her car and insurance payment while still juggling rent. Maybe she should just look into having a roommate. But even as she thought this, she knew it wasn't going to happen. Robin's shyness made being comfortable around strangers almost impossible, so living with someone she didn't know well would be a nightmare.

Besides, she valued her space and solitude. Some people liked being in crowds or partying; Robin liked listening to music and reading a good book. Others might think of it as boring, but to her it was satisfying.

The want ads were a bust; the same jobs that promised great pay but only made the company owners rich. Again, she considered college. But no one understood how much she had struggled in school. Math was hard, English was hard, being social was hard; nothing came easy to her except American Lit.

She became the characters in the books. Did she know anything about conjugating verbs? Not at all, she just enjoyed the fantasy of being someone else.

She sat quietly, just contemplating how to find an enjoyable career if one didn't go to college. She supposed that she would have to find something that she enjoyed doing. And what did she like doing? She liked reading; maybe she could become a writer or journalist. She liked art, but couldn't see herself doing anything artistic every day, all day. She liked cooking, but that didn't mean she wanted to make a career out of it.

Frustrated, she came to her feet and tossed the paper into the trash. Hell, a job was a job. There was nothing that she liked doing that would pay her good money. With a sigh she opened her laptop, navigating through YouTube until she got to one of her music playlists. Later, she would be working the night shift until closing, which meant that she had several hours to kill. So, she did the thing that she loved best; chilling out to her music.

She selected a playlist that included a little Jaheim and Sade, as well as some other singers that put her in a relaxed mood. There was some Erykah Badu and

5

some old D'Angelo from his *Voodoo* and *Brown Sugar* albums. She opened up the Kim Harrison novel that she had just begun, and curled up in her old comfy armchair that had once belonged to her dad. And then Robin proceeded to zone out.

When the playlist ended, and she dragged herself out of the story of witches and vampires, Robin was alarmed to see that she only had about half an hour before work. Cursing, she jumped up and rushed into her small bedroom and quickly stripped out of her jeans and shirt.

She pulled on a clean work shirt and found a semi-clean pair of polyester work pants that had been tossed carelessly onto her bedroom chair. Robin's hair was already pulled back into a neat ponytail and she checked it in the mirror, seeing a dark brown face with slightly rounded cheeks and dark brown hair tamed by hair gel. She wasn't short, she wasn't tall; a bit stocky but nothing one less scoop of ice cream at desert wouldn't solve.

People always took a second look at Robin, not because she was any great beauty, but because of her eyes. Her eyes were a strange mixture of green, brown, and grey. And it wasn't just the color. She had permanently half-hooded eyes; bedroom eyes, beneath long dark lashes. She either looked mentally retarded, sleepy or horny; depending on whom you asked. She knew she was a confusing mixture; a dark brown girl with the last name Mathena and eyes that could almost be Asian. Her hair was not silky and smooth and she wasn't Hispanic. As far she knew she was just black, despite having eyes that indicated otherwise.

Unfortunately, having bedroom eyes did not equate to the experience that those eyes tended to suggest. She was a virgin, but not an unwilling one. Unlike most of her friends she wasn't in a rush to have sex. It wasn't that she thought a woman had to save herself for marriage, she didn't even know if she would ever *get* married. She certainly enjoyed the explosion that happened between her legs when she touched herself in just the right way, so she wasn't a prude.

Still, the fact remained that Robin had never had a boyfriend — ever. For a girl who was shy around new people, dating had always been a disaster. She had once had a panic attack because a friend had told a guy that she'd had a crush on that she liked him. He came over to talk to her and she'd had to hide in the bathroom until he walked away. She referred to these panic attacks as her 'nervousness', and they occurred whenever she was placed in awkward situations with people she didn't know.

If she could be friends with a guy first, then maybe it would happen, but blind dates were a no-no. And therefore, making male friends just never happened.

She hurried to her Volvo and tried not to break any laws getting to work on time. She loved her car. Her parents had bought it for her when she graduated from high school. But then, when she had revealed that she wasn't going on to college, they had taken it back. She'd quickly promised to make the payments herself. And that seemed to mark the period when everything had begun to go downhill. Her Dad had been diagnosed with cancer about a year later and after he died, living with Mama had become intolerable and she'd had to move out.

Despite the financial struggle, the idea of giving up the car had been too much. She remembered when Daddy had been so sick, but still insisted on doing the oil changes himself. He and Robin would sit for hours while he tinkered away under the hood on some non-existent problem. They talked about everything; almost like he was trying to make up for the shortened time that he had on earth. So yes, there were times when it would have been better to just give up the car, but it was her connection to the good times with her Daddy and she would keep it at all costs.

Robin saw that it was six o'clock on the dot when she finally pulled into a parking lot at the restaurant. It was five after when she finally got clocked in and still Linda rolled her eyes at her. She mouthed an apology to the older, tired looking woman. Linda couldn't leave until her replacement showed up.

"I gotta get to my second job," Linda explained as she counted up her register. "They're shorthanded and I have to give the old man his medicine before he can go to bed."

"You're a nurse?" Robin asked. Linda took a moment to jot down a figure before answering. "No, I'm a home health care aide." There was an order coming through at the drive through window and Robin took it quickly.

"They're hiring." Linda spoke absently as she jotted down another figure.

"Oh? Well, I don't know anything about administering medicine or anything." She quickly put together the order. Linda paused in adding up each figure to look at her.

"You don't have to know anything. Hell, I go there just to get some sleep. After I give the old man his medicine, I put him to bed and I'm getting paid while he sleeps. I give him his medicine once in the middle of the night and then again when he wakes up." Linda hurried to the back office with her envelope of cash, but before she disappeared she said over her shoulder. "I make way more there then here and I hardly do anything."

Robin paused. She had never thought about having a second job. She didn't want to live to work, but if she could read a book and listen to music while she took care of some old person, then maybe she should look closely at the idea.

When she saw Linda hurrying out the door she called after her, "I'm interested. Tell me more when you get a chance!" Linda gave her a backward wave and disappeared out the door. Robin turned her attention back to the task at hand and taking a deep breath, dove into her w

CHAPTER 2

"Robin, phone." Robin pulled herself out of the small booth at the back of the restaurant, closing her finger over her place in the book. The first thing she thought of was her mother. Who else would be calling her at work? She hurried to the phone.

"Hello?"

"Robin." It was Linda.

"Hey, how's it going? I'm sorry I made you late."

"No worries, I got here on time. Guess what I'm doing?"

"Um, changing an old man's diaper?"

Linda laughed. "No! I'm watching this guy's big screen TV, and eating Chinese food. And guess what else? I'm getting paid to do it."

Robin raised an eyebrow. "Okay, so I'm interested, tell me more."

Linda gave her the name and phone number of her supervisor and told her to call him the next morning. The next day Robin did just that. After a brief phone conversation, the supervisor asked Robin to come to the office to put in an application.

She lightly rapped on the door, dressed in a skirt that she had only worn to church and a simple sweater. PINNACLE HEALTHCARE PROVIDERS was stenciled across the glass of the door. She nervously wiped the palms of her hands down her skirt. She had never been comfortable with interviews.

"Come in." A middle aged man stood and offered her his hand. He was tall, silver haired and had a smile like a television evangelist.

"I'm Ben Kennedy; one of the managers here. And you're Robin Mathena, correct? How old are you?"

Robin nodded, taking his hand. "Oh, I'm twenty-one." Robin was aware that her round face and relatively short stature made her look a lot younger.

Ben spent a few minutes asking her about previous experience, criminal history, her available hours and then had her put in a brief application and disclosure form. He seemed rushed but nice and less than half an hour later she was back in her car. It was just that simple. One minute she was talking to him on the phone, the next she had her application on file waiting for her first assignment. She guessed that she was now an employee of Pinnacle Healthcare Providers.

She drove home confused but excited.

At work that night her cell phone began to ring. She asked one of the women to cover for her while she snuck away to the bathroom to listen to the message.

"Hello, Robin this is Ben at Pinnacle Healthcare Providers. Call me back tonight if you can fill in for someone. I know this is sooner then you had expected and we would normally train you with a coach to walk you through your first time. Unfortunately someone just quit on me and we have a client that needs someone to administer meds, and to do some monitoring. She is a female patient, seventy-eight. Call me back to let me know yes or no."

She called back. "Hello, Ben. This is Robin, I got your message. But, well, I'm at work right now and I close so I won't be done until late-"

"Not a problem. Can you get here by one am?"

"Well yeah-"

"I can get the girl on duty now to stay over by a few hours if you can relieve her by one. Plus she will stay long enough to instruct you on what to do."

"At one-?"

"It will only be for four hours. Your replacement will arrive at five. And it pays you seventy-five dollars. For four hours, that's pretty good money."

"Okay." Robin said. "I'll be there."

"Do you have something to write with? Just go directly to this address." He gave her an address and she keyed it into her phone. "Don't let me down, Robin."

"I won't, Sir."

"Once you get there, call me to check in."

"Ok."

Robin hung up the phone, a nervous wreck. Was she ready for something like this?

After work she needed to rush home in order to change out of her work clothes and to do a MapQuest search of the address that Ben had given her. It was in a part of town that she wasn't familiar with. As she drove through the quiet streets and into Indian

Village; an upscale community in Cincinnati, she wondered how she had gotten here in such a short amount of time. But the seventy-five dollars would do her good that was for sure!

It was five 'til one when she hurried up the stairs of the nice townhome and rang the doorbell. Immediately a young Hispanic woman, not much older than herself, yanked open the door.

"God, man! Why'd you ring the bell? Do you want to wake her up?"

Robin's face felt hot. "Oh, I'm sorry. I wasn't thinking."

The girl smiled suddenly. "No problem. Come on in."

The house was really nice, even if it was decorated in floral prints and there was plastic on the two sofas.

"Look, I need to get going, so let me show you the ropes." She led her into the kitchen and opened a cabinet. "Be sure to put the medicine back in the exact same spot, okay?"

"Okay."

"She takes fourteen pills a day." The woman picked up three bottles. "She needs two of these every four hours. Wake her up at three to give them to her." The woman picked up another bottle. "She needs one of these with a glass of orange juice. The orange juice has her other medicine in it so only give her half a glass. Give her the insulin injection then-"

"Insulin injection?! I've never given anyone an injection!"

The woman gave her a long look. "Are you squeamish?"

"Not really, but-"

"It's easy." The woman moved to the fridge. "It's already pre-measured. Just pinch her flesh and stick. First swab with an alcohol pad which is on her side table, and then toss the needle in the dispenser in the bathroom. Easy, ok?"

"Um...no. Not okay." Robin's hand felt sweaty, and her stomach began to twist into knots. She didn't want to give anyone a shot!

The woman chuckled. "Millions of people give themselves insulin shots each day. If they can do it to themselves then you can do it to someone else. Now, I need to go so if you're going to write any of this down then you best do it. I still need to show you her breathing monitor."

The woman headed down the hall and reluctantly Robin followed. The bedroom door was closed and when they entered the dimly lit bedroom, Robin could hear the steady beeping of a machine and the slight swooshing sound that came at regular intervals. The room was cooler than the rest of the house. She saw the bed and a lump of blanket that must have contained a human being though Robin couldn't see anyone.

Quickly, the woman ran through the purpose of the machinery, how to reset it, what to do if the red light went off, and last, how to put medicine into the breathing apparatus.

"And that's it." Robin was silently repeating the information as she jotted it down on paper. "You'll be okay. Call Pinnacle if you have any problems, okay? Someone is always there, morning noon and night."

Robin sighed. "Okay."

"I gotta go. I have kids and I need to pick them up from my mom's so that I can get some sleep before its time to get them up for school."

It was one thirty and Robin suddenly thought about something other than her own confusion. "You go on ahead. I'll be okay."

The woman pulled out her cell phone. "Ben. Yeah. I got her trained and I'm heading out now. Yeah she got here at one." Oops, forgot to call. "I'll tell her." The woman turned to her as she gathered her things. "Ben's going to need you to work until seven but he'll give you one hundred twenty-five. Write down in the log when you give her medicine and check the log for the schedule."

"What log?" Robin was scratching her head and thinking about the extra hours that had been dropped into her lap and now something about a log. She followed the girl nervously to the door.

"I didn't tell you about the log? Shit, I'm sorry, it's on the fridge. Initial what you do. I gotta go. Everything will be good. You take care, *chica*." Then the nameless woman disappeared.

Robin closed and locked the door. She turned slowly into the room. It was just one day ago that she'd even heard of this job and here she was looking after a senior citizen that needed a boatload of care.

She knew that she'd been suckered, but it still needed to be done. She pulled some of the pamphlets from her purse that Ben had given her, and she sat down on the plastic covered couch and began reading. She still wasn't comfortable with what the woman had told her, but she would be gone in a few hours and she'd tell Ben that he could shove his job.

At about three o'clock, Robin stood stiffly. She had been entirely too anxious to read the book she had brought or to even relax, less she fell asleep and missed administering the medicine. She went to the kitchen and gathered the pills that the woman had pointed out. Then she checked the fridge for the schedule just in case she hadn't been told everything necessary. One medicine she couldn't find until she remembered that it was probably the one hidden in the orange juice. She went to the cabinet for a glass and hesitated. She said half a glass but did she mean a half cup of juice? Robin measured it carefully into a glass and then carried the items into the darkened room.

Damn, she didn't even know the woman's name. She stood quietly over the woman's slight form. She was pale, wrinkled, and had strikingly white hair done up in a single braid. Dear God, what was she—one hundred years old?

"Ma'am?" Gently, she placed her hand on the woman's birdlike shoulder. "Excuse me, ma'am?" After a few moments of this, the woman finally opened her watery eyes and looked in Robin's general direction, though she didn't seem to be focused.

"I'm Robin. It's time for your medicine. Can you sit up?" The woman closed her eyes and went back to sleep. Uh oh. She wasn't sure what to do. She gently shook the woman's frail shoulder again until her eyes again opened, and this time the woman mumbled sleepily. Robin lowered her oxygen mask and propped her up gently. "Medicine time."

Terrified that the woman would choke, she slipped the first pill into her mouth and pressed the glass of orange juice to her lips. But she seemed to know what to do and she placed her hand on the glass and expertly swallowed the first pill even though she was still partially asleep.

The OJ was gone and there were still more pills to take. Robin saw a glass of water on the bedside table and she slowly gave her the rest of the pills along with the tepid water.

With that overcame the hardest task; the injection. She found the alcohol swabs and lifted the bed covers and hiked up her gown. Her leg was so thin that she didn't want to pinch it for fear of injuring her. Carefully she gathered her flesh and then used her teeth to uncap the syringe. Robin eyes squinted and she silently counted to three. Then she quickly stabbed the gathered flesh and waited for the woman to jump and yell. She barely moved and Robin quickly depressed the syringe.

When that was over she could finally breathe. She helped the old lady lay down, and got her tucked in. It had taken her half an hour to give the older woman a few pills and an injection. She marked the log, replaced the pills and then sank down onto the plastic covered couch. She had made that harder than it needed to be. And now that it was over, fatigue overwhelmed her. She had worked hard at the restaurant and did a lot of ripping and running to interview in order to put in her application. Her eyes drooped and she yawned. And despite the fact that the plastic on the couch squeaked and caused her to slide around, before she knew it, Robin had fallen asleep.

"Help...me!"

Robin lurched awake and then jumped off the couch as if it was on fire. She ran into the bedroom only to see the elderly woman halfway out of bed. Her tubes were pulling and the machine was beeping loudly and flashing red.

Oh God. She placed her hand on the woman's shoulder. "You shouldn't be getting up, Ma'am. Please let me help you-"

The woman slapped her hand away. "Do you want me to pee myself?!"

"Okay." Once she made sure that the woman wasn't going to fall and break a hip she rushed to the machines and tried to remember how to stop the red light from blinking and buzzing.

"Hit the top button!" The woman yelled weakly. "Then the bottom one twice." She coughed and Robin did as instructed. She hurried back to the woman and placed the oxygen back on her face.

"Take a few breaths ma'am and then I'll take you to the restroom." The woman placed her hand over the mask and took a few breaths. Then Robin removed it and helped her to walk way across the room to the restroom. She was so small and thin that she probably could have carried her.

The woman brushed her hand aside and lowered herself down onto the toilet with the aide of the handrails. Robin listened as she peed for damn near five minutes. Her stream would stop for a few moments and when Robin thought she was done it would start again. The white haired woman gave her a long look.

"Is this your first caregiver job?"

"Is it that easy to tell?"

The woman smiled. "Where's the other girl?"

"Um...I guess she quit."

"Hmph, that girl didn't do anything right."

The lady used a wad of tissue to pat herself clean and then she got up and washed her hands. When Robin tried to give her a hand back to bed, she brushed her aside.

"Well, help me get dressed."

Robin glanced at the clock on the bedside table. It was just after six am. "Okay, sure." She moved about the woman's room pulling out underwear, clothes, and socks. She helped her put on a huge bra. Robin wasn't squeamish, but it wasn't pleasant. Next came some granny panties and then a comfortable dress. During this time she found out that the woman's name was Lucille. Lucille didn't ask her name.

Lucille talked about her son who was a doctor and her grandchildren. She talked about some women who were in a group with her. She talked so much that she lost her breath and Robin had to give her oxygen.

Seven o'clock came and went and her replacement still hadn't arrived. She led Lucille to the living room and set her in a comfortable chair.

"I guess it's time for your medicine. " Lucille turned on the television set to watch an evangelist, paying her very little attention. Robin covered her mouth as she yawned again and checked the schedule. Four pills.

Lucille wouldn't hold out her hand for the offered pills. She looked at Robin and scowled. "I can't take these on an empty stomach. I need food."

"Oh...Um. Ok. What do you want?"

"Coffee, toast no butter, soft boiled eggs; two.

Really tired now, Robin headed back to the kitchen and started coffee. She dug through the refrigerator for the carton of eggs and set two to boil. She checked the clock again. Seven-thirty. Damn, where was the replacement?

"Miss Lucille, do you want to come in here to eat, or do you want a tray pulled up to the chair?"

"A tray, please. And I like cream and heavy sugar." Yawning, Robin prepared everything and carried it into the living room. It took her a long time to eat and finally she could take her medicine. She marked everything into the log.

At eight-fifteen she called Ben's number but didn't get an answer. Of course not, he was probably sleeping. At a few minutes after nine, the replacement finally strolled in. Robin was so mad that at first she couldn't speak.

"Hey there. Who are you?" It was an older woman about forty.

"Robin. And you're late." She spoke, uncharacteristically rude.

She scowled. "Five minutes. So-r-r-r-ry."

"Try two hours. You were supposed to be here at seven."

"No." The woman put her stuff in the kitchen. "I always start at nine. "

"Damnit." Robin whispered. Ben was such a liar.

Lucille smirked. She had known all along. This was a full shift. Ben had tricked her here with promises of a half shift.

She went into the kitchen where the replacement was looking at the log. "Hey, I'm sorry for being a bitch. Ben told me I'd be working for just four hours."

"Yeah. Look, this is a good job but don't let Ben push you around. Get a shift and stick with it. If he asks you to fill in for someone then do it at your own risk and ask for a shit load of money. He'll have no choice but to give you what you ask for." She held out her hand. "I'm Jodie."

"I'm Robin. Um, how much do I get paid for working a full shift?"

Jodie gave her a curious look. "Girl, you get paid by the hour, don't let him try pulling that 'I'll give you X amount for X amount of hours worked.' We get paid 18.50 an hour and 23.50 for overtime and they don't take out for taxes." She gave her a sly look. "It's like getting paid under the table! Your shift is no longer than 8 hours and after that you charge him at the overtime rate!" Robin did the calculation in her head taking a painfully long time to come up with the figure before Jodie jumped in with the answer. "You get paid one hundred-forty eight dollars a day. That's not bad money because any other place would be taking a shitload of taxes out on you, especially for people like me that don't have kids."

One hundred-forty eight dollars a day for eight hours work wasn't anything she could sneeze at, even though she had every intentions of doing the proper withholding. Having a CPA for a mother had put the fear of the IRS in her.

Was she really considering working two jobs? The idea was daunting, but being able to afford her insurance *and* monthly car payment would be wonderful.

"It's not a bad job if you make it work for you, and not the other way around. And there is always overtime. Also, go over and pick up your money, don't let him mail it to you. It will take him days to put it in the mail."

Robin nodded, thankful for the information. But she was simply too tired to pick up her money and instead she drove straight home. She collapsed into bed after kicking off her shoes, still fully clothed and was asleep within seconds.

CHAPTER 3

Robin drove to Ben's office without calling first. After putting things into perspective she realized that she didn't want to lose an opportunity to make that much money for eight hours of work. But she had to be smart about it.

Ben jumped up quickly when she entered the room. "Hey Robin, I hear you did great last night. Sorry about the mix up with the times. Here, have a seat."

"I can't. I need to leave. I just came to pick up my pay."

He reached for a large ledger book. "You know I still haven't replaced the other person." Robin peeked at the check.

"That looks like you are about to write that for one hundred twenty-five dollars. But I did work eight hours and if I'm not mistaken that should be one hundred forty-eight."

"One forty-eight?"

Robin frowned.

Ben smiled. "Sorry. My mistake." He wrote her two checks. "So do you want the shift?"

"One until nine?"

"Midnight to nine."

"That's more than eight hours."

"True, but it *is* regular money."

"How many days a week?"

"Monday through Friday."

"I want twenty-three fifty for each hour over eight that I work."

"Ouch." He smiled at her after a moment. "Prorated on fifteen minute intervals?"

She thought about that. "You have a deal." Robin held out her hand and Ben shook it.

After work at the restaurant, she went straight to Miss Lucille's house. The Hispanic woman from the night before greeted her when she let herself in. Ben had given her a key and a log that she needed in order to chart her hours.

"Hi, *chica*. Back again." The woman headed for the kitchen where she had left her things and Robin followed her. "I guess you liked it, since you're back. Are you on this shift permanently?"

"I think so."

"Hard shift to work. How people stay awake is beyond me." She gave her a brief, knowing look. "Do you have an alarm on your watch or cell phone? If so, set it. Oh yeah, Jodie was complaining that you didn't do up the dishes at the end of your shift."

Robin winced. "I wasn't aware that we had to cook meals."

The woman stopped. "We don't." She put her hands on her hips. "You can always tell that little old lady to go in and make her own breakfast."

Robin's face felt hot. "I don't mind, as long as I know."

"Also, it wouldn't hurt to make up her bed." The woman whisked past Robin. "Nighty- night, *chica*. See you tomorrow."

With a relieved sigh that the other lady was gone, Robin went in and checked on Miss Lucille. The small, bird-like woman was sleeping peacefully.

Things ran much more smoothly now that she knew what to expect. She read until it was time to give Miss Lucille the first dose of medicine. Afterwards, she nestled down in the one armchair that Miss Lucille had used; the only one not covered in plastic. She took the girl's advice and set her cell phone's alarm to ring at 5:45 then she roused herself and set the eggs to boil and got the coffee going.

Miss Lucille was already awake when Robin walked into the bedroom and helped her to the restroom. While she peed, Robin turned off the eggs and set them in the sink to cool. She got her dressed while the older woman repeated the same story about her son the doctor, her grandkids and the woman's group.

Robin set the TV tray up and brought the woman's breakfast as she watched the television evangelist. This was going a lot smoother. Robin smiled, stretched then went back to the bedroom. Yawning, she began to make the bed before discovering that they badly needed changing. She squinted and looked around. The room was dusty. Did anyone actually come to clean?

"Miss Lucille, do you have a cleaning lady?"

The old woman gnawed on her toast, eyes glued to the TV. "No."

"Who does your laundry, the dusting and your shopping?"

"My son brings me one dozen eggs a week along with one loaf of bread. When the sugar, creamer and coffee runs, out he buys more. He brings me seven chicken lean cuisines, and seven meatloaf Marie Calendars." Robin retreated to the kitchen and checked the freezer. There were two chicken and two meatloaf frozen meals left, as well as a tray of frosty ice cubes.

She checked the fridge for butter or jam. None. She checked the pantry. There were can goods that were years old, and spices that had dust on them. Yikes.

"Miss Lucille, who cleans?"

She turned her light grey eyes to Robin. "My son is a very busy man. He comes over and does the laundry for me once a month and does the dusting and vacuuming then." Robin hid her doubtful look, but accepted the woman's words.

Robin whisked away the dishes, washing them and replacing them quickly. She was on time with the next dosage of medicine. She still had another two hours, so she returned to the bedroom, changed the bedding, and dusted the furniture. Poor old lady probably wouldn't need oxygen if she could breathe past all of the dust.

Robin then returned to the living room and sat down on the couch, trying to keep her arms from sticking to the plastic. She tried to watch TV with Miss Lucille but it, more than anything else, made her sleepy. She thought about making small talk, but the woman seemed very preoccupied with her show, so Robin didn't want to interrupt her. She picked up the book and began reading.

"What is that?" Miss Lucille was trying to see the cover. She reached out her hand for the book.

"It's a story about a world where witches and vampires exist alongside of humans."

Miss Lucille scowled. "That's blasphemy!"

"Huh?"

Miss Lucille looked at the cover with disgust. "It's probably all about sex; vile sex with devils."

"No! Not at all." She slipped the book out of the older women's hands. "It's just a story about a nice girl who was born a witch."

"Hmmph!" Miss Lucille snorted. Robin sighed and checked her watch. *Just another half an hour.*

CHAPTER 4

The next day, when she went to Miss Lucille's she carried a bag containing butter substitute and no sugar added jam. She spread butter and jam onto her morning toast and set the tray along with the two soft boiled eggs and coffee with sugar and cream. The tray went in front of the elderly woman before Robin hurried out of the room to make the bed.

When she returned, every bit of the toast had been eaten. Robin picked up the tray to carry into the kitchen to wash and Miss Lucille's eyes moved from the television screen to stare at the young woman.

"Did my son bring that butter and jam?"

Robin paused. "I guess..."

Robin fell into her routine easily, despite the fact that she now had to eke out her sleep time during the part of the day when neighbors ran their vacuum cleaners and babies cried for breakfast and toddlers watched the same episode of SpongeBob Square Pants until she thought she'd jam a pencil into her ears if she had to hear that damned song one more time.

She went to Pinnacle each day to pick up her wages, and when her bank account actually showed an amount that contained two zeroes instead of one, Robin did a happy dance. Nothing could put a damper on her mood except one person; mama.

The two women met for church each Sunday. It was a routine that was solidified after daddy's death. Mama wouldn't have to keep hinting that she didn't come by enough and Robin was undoubtedly saving her immortal soul each Sunday, so it was killing two birds with one stone.

After the service, they went to brunch. Mama always treated, so she always chose the location. "I'm planning a cruise to Jamaica this winter. I can use a vacation." Betty spoke as she sliced into her Belgium waffles.

"That sounds like fun, mom. You haven't had a vacation in years."

"Well, I want you to come with me." Robin looked up in surprise. "I want to make it for seven days. I'll pay; I just want us to have some time together." Her mother smiled nervously.

Robin's food stayed frozen in her mouth. She didn't want to be alone with her mom for seven days.

"Take off work for seven days?"

"Well, it will be months from now. If you ask now, then I'm sure they will be able to accommodate you."

"Well, I just picked up a second, part time job." She lied about it being part-time, and about it being 'just'.

"Oh?" Betty picked up her glass of water and sipped while waiting with interest for her to continue.

"Yes, I started working at a home health care service; night shifts. But they are awfully short staffed-"

"Home-healthcare," she gave Robin a confused look. "You want to be a nurse?"

"No, no, not at all. All I do is monitor people in their homes-"

Betty sucked in a loud breath. "Are you telling me that you are going to people's homes, taking care of them?"

Robin gave her a surprised look. "Well, I guess."

"Jesus, Robin!" Betty threw down her napkin in annoyance. "It wasn't bad enough that you work in a low paying, fast food restaurant, but now you want to wipe the asses of old white people, clean their houses, give them their medicine?!"

Everyone in Perkins turned to look at them; mostly white people and Robin wanted to sink in her seat.

"Mom, please..." She begged, hoping she'd calm down. She could already feel the familiar pounding of her heart in her chest and the way that the sweat was beading on her forehead was an indication that she was going to probably have a nervous attack, and she didn't want to do it in front of mama and all of these strangers.

"Oh, Robin! You know, I give up!" Betty stood up and tossed several bills onto the table. "If you want your life to amount to nothing, then fine!" Hot angry tears sprouted in Robin's eyes. She was shaking as she stood and followed her mother out of the restaurant. How dare she judge her? How dare she say that her life amounted to nothing?

"I, I give up too!" They were in the parking lot and Betty looked at Robin somewhat surprised. The hot tears made her colorful eyes big. "I wouldn't *want* to spend seven days with you, okay?! The idea of it makes me sick, mom. I'd rather spend seven days wiping Miss Lucille's ass then in Jamaica with you!"

Robin got into her car and drove off, leaving her mother staring after her.

Robin sat slouched in her armchair in her small apartment, staring at the computer screen of her laptop. Nothing felt right to her anymore. She was just a simple person that wanted a simple life of no complications. How is it that she had killed the one relationship that meant anything to her?

It had been two weeks since she had spoken to her mother. She hadn't even gone to church, her stomach was in knots and she was constantly in the bathroom with irritable bowel. She picked up her telephone before she could think of excuses not to, and dialed the familiar number. Her mother picked up on the second ring and Robin knew that she had checked the caller id before answering by the wary tone of her voice.

"I'm sorry, mom."

There was a long pause. "I should never have yelled at you like that Robin."

"I know that I am a disappointment to you-"

"I know I've made you think that-"

"I'm sorry, mom, that I'm not outgoing and-"

"But you are perfect the way you are!"

Robin swiped away her tears. "No, I'm not." I'm afraid of my very shadow, I'm lonely, I'm sad all of the time and my life seems pointless. She thought these things but didn't dare say them, admitting them to herself was hard enough.

"Robin," her mother said softly. "I don't want you to ever struggle and I want you to be happy. You're my only family." An only child, Betty Mathena's mother had passed away long ago and she had never known her father. No one else that she was kin to meant anything to her. There was no one but Robin. "You are not a disappointment to me! I just want more for you. I just want you to have a life that's not filled with struggles, and baby I am in a position where I can help you — in a way that my mama never could help me." Money had been tight for her and her mother so there was no question of her mom paying for college — if she wanted it she would have to pay for it herself. And pay for it herself she did; by working very hard. She had always sworn to herself that she would give her daughter what her mother couldn't.

"I want to find my own life, mom, like you did. You're pushing and it doesn't push me towards what you want, but away from you." There, she had finally said it. She held her breath and heard her mother swallow back her own tears.

"I know."

And then the two talked, really talked, for the first time since daddy's death and maybe for the first time ever. When Robin hung up the phone an hour later, she wasn't sure if her mother would change, but she already knew that she couldn't continue a relationship with her mother where she had to hold everything in. She breathed a sigh of relief.

CHAPTER 5

Robin was kneeling, putting the older woman's feet into her underwear as she sat on the side of the bed, now containing clean sheets. "What's your name, dear?"

Robin looked at her, not sure if the question had been directed to her or not, even though there was no one else around. She had been Miss Lucille's home health care aide for over three weeks and the woman had never asked that one question.

"Robin."

"You're a pretty girl, Robin. Such pretty eyes you have."

Robin smiled at the compliment. "Thank you." Miss Lucille struggled to stand and Robin pulled up her panties.

"My son will be coming over today. Can you pick me out something nice to wear?"

Robin stood and went to the closet. "Sure. Would you like pants or a dress?"

"There is a navy blue dress. Bring that to me." Robin draped the dress over the bed. There was dust on the shoulders and she brushed it off quickly. "I have a doctor's appointment today. Bentley will probably take me to lunch after. We go to the Brown Derby. I usually have the chopped steak and baked potato. They use fresh mushrooms, you know. Not all restaurants do; even those expensive steak places-". Robin listened to her as she talked about her son, her grandchildren and the ladies from the women's group. She pretended that she hadn't already heard this story thirty times and commented in all of the right places.

When Jodie arrived to replace her, she called over her shoulder. "Bye, Miss Lucille. See you tomorrow, and have a pleasant visit with your son."

Jodie frowned. "Is that why you put her in that party dress?"

Robin shrugged. "Well, she wanted to wear it when her son takes her out to lunch."

"Her son doesn't take her out. He's a busy doctor." Jodie's voice wasn't low and Robin looked over at Miss Lucille to see if she had heard. "He drops off her food, and pays whoever is on duty to do some cleaning and laundry. And then he leaves."

Jodie moved to the kitchen but Robin stopped her. "Well, who's going to take her to the doctor?"

"Nobody. The doctor comes here, if ever. Look, these old people are delusional. They think all kinds of things because their reality sucks for them. Just play along, okay?" Robin nodded her head and left. She felt gullible and saddened.

"Robin, I want to know if you will take on a new client ASAP while Miss Babbs is in the hospital." Robin was on her way to work her first job. She had been informed only a few hours before that Miss Lucille had been admitted to the hospital with a case of pneumonia and was still reeling from that news. She wanted to visit her but her need for sleep had prevailed; she intended to visit her first thing in the morning, though. And now Ben was calling, asking her make a decision on replacing her with someone else.

Over the course of two months, Robin had grown more than fond of the older woman. Initially she had looked at the job as a just a means to bring in more money, but seeing the other woman's life as a series of caregivers and evangelist shows had caused Robin to put forth more effort. Though it wasn't like her to reach out, she did with Miss Babbs.

At her morning breakfast she sometimes placed a fresh muffin that she'd picked up from a nearby bakery on her plate instead of the usual toast. Miss Lucille never said thank you but she ate every crumb of the treat. She'd taken to brushing the woman's beautiful white hair while they talked about new things; like what it had been like for Miss Lucille as a young woman. These stories interested Robin the most and she listened intently as she brushed the woman's hair before finally giving her the usual one braid that she pinned up into a bun.

Miss Lucille was a natural born story teller. Robin always thought about "The Autobiography of Miss

Jane Pittman" when she sat there listening to tales that ran the gambit from ghost stories to revenge tales, and of course, stories of segregation.

"Ben, I want to go back to Miss Lucille-"

"It's just temporary," he assured her. "So, are you interested?"

She had clicked very well with Miss Lucille. She wasn't sure if she would be able to do that with just anyone. "Who is the client?"

"A young man with cerebral palsy needs an aide. This job is a little different. You will need to transport him to and from school. You will need to do some light lifting, and other than that, he is very self-sufficient and can do most everything else himself."

"Transportation? You mean use my own car because-"

"We'll reimburse you for your mileage."

She had become smarter in her dealings with Pinnacle. "And wear and tear?"

Ben chuckled. "You're a savvy business woman. I'll throw in an extra fifty per shift to cover both wear and tear and mileage. Do we have a deal?" God, she just knew there was something he wasn't telling her.

"Deal," she said reluctantly.

"Okay. Got something to write with and I'll give you his address. "Be there at seven a.m. in order to get him to class by eight. Got it?"

"Got it. And when does the shift end?"

"As soon as you get him home from school."

"Okay." Sounded a bit vague but, ok.

"Ok, Miss Mathena, I think we have a deal. Please start in the morning."

The additional fifty dollars would be good and she'd be able to sleep at night like normal people. It hadn't been easy to make sure she left the restaurant by 11:30 in order to get to Miss Lucille's by midnight. Fourteen-hour days took their toll. Even after months of it, she still found it hard to sleep through the day. She had to keep her music going in order to counteract the noise of her neighbors. And even though she really had no life to speak of, she felt less so when she went to sleep until four o'clock only to be back at her first job by six. Reluctantly she admitted to herself that it would be nice to sleep through the night again.

CHAPTER 6

The next morning, Robin stretched in her bed, reveling at the feel of luxuriating there. She showered, and keeping in mind that she would have to do some lifting, put on jeans, a sweatshirt, and tennis shoes. She then brushed back her wild hair, pulling it tight into a ponytail at the top of her head; the ends springing out wildly.

She hurried to her car, a cup of coffee in her hands. It would be nice taking some kid to school, and then she could get caught up on her grocery shopping. She wondered if he had a pager or something. She checked the address as she pulled up into a parking lot of a nice condo.

It was just a little before eight as she hurried up the walkway and rang the doorbell. A man in a wheelchair opened the door and the smile she had plastered on her face drooped. Man, not kid. He stared at her, his head bobbed a bit on his neck. Unruly red hair flopped into his eyes; eyes that were cold and unfriendly as they appraised her.

"Thanks for fitting me into your busy schedule." His voice was as cold as his eyes, slurring enough that she had to strain to understand him. His mouth twisted and he gulped in a breath. "So happy that you could make it, even if you're twenty-four hours late and I had to miss a day of classes."

"Um..."

He rolled his chair back into the apartment in stiff, angry movements and Robin stepped inside uncertainly. "I'm not sure if I understand you. I just got called on this job last night-"

"Well, Pinnacle is so fucked up!" He wheeled around, coming toward her. She almost took a step back. His pale skin was mottled red from anger and was covered in millions of freckles. Although he obviously had some muscle control issues, he had no problem pointing his finger at her accusingly. "They got paid a week ago, promising that it would be no problem getting me an aide. Then you cancel at the last minute leaving me in a lurch!" The last slurred words were shouted in a spray of spit.

Robin was not one to easily anger, but his rudeness pushed her into that direction. How dare this asshole shout and spit all over her. Angrily, she wiped his spit spray from the back of her hand.

"Well first of all, I had nothing to do with the deal you had with Pinnacle. Like I told you, I accepted a job just last night!" She began to shake with anger, but her voice stayed steady. "It couldn't have been me to cancel out because before that I was watching a little old lady that just went into the hospital with pneumonia. So-don't you yell at me!" She put her fists on her hips as the man in the wheelchair quieted.

He watched her silently. "I'm sorry, then. I thought it was you." Now that his anger was no longer directed at her, his head didn't flop and lurch around as much, and his voice became clear and quite easy to understand. His breathing slowed as he continued watching her. "What's your name?

He'd switched gears so fast that she didn't know how to respond. She was still ready to chew his ass, and now he was speaking calmly. "I'm Robin. Robin Mathena."

"I'm Jason, but I guess you know that." Actually she hadn't. All she had was his sex and address. She didn't admit that, though. He was her age, so if he was going to school then it meant college. Shit.

"What can I do to help you, Jason?"

"I can use help getting breakfast. Follow me into the kitchen," he demanded. He didn't seem mad at her any longer, but that didn't mean that he was being nice. She followed him from a large living room that contained one couch, an armchair next to a side table, and lamp and all kinds of electronic equipment. She could tell that it was a nice apartment containing expensive things, but it wasn't set up like a person's home. It seemed more like a studio.

The kitchen had a big butcher's block table; very nice. But it too wasn't what one would consider homey. There was a commercial feel to it, as if this room should be in an exclusive restaurant. He opened a lower cabinet and retrieved a bowl and spoon.

"I need you to make coffee, please." He moved to the fridge next and retrieved milk which he placed in his lap. He had the type of wheelchair that required him to actually wheel himself. He then went to a pantry where he retrieved a box of Cheerios.

Instead of a coffee pot he had a coffee press. She studied it while chewing her lip. She had no idea how to use it.

"Forget about the coffee," he said noticing her confusion. "We don't have time to fool with it, anyways." She put the contraption down and moved to the table, reaching for the cereal. He snatched it and glared at her. "I can do it."

Okay. What was he, four? She stood back and waited for him to tell her what he needed. He spilled cheerios on the table as he poured them into the bowl, but she wasn't going to offer to clean it up and risk getting yelled at again. He carefully poured the milk, not spilling any. It obviously took a lot of work because his tongue peeked through as he concentrated on his task. She smiled. He looked like a kid that was working out a puzzle; a cute little ginger kid with wild crazy red hair. He glanced up at her and caught the smile. He scowled.

"Please put this away for me, Robin." He said in a neutral voice. His words were slightly slurred but she could still hear the dislike in it. It was on the tip of her tongue to tell him that she wasn't his maid. He had gotten it out of the fridge with no problem, so she was sure that he could return it. But, it was also eighteen fifty an hour and for now, he was the boss. She returned the milk, and then put away the cereal.

A newspaper was on the table and for a moment he ignored her as he read and ate; scooping cereal into the gaping hole that was his mouth and not doing a good job of keeping it all inside. She looked at anything other than him eating.

"Have you ever worked with anyone with Cerebral Palsy?" She looked at him quickly. He was still holding the paper but now watching her.

"No."

"Have you ever *known* anyone with CP?"

"No."

"Figures," he muttered. "First, let me explain that there is not just one symptom associated with my disorder. Even though I slur my words and have less muscle control doesn't mean that I'm mentally disabled. Please don't make the mistake of thinking that I am. I'm probably more intelligent than you."

"You're certainly ruder." She glared at him.

"It's not my intent," he said calmly. "I'm just making sure that you understand. Food falls out of my mouth not because I have no table manners but because I have little muscle control." She guiltily bit back the sarcastic response that she had prepared. "When I eat I sometimes choke. You do know how to give the Heimlich maneuver, right?"

She nodded.

"Okay." He sighed. "So I need you to watch me eat." He gave her an icy look. "Hope it doesn't disgust you much." Her face warmed.

They had started out on a bad note. She decided to be the bigger man and set things right. "Jason, I apologize for calling you rude." She blew out a tense breath. "I won't judge you if you stop judging me." His eyes flinched. He turned back to this cereal.

"Fine," he said between bites of food.

When he was done eating, he placed his dishes into the sink then wheeled out of the room. "I need a shave but there's no time for that. I need you to pee me." Her heart jumped in her chest. Pee him? What in the hell did that mean?

"Um, how do I do that?" She followed him to a large bathroom.

"You need to hold my penis while I piss."

Oh my God, this was a nightmare. She'd never been around a penis before. Her face was hot and sweat sprouted from her arm pits and dotted her forehead.

"I-uh, you were holding that spoon just fine, Jason."

"I'm just messing with you Robin. I can hold my own penis just fine." He gave her a long look and she almost fainted from relief. He smirked. "Have you ever been an aide for a male before?"

She wanted to kick him in his smirking face. "Don't worry about me," she snapped. "I'm a fast learner." She tried to hide her displeasure that he had known just what to say to cause her to shake in her shoes.

He stopped the chair as close to the toilet as he could get. "I only need to use the bathroom three times a day. My body has been- I guess you would say, 'trained' to go once in the morning, once in the afternoon and then before bed. But I can't use my legs much. If you can help me to stand, then I can take care of the rest myself."

Robin squeezed past the wheelchair and got in front of him. "How do we do this?"

"Lean forward, bending at the knees. Use your legs not your back. I'm going to put my arms around your shoulders; your arms go around my body under my arms. Pull until my legs are locked beneath me. I'm wearing braces, so once I'm standing, I'm ok."

She leaned forward and Jason's eyes stayed glued to her lighter ones before his arms went around her. His long, red hair was in her face. It ran down in unruly curls over his shoulders. It was beautiful hair. He was a ginger; red hair, green eyes, freckles dotting pale skin. Too bad he was such an asshole. She might have thought he was cute.

She began to lift. "Don't use your back," he said with lips very close to her ear. She paused and then used her legs to lift. "There you go." She was hugging him, he was hugging her and the timber of his words vibrated through her body, creating goose bumps that ran down her spine. She had never been so close to a man that was not directly a part of her bloodline. Beneath his loose fitting shirt, his muscles were tight and tone. Her mouth felt suddenly dry as she nervously took a step away from him. Standing, he towered over her. She had to look up at him. He was looking down, but not at her, at his legs.

She looked down, as well. They seemed to be supporting him ok. She backed up again, bumping the toilet and he placed one hand on the sink counter while the other remained on her shoulder for balance.

She gave him a surprised look. "Can you walk?" And then she blushed that she'd asked such a thing to a man in a wheelchair.

"A little." He swung his left leg out and she stepped out of his way, still remaining close enough so that he could continue to hold onto her for support. He leaned his body to the left and then swung his right leg out.

"You're walking." He wobbled a little but righted himself. "Jason, if you can do this then why don't you get a walker or crutches?" His expression grew dark and he didn't answer. Shit, she'd put her foot in her mouth. He had reached the toilet. Now what was she supposed to do?

"Lift the toilet seat." He said while he moved to undo his pants. She did it quickly. He wasn't holding on to her for balance but he wasn't wobbling either. "Bring my chair behind me so that I can sit when I'm done."

She did as he demanded, wishing that he could be a little nicer. As she moved to get the chair, she heard the loud patter of his urine stream hitting the water within the toilet. She blushed. Well there was no shame in his game.

After urinating for an ungodly long time, he checked behind him for his chair and then using the cabinet he lowered himself into the chair, flopping down in it. He picked up his left leg and then his right, setting his feet into position. She watched as he reached forward and flushed the toilet, and then wheeled himself to a pedestal sink, where he washed his hands.

He sighed and looked at her. "Well, we'll be late but I guess that can't be helped. Wheel me out to the living room so that I can get my things."

"I got here at seven on the dot." She said, unwilling to take the blame for his tardiness to school.

"You're supposed to be here at six am."

She sighed. "Well, I won't be late again." He didn't speak, and she silently cursed Ben for making her look so stupid for this job.

He instructed her to get his book bag out of the closet while he went to his computer and unplugged something from the modem. He pocketed whatever the thing was and then rolled to the door waiting for her to open it. At her car, she helped him to stand again.

It took a while, but she got him folded into the small car while he looked at her like she was an idiot for not having a mini-van. After opening the trunk she tackled the chair. It was light weight, but still big and awkward. And because she'd never done anything like this, it seemed to take forever. Jason had eventually bellowed that there were latches that would need to be undone. She found them and lifted the suddenly collapsible chair. Something metal scraped against her bumper and she cursed. It had left a mark. Now she was really in a foul mood; a rude client, Ben lying about the job, and now her car was scratched.

Robin climbed behind the wheel, refusing to look at Jason. "Where to?" He pulled out a cell phone and checked the time before answering.

"Head to the main campus. I'll direct you from there."

"Which main campus?"

"UC. " He raised a surprised brow that she didn't know. He put on headphones and proceeded to ignore her for most of the ride.

Robin was not particularly happy to navigate through the congested early morning traffic as Jason directed her through the maze of buildings. She would have to draw a map in order to find him again. He directed her to a parking spot, scowling again because she didn't have a handicap sign. Silently she retrieved the bulky wheelchair from the trunk. Jason had already unbuckled himself and had his feet positioned on the ground. He stood without her assistance, using the door to steady himself.

She came around to the side of him with the chair and he turned his body and again flopped down into it. "Okay, can you take it from here?" She asked, already counting down the seconds when she could be done with him for a while.

He eyed her.

"I can wheel you inside if you want-"

"God," he sighed in exasperation. "You aren't dropping me off. You'll be spending the day with me."

She frowned at him in disbelief. "I-uh...I thought-"

"What? That you'd just drop me off and go off somewhere and do your own thing and still get paid? No, you are my aide for the entire shift." Her heart dropped as she glanced nervously at the other students moving about. She did not want to be here — more, she didn't want to be here with this asshole.

Swallowing back her disappointment and trying not to become anxious, Robin wheeled him to the entrance of the building. Jason suddenly stopped the chair by gripping the wheels. He turned his head to look at her. He had a frown on his face and his muscles jerked so much that it caused his unkempt hair to flop around him.

"You do know why I need an aide, right?"

Robin did not want to answer that question and appear even more clueless then she already felt. Yet she did need the answer to that simple question.

"No. No one explained-"

"Damnit," he turned back in his seat, straining to look at her. "I don't have time for this." He was back to being annoyed, which made his speech even more slurred and hard to understand, and his movements even more jerky and spastic. She wanted to roll her eyes and was on the verge of telling him to just shove it.

He was digging for his cell phone. "I have seizures; about two a day — maybe less maybe more. I need you to help me with my seizures, help me with my books and my laptop. I can do pretty much everything on my own. But if I have a seizure, then I do need someone with me. Um, mind coming around

49

in front of me so that I don't crane my neck looking at you?"

Robin moved from behind his chair to stand in front of him. People looked at them curiously. He was jabbing at his phone. "The duration of a seizure is anywhere from one minute to three. They don't hurt me, but sometimes I'm tired afterwards — Hello? I need to speak to the manager in charge. This is Jason Hamilton. "

He ignored her momentarily as he focused on his call. She felt stupid, just standing there as people moved around them. UC was a huge campus and a guy with Cerebral Palsy in a wheelchair and a black girl standing in front of him looking like a kid about to be punished by her parent; it garnered a lot of attention.

"Who am I speaking to? Mary Louise. This is Jason Hamilton. JASON." He said distinctly, obviously attempting to control his enunciation. He talked as if his tongue was half a second behind the movement of the rest of his mouth. "Yeah, I'm not doing very well at all Mary Louise. Pinnacle lied to me." Robin's eyes widened. She listened intently to the one-sided conversation.

"First you took my m-money promising that you could do *all* of the th-things I asked." He stuttered a bit, face turning red. He suddenly sucked in a deep breath and closed his eyes, seeming to gain a bit more control of the movement of his neck and the jerking of his head and facial muscles. "Oh yes, it was a lie. You didn't have an assistant lined up for me. You threw this inexperienced girl into the job, probably lying to her the same way that you lied to me."

His eyes flashed. "Mary Lou-Louise, don't patronize me! I've already missed a week and one day of school, I'm late today and it's all Pinnacles' fault! You will be crediting me for the loss of my time." He sighed. "The only thing I want to hear from you is, 'Yes, Mr. Hamilton.'" He snorted. "Then I'll just stay with the state or I'll just keep looking elsewhere-" Jason suddenly looked at Robin. "Fine. That's acceptable. Robin needs a course in seizure emergencies if she's going to assist me."

Robin tried not to stare, but couldn't help it now that the conversation had turned to her. "As soon as possible or she's no good to me. Because I can get the Access bus to drive me around—but I *need* someone who knows how to handle seizure emergencies." He listened quietly. "That's not good enough. No. I need you to tell me something today. Find out today and call me back this evening. Let me make sure we understand each other; you are crediting me two full days—today and yesterday, you're providing Robin with training in a certified seizure emergency course. No. That's not good enough. Oh my God, you should know this! Contact the Epilepsy Foundation, or the National Institute of Neurological disorders and they will tell you exactly where—"

He winked at her suddenly and she almost jumped. A slow smile crossed his lips. "Thank you, Mary Louise. I don't mean to be an ass, but this is a job for others; for me this is my life." He disconnected the call and replaced it in his pocket. He gave her an intent look.

"Okay, so I guess your boss will be contacting you to set up training." She nodded stunned. He had handled himself so well; better than she ever had with Pinnacle and he made a good point. Obviously he had every right to be aggravated because to her this was a job that she'd leave behind at the end of the day. But this was his life.

CHAPTER 7

Robin felt guilty for her impatience. She moved back to push his chair but he had already begun rolling himself to the entrance. She hit the automatic door opener for him and followed him silently down several hallways.

They reached a set of double doors and Jason stopped abruptly. "Please don't disrupt class. If you have questions, then write them out on paper. As soon as we get inside, I will need for you to get my backpack from behind my chair and set up my laptop."

Set up his laptop?

"If you have a cell phone, then set it to vibrate. If I have a seizure, don't panic, I will tell you what to do. Got it?" She nodded, nervous at the instructions he gave and how quickly he delivered them. "Open the door Robin."

She moved ahead of him and opened the door. She could hear the voice of a male teacher who paused to watch her as she stepped inside of the auditorium, using her body to hold the door for Jason to wheel inside.

Her face burned as the attention fell on her. It was a large auditorium and she calculated that there was close to seventy bodies there--all focused on her. And then Jason wheeled inside, and they one-by-one dismissed her as they recognized a routine.

A tall, white-haired man looked over his glasses at Jason and continued his lecture. Jason moved to the front of the room. Robin would have definitely moved to the back, but the back was up on risers.

He locked his wheelchair in place directly in front of a long table that looked like it was used for nothing more than to hold books and other things that no one needed. No one else sat at the table and it awkwardly positioned Jason at the front of the class; away from the rest of the students. But, she supposed he needed the space for his laptop.

He gave her a look and she jumped into action, grabbing his heavy book bag that had been hanging behind his chair. She put it on the table in front of him and waited for him to unzip it and retrieve the laptop. He handed her the power cord and gestured where she should plug it. Once that was done he ignored her. Another student gestured to a spare chair and she smiled her thanks and pulled it up next to Jason.

Robin listened quietly. But she had no idea what was going on, or what the teacher was talking about. She heard phrases like 'analyzing diversity', and 'rational argument'. She wondered what those things meant in connection with the types of classes she was familiar with from high school. She just watched Jason typing up his notes; his fingers pecking out quickly. The teacher talked a lot but so did the students, including Jason. He was a constant contributor to the conversation, but again, the topic was completely out of her realm of understanding.

Was she really expected to sit through his classes with him every day? Not to mention the fact that she was hungry. She'd only had coffee all day, which led to her next dilemma; she had to pee. And what was she supposed to do if Jason had a seizure? He would have two a day. Maybe he wouldn't do that until after her shift was over. She prayed that she could end this hellacious day without any further embarrassment. Then she intended to get her shift changed back to some little old man or lady where all she needed to do was giving them medicine and maybe make them something to eat!

No bell rang, but about twenty minutes later the teacher dismissed the class, reminding them about an upcoming writing assignment. After unplugging his laptop, she replaced his backpack behind the wheelchair. He led them out of the class and several students high fived him. He ignored her as he took a few minutes to joke with them. They looked at her curiously, if they looked at her at all, and when he was done with his friends he just moved on towards the next class, never introducing her.

She was quiet for a while as she followed, but then curiosity got the better of her.

"Jason?"

"Yep?"

"What class was that?"

"That was a humanities class." He said blandly. "Western philosophy." He looked at her. "How old are you?"

She hesitated. "Twenty-one."

"You never went to college?"

"No." She fidgeted with the sleeve of her sweatshirt. "How old are you?" She asked as an after-thought.

"Nineteen."

"Is this your first year of college?"

"Second."

"So, what's the next class?"

"Business."

"Um, Jason, I need to use the restroom."

He didn't respond for a moment and she was just about to repeat herself when he finally spoke. "You're going to make me late for class. You should have said something earlier."

Yeah and he should have introduced her, and he should accept the fact that she did have biological needs. "I'll be quick, I promise." She craned her head searching for the facilities.

"Follow me."

They rounded a corner and she saw the female facilities and hurried to it. "Be right back!" She yelled over her shoulder.

She didn't dally and when she returned he was listening to his headset again, bobbing his head to the beat of some unheard song. When he saw her, he began wheeling down the hall, forcing her to hurry in order to catch up.

The business class was incredibly boring, but at least there were several good looking guys that she could peek at since he wasn't positioned at the head of the class. After that, they could finally stop for lunch. Her stomach was a big empty hole.

The cafeteria had a smoking and non-smoking area, and then further there was an upper and a lower level. It was huge. He went right to the hot food line while she tried to take in everything to decide what she wanted to eat. She caught up with him. Man was he good at ignoring her. She reached for a tray and he looked at her.

"Are you going to eat?"

"I was planning to, why? Am I not allowed because I'm on your time?" She replied sarcastically.

"I don't use a tray, too hard to maneuver a wheelchair if I'm carrying one."

"Oh," she said sheepishly.

"But since you're carrying one then just put my things on it, too." He pointed out things that he wanted; ham sandwich, potato chips, pudding, and a fountain coke. She got a cheeseburger and fries and a fountain drink as well.

She was sliding the tray down the aisle and reaching into her purse. "I got it." He pulled out a wallet and then withdrew a card with the UC logo on it. She thanked him; surprised at the kindness.

"What's up, Top?" A girl with punk hair was working the cash register. "Got any new mixes?" She asked while ringing up their order.

"I'm working on something."

"Ooo," she scanned his card. "What is it?"

"And you know I don't tell anyone what I'm working on-"

The girl looked at Robin. "You can tell me, I won't blab." The request was directed at her and not him. Robin gave her a confused look.

Jason just chuckled and rolled away, leaving her to follow behind with the tray. What in the hell were they talking about? Top? She'd called him Top. Was that his nickname?

He wheeled up to a table with other students and Robin's step faltered. Normally at lunch she would find a corner where she could be alone and read a book. Being around crowds had always caused her to clam up. She ignored the knot forming in her stomach and followed her client. She saw another student in a wheelchair but he didn't seem to have any problems controlling his muscles the way Jason did. He was joking and talking loudly without any slurring.

"Hey, Top."

"What's up, Link." They slapped hands.

"You got one hundred thousand-eight hits on the *More Love* mix!" A guy with hair as long as Jason's spoke.

"I saw that this morning!" Jason said in excitement. "Dude I'm hyped!" He looked at Robin and his eyes were bright and happy. "Put the tray down and pull up a chair."

She placed his food in front of him and no one paid much attention to her. She just wanted to stay out of the way. They were young, animated white kids that didn't even look at her. She ate her burger quietly and tried to pay only enough attention to Jason so that she could be sure that he wasn't choking.

There were a total of eight people present. Link was in a wheelchair. She didn't know the name of the other guy, the one with the long hair. Then there were two girls; one had the same disorder that Jason had, but she wasn't in a wheelchair. She didn't have an aide either. The other girl was very butch and it was hard to tell that she was even female. The other students left one by one; their vacant chairs filled with different butts. However the three original people seemed a bit closer to Jason; almost like they were in a club.

They talked music and beats and mixes and not much of anything else. They surprised her by bringing up names like J Dilla and Common. Obviously, they were heavy into hiphop. He looked at her for the second time in twenty minutes. "Ready?"

She nodded and gathered up their trash, dumping it in the bin. He then led her out of the cafeteria. "Robin, it's time for the bathroom."

"Ok."

When they reached the facilities her mind was already in a blank place. Would she need to go into the men's room with him? "Just stay out here," he said. "If I need you, I'll call you."

"Ok."

"I'll be a while. I'm not super-fast when it comes to cleaning myself, but I can do it." He seemed to be waiting for a response so she nodded, not offering to help if he didn't ask for it.

"Ok."

He snorted and then rolled into the restroom. He was right. It took forever; almost as long as lunch had. She checked the time. It was almost one p.m. and she was really tired.

When he returned he took in her slouched posture. "What's wrong, college doesn't agree with you?"

That comment had hit so close to home that she was momentarily speechless. Then her green eyes flinched and she looked at him coldly. "I'm fine. What's next?"

He didn't say anything immediately. "One last class; computer science." This time he had his own table, as did everyone else. His was empty while others had computers. She set up his laptop quickly and then sat down in the chair next to him.

He put on headphones, but so did others. She watched him pull up YouTube and navigate to an account; the name of which she was unable to catch. His head began to bob as he began moving around the screen. Everyone was quietly working and the teacher hadn't even told them to do anything. She couldn't hear anything since she didn't have headphones, but at least she could tell that he was building a web page. He was pulling images and music from other sites, moving confidently around the web.

Robin didn't have much interest in it and she began to zone out again. Soon her eyes closed without her realizing. She was in a place that was next to sleep and probably would have been in the middle of snores, but for the constant and irritating tapping sound that woke her up from her dazed state. Her head popped up and she looked over at Jason to see if he'd caught her napping.

Jason's eyes were rolled to the top of his head. His body was taut and stretched. It was his hand that was drumming rhythmically against the table, creating the low tapping sound. Robin jumped up in alarm and everyone in the room looked at her. For a second she was near to panic. For a moment she forgot everything she knew. She wanted to call for help, except that she was the person that was supposed to be helping him.

His head was thrown back and his Adam's apple bobbed as the tendons in his neck stood out. He was making a low guttural sound and she placed one hand on his chest and rubbed him there lightly. The other was placed against the side of his face. Her heart still hammered in her chest and she glanced up at the class instructor who quickly averted her eyes. Why wasn't she doing something?!

Robin continued to rub Jason's chest. "It's okay. I'm here, Jason. Everything is ok; you're ok." She continued to murmur reassurances and after what seemed like forever, his body suddenly relaxed. He hadn't opened his eyes yet, but he was taking in deep breaths. Her body relaxed some, as well, but she could not completely relax until he opened those mean green eyes and stared at her with his usual coldness.

Oh my God, he wasn't moving. Was he unconscious? She was about to panic again when his eyes opened and stared at her. It took him a moment to focus and he blinked repeatedly. He had lashes longer than any man should be comfortable with. Of all the thoughts that she could have, that one was surprisingly at the top of the list. She moved back, realizing that she was in his personal space. Then she realized that she was still rubbing his chest and cradling his face and she quickly moved her hands from his body. No wonder he was staring at her.

And his muscles weren't jerking. He was just staring at her calmly.

"Are you okay?" She whispered.

He smiled slightly. "You look like you've seen a ghost. You're as pale as a sheet. Bet you haven't heard that before."

She chuckled softly. He was very strange. But at least she felt better. "You didn't answer my question."

"I bit my tongue; pretty bad this time, but at least I didn't fall out of the chair and break my nose."

Her eye grew large. "Are you serious?"

As if in response to her disbelief a bit of blood appeared at the corner of his mouth. She quickly reached into her purse for tissue.

"Let me see your tongue," she demanded.

Jason slowly opened his mouth. It was a bad bite; blood was coming up out of the torn flesh.

"Put this in your mouth and hold it against the bite." Again he did as instructed. Then his head began to bob slightly and his fingers began clicking against the keyboard of this laptop. She gave him an amazed look. Still wearing his headphones, he was bobbing his head to the beat of the music streaming from his webpage and making adjustments while her heart was still beating a mile a minute.

CHAPTER 8

Jason watched the numbers on his recent mix. It had broken the elusive one hundred thousand views mark on YouTube and the feedback was awesome — not considering the few jerks that made stupid comments about his use of hip hop beats. He went through the comments, checking to see if any needed to be removed. He didn't have a problem if people just didn't like what he put together, but things like dropping the N-bomb because his influences were mostly black artists or petty arguments just got deleted.

He didn't even bother removing the negative comments about him being crippled or using a wheelchair. He didn't have to bother; people that followed Wheels of Steel always fought those battles for him. The beats spoke for themselves. There were haters that couldn't understand how he chopped an Amen beat and put it back together mixed with James Brown or Curtis Mayfield and said that he was ripping off Madlibs or Dilla. But then his listeners would jump down their throats schooling them that reforming the familiar drum beat known as the Amen break had been done for over a decade over in the UK and to stop talking about shit they didn't know about.

Wheels of Steel was not just Jason, nicknamed Top—for his carrot-top hair. The group's name was representative of the four friends; their logo was an upside down wheelchair over a turntable. The group's name was a play on both; their ability to mix music and the fact that they embraced their perceived disabilities. However, the nicknames were a different matter. Jason hated the reference to his red hair, as well as any connection to the stand-up comedian. But really no one in the group loved their nickname. Each of the four members had a pseudonym given to them by the other members.

There was Peter—better known as Link. He was also in a wheelchair, though not because of CP but because of an unfortunate drinking and driving accident that had left his legs useless. Link was a beast as a human beat box as well as a damn good singer and he could play just about any instrument, therefore he was considered the missing link. Next was Belinda nicknamed Patty—as in Peppermint Patty; for the girl from the Charlie Brown cartoons that had the questionable sexual orientation. Patty and Amberly both put together the music videos; editing them in a sharp, funky way that showed an artistic quality that enhanced the music. In other words; the music was made better by watching it with the video. And as far as Amberly's nickname; no one dared to call the sweet, overly protected girl by the name that had been given to her; Tramp Stamp. It was almost audacious to call her something like that, considering that the reason she had gotten the name was because she hadn't even known what one was. Amberly had cerebral palsy, as well, and as is common of parents with children inflicted with the disorder, Amberly had led a very sheltered life.

Jason concentrated on responding to the YouTube questions and comments. Someone asked; 'I always thought to "flip" a sample meant to take one measure of a piece of music and just replay it backwards. More LOVE seemed that way to me. Is that what you did?'

'No,' he wrote. 'If you use your computer, find a slicing program that can slice up parts of a long sample -not necessarily a loop, and each key on a keyboard or piano roll (if you're using software) is a different part of the song. You can double certain parts up, rearrange parts that you think go together, reverse certain parts, and raise the pitch to certain parts. What I'm talking about is what the old pros did like Afrika Bambaataa or Pete Rock.'

He spent a while longer responding to comments, and then anxious to get back to the beat that he was currently working on, he pulled up his slicing program and pressed playback. Momentarily, he felt a dull pain on his tongue where he'd bitten it earlier. This was the song he'd been working on when he had the seizure and it caused him to be transported back to that moment.

He pictured the girl; the new aide – or 'possible' new aide. He didn't think she'd stick around for long. He didn't care one way or the other, except he kept picturing her eyes. He thought she had the strangest grey/green eyes that he'd ever seen on a black girl – or any girl, for that matter. He couldn't stop seeing the look on her face when he opened his eyes after the seizure. Her hand rested on his chest, the other cradled his face. And she actually looked like she cared. Really, she looked scared to death. But beyond that was a concern that he wasn't accustomed to. Good aides cared but they stood aside and let him go about the seizure as if waiting for a small kid to finish using the potty chair. They were a witness and a presence in case something went wrong, but he always knew that there was a distance between him and them.

The new girl was different. He knew instantly when he opened his eyes that she was right there with him in the moment. The phone rang then and he almost jumped. He turned down the volume on the repetitive beat and pressed the speaker phone mic. Before he could even get out a hello, Link was already talking.

"Dude, I want you to listen to this! We might have a hook for the new one!" He heard his Skype begin to ring and knew it was Link, so he pressed disconnect on the phone and picked up the Skype. Link came through on video cam and Jason pressed his cam feed as well, then he hit record. All without ever saying a word, he was already beginning the process of capturing Link's newest beats. He worked with a FL Studio as well and immediately he heard a snare roll and then a hip hop drumbeat. Next was Link's adlibs.

Jason's head began to bob to the beat. He closed his eyes and when it was over he wore a big grin.

"That was tight!"

"I know! Can you use any of it?"

"Hell yeah." He began to do some rewinding and playback. It wouldn't be crisp but Link would know what he wanted. Then he played about six seconds of Link's recording. Link listened and then his fingers moved deftly over his keyboard. Soon the small bit that he wanted began to play back.

"Yeah, that's it!" Jason exclaimed. "Send me about six seconds."

"I'll email it to you."

"Cool. I'm going to try to work on it tonight."

"Give it a break Top."

"A break?"

"Not the music; yourself. You need to take a break."

Jason chuckled. "Flipping beats *is* my break." But yeah, he could stand getting away from the computer for a while. "What do you have in mind?" He wouldn't mind catching a movie or even having something more substantial for dinner than a nutritional shake. Anything more than that caused a choking hazard which he couldn't risk while living alone.

"There's a party at the Omicron house and they want me to DJ. It's later tonight-"

"Frat party...dude, you know I can't drink." Alcohol wreaked havoc on his kidney function.

"No shit." Link said stiffly. "And I'm not going there to drink either." He was very touchy on the subject of drinking and driving. Link still enjoyed drinking despite the fact that it had led to his paralysis as well as the death of many of his good friends. Because of this he never went out drinking unless there was a designated driver.

Jason felt bad for his thoughtless comment and wanted to kick himself. That, more than anything else, is what caused him to agree to go along, even though he didn't care for frat parties. He wasn't big into parties; *period*. Wheelchairs made it tough to maneuver around and you never knew what to expect inside of someone's house. Nine times out of ten, it wasn't wheelchair friendly.

But he'd been to the Omicron house often enough. And besides, he enjoyed listening to Link put together beats. He could use the turntables to scratch whereas Jason's cerebral palsy did not allow him full muscle control in which to manipulate them. The cerebral palsy also prevented him from playing the musical instruments that he loved so much. His muscles had a mind of their own and when he tried his hardest to control them is when they betrayed him the most. The most that he could do was to tap out a simple rhythm on a piano keyboard.

Jason didn't much mind having CP. When it's all you know, then there is no other life for you. Unlike Amberly, his mother had pushed him to be like others and therefore he didn't see limitations just obstacles. The biggest obstacle was other people. Jason remembered something that Yoko Ono had once said about why she never smiled. She said that everyone expects you to be that smiling Japanese caricature that nods and bows; so she swore to be the opposite. And that is what Jason decided. Everyone expects a person with muscles that jerk and lurch any which way and a tongue that moves two seconds behind the rest of his mouth to be happy and thankful for their careful attention and pats on the head. But he was quick to tell them, 'I am not fucking retarded!'

After his phone call, he shut down his equipment, his mind still preoccupied with the new beat Link had sent and the things he wanted to do with it. Soon he was outside in the parking lot, waiting for his friend. Link drove up in a minivan that had been custom painted with flames and a burning skull. Jason just shook his head. Link was so dramatic. The van had been outfitted with hand controls so that an individual with no use of his legs could drive it. Link had actually taught Jason to drive it—not that he could ever get a license, not with the seizures. He watched Link pull up alongside of him.

"You need me to get out?" Link called after rolling down the passenger window. Translation: 'Do you need help getting in?'

He gave him the finger and then made a rolling motion with his hands. "Roll it down, son," he replied. Translation: 'No.'

The mechanical door slid open and a lift suddenly appeared. When it was in position, Jason expertly rolled his chair into place and then reached down to secure it. "I'm in," he said. The lift rose and slowly slid into position directly behind the passenger seat.

He put on his seat belt and was in position. Next to him was Link's titanium racing bike. Link didn't behave like a man who was paralyzed. He was on a basketball team, he drove, and dated, DJ'd, and did anything else that a person with full use of his legs could do. Despite the fact that he was in a wheelchair, Link was outgoing and popular. The two had become friends during a time before he had accepted his condition; back when he wished the accident that had taken away the use of his legs had taken his life instead.

Music was blaring from the speakers and Jason thought with amusement, 'Yes, we are those white kids that drive down the street blasting rap music.'

"Who's that, Mos Def?" He asked, digging the mash-up as his head bobbed to the beat.

"And DJ Krush." They pulled out of the parking space. "I made up some mixes to get me in the mood." They listened to music and talked beats.

"Where are the girls? You invite them?"

"Nah. This ain't Wheels of Steel. This is all about me, son."

Jason gave him a curious look. "You're not playing any of our stuff?"

"No, I got some good shit I want to try out."

"Cool." They were a loosely organized group. They sold mix tapes and made decent money on it, nothing to get rich over. But now that everyone had heard the *More Love* mix, they were more popular than ever. Yet Wheels of Steel wasn't just Jason and Link just because they were the two that made the actual music. It was an equal endeavor between the four of them, as the videos certainly added to the entire effect.

It would make Jason feel very odd if Link played any of their music and Amberly and Patty weren't around.

Link pulled the van up to the curb and blew his horn while Jason undid his seatbelt. The side door opened and the lift gently maneuvered him down to the ground. After a moment Link moved out of his seat and using nothing more than his upper body strength, he maneuvered himself into his wheelchair behind the driver's seat. Then the side door opened and he was maneuvered out of the van with the use of a second lift.

Two guys hurried out of the frat house. The party could be heard clearly from the street. Several other people spilled out of the large house holding plastic cups of liquor, including two very drunk women.

"Link!" One of the girls screeched. Jason didn't particularly care for drunken girls. They were either curious or cruel. He speculated that there was something about a man in a wheelchair that made drunken women curious about the function of his penis. He'd gotten felt up more times that way, but they always stopped short of allowing him to actually do them. Therefore he'd had lots of sexual contact, but was still a virgin.

He pressed the button to send the lift back up and then he slammed the door shut. The two guys were already at the back of the van unloading the equipment while Link supervised and 'greeted' the drunken woman.

While Link's lips made their acquaintance with the pretty blonde, the pretty brunette pointed at Jason.

"Top? You gotta be Top with that red hair!" She came over and quickly hugged Jason, stumbling and spilling some of the beer on him. He jumped as the cold fluid slushed down the back of his neck.

"I'm sorry. I'm sorry! I'm so sorry!" She exclaimed and then laughed. For some reason she began trying to sit on Jason's lap and he grimaced when he realized that she wanted a ride on his chair.

His back stiffened and he quickly wheeled away from her and up the ramp to the house. Link was following behind him. The blonde was in his lap; ah so that's where she had gotten the idea. But how he managed to wheel the both of them with his tongue half buried down her throat was beyond him. The drunken brunette positioned herself to sit on his lap too, and the blonde made room for her friend.

Once inside Jason saw that, just as he had feared, the house was crowded with drunken bodies and because of this, not very wheelchair friendly. He followed the 'roadie crew' into a large dining room that was empty of the big dining table and chairs. A staging area had been set up; just two long tables pushed together and the crates of music and equipment were placed carefully there. Not many people had gathered in this particular room as all of the booze and food was elsewhere, so Jason didn't fear running over drunken people's toes.

"I want a ride!" Another girl cried out when she saw that Link had set himself up as an impromptu shuttle. She ran over to Jason, who stopped her with a withering look. Most might not always be able to understand his words but the look he gave held no mystery. The girl pouted but wisely chose to turn her attentions elsewhere.

With nothing better to do, he wheeled behind the table and began hooking up the equipment. Link joined him after a few minutes, sans his entourage. Suddenly several people began chanting 'Wheels of Steel!' Jason and Link exchanged looks. He was grinning, Jason wasn't. This wasn't Wheels of Steel. He quickly moved back away from the stage area and Link began spinning a few practice beats. People began crowding into the room chanting, 'WHEELS OF STEEL! WHEELS OF STEEL!' Jason was amazed as he looked around.

He knew how to mix beats but that didn't mean that he had ever gone out in public to DJ. His gauge to popularity was YouTube and the few people that approached him at school as Top. So what was happening tonight at Omicron house was on a totally new level.

Link began playing a drumbeat that Jason knew was James Brown's *Funky Drummer* but chopped and screwed. And once he had people moving to the beat he threw in some rhythm. He kept building on it until he finally moved to the turntable and began mixing in a techno record.

Jason's eyes were glued to his friend's fingers as they deftly moved along the vinyl. He had taught Link to do this and he was a proud papa, despite the fact that Link was the older of the two. But still; watching his friend's hands move in a way that his never would made him feel cheated. For the most part he accepted his CP. It was just times like this, when his mind could do what his body would not allow, that he felt like a prisoner within himself.

They were going crazy as more and more people tried to squeeze into the room. Even he was dancing in his seat; head thrashing as his unruly red hair fell across his face. He saw a girl watching him. She was holding a cup and seemed more interested in him than in the music. When he met her eyes she quickly looked away. He continued with his head bangers dance and then felt something move his chair forward an inch. He looked behind him and saw a guy and a girl talking. The guy was leaning against the back of his chair as he tried talking his way into the girl's pants.

Jason tried not to become annoyed by it. People didn't always understand that leaning against his wheelchair was like leaning against him. The wheelchair was an extension of him. He fought to ignore it but soon both the guy and the girl were leaning against it. Jason would have wheeled forward but there was absolutely no place to go since the crowd had thickened. So Jason decided to just roll backward.

"Fuck! Dude, watch it!" The guy yelped when his foot was crushed beneath the wheels of the chair. But he and the girl backed up. Jason smiled to himself and from the corner of his eyes he saw the pretty girl watching him with open curiosity and a hint of a smile on her lips. He continued to dance and wondered if she was drunk enough to approach him.

Link went nonstop for an hour and then he let a techno song play out as he wheeled back onto the floor. People crowded around him; high fiving him and telling him how good he sounded. The two friends were finally able to slap hands.

"Top!" He yelled over the noise of the crowd and music. "I want you up there man! You need to play one of your mixes." Jason didn't know what to say. He'd never DJ'd at a house party before. And besides, he wasn't sure if he wanted to do that. It was too close to what he'd thought earlier; Wheels of Steel performing without Amberly and Patty. Somehow it didn't seem right.

But the contagious music and watching his friend doing something that he himself loved became overwhelming. Jason wheeled behind the table where the equipment was set up and studied the crates containing albums. Link had picked some good ones.

And he suddenly knew what he wanted to do. He hadn't even shown it to Link yet, so it wasn't Wheels of Steel, just his own creation. He grabbed Portishead's *Only You* vinyl and set it up on the deck. Then he put on headphones and made a flip, just cutting a portion out of the song using the mixer. No one could hear what he was doing but with the flip he could scratch on the FL mixer instead of using the turntables.

When Link's song ended, Portishead began. The familiar sultry yet hip beat caused the partygoers to change tempos. And then Jason used the controls on the mixer to scratch a beat that complimented the song. Now that he was doing something that he loved, he almost forgot the crowd. It wasn't until they began applauding at each of his scratches that he remembered that he was doing this for them. He continued; slowing down, speeding up, and moving backwards until it was like he was doing acrobats on the system.

Before he knew it, Link had joined him. He placed a record on the second turntable and an ambient/electronic beat could be heard. Jason continued doing his thing with Portishead and Link began mixing in his electronic beat while the crowd chanted 'WHEELS OF STEEL!' over and over. It was so perfect that Jason felt himself becoming the music. It sometimes happened when everything came together just perfectly. His body knew what to do, his ears counted the beats, and his fingers found the right breaks, his mind soared ahead to put everything in its proper order. And Link was right along with him, bobbing his head and spinning, and looping and mixing.

They played together for nearly an hour and then he felt the familiar pull of his limbs and then the light-headedness that told him that he was going to have a seizure.

'*Oh fuck, oh fuck, oh fuck*', he thought. Carefully, he backed away from the table and gave Link a warning look. Link's brow rose in a question, then he got it when Jason's eyes began blinking rapidly. He knew what was up and he kept one eye on the younger man and one eye on the records that he was spinning.

A seizure was not something that he relished having in front of fifty people and yet he had them so often that he had no choice but to accept the inevitable whether he liked it or not; he was going to have a seizure with all eyes on him.

Jason allowed his head to fall back and he gripped the wheels of his chair. *'Don't fight it'*, he said to himself. It would be less violent if he just rode along with it. He knew Link was watching him in case he fell forward, but hopefully that wouldn't happen this time. He'd had a seizure in the van once and had slammed his head onto the dashboard before he'd gotten himself buckled in. His nose had bled profusely from a gash. He thought he'd broken it, but it was just cut up pretty good. If he fell forward, he would destroy Link's Fruity Loops Studio.

His heart suddenly began to race and Jason's muscles quickly seized. His hands gripped the wheels and his legs thrust outward. His head strained back and he looked like a man that was receiving an electrical shock. His body stretched outward, as if searching for a way to extend itself beyond its packaging of skin and bones.

Every muscle in his body was taut, including his penis. He froze there for a moment, all stretched lines and tight muscles; just as suddenly as it began, his body collapsed, relaxing back in the chair. Next came the muscles jerks; the tapping of his feet, his fingers. Sometimes he kicked or thrashed but if he allowed the seizure to work its way out of him then that did not always happen. Soon his body quieted. Link's music continued and the crowd's appreciation for it continued as well as Jason lay semi-conscious in his chair. When his green eyes opened once again, he found that he wore a broad smile on his face and was chuckling.

That was something that happened at times; he would regain consciousness to find himself chuckling. He'd never heard of anyone else doing that and he'd looked it up on the internet. Maybe self-consciously he realized the ridiculousness of how he must look to everyone around him. Or perhaps he was just amused by it all. Whatever the case, when he sat there in his chair chuckling to himself, still half sprawled he heard a girl yell.

"You big faker! You were faking all this time!" And then all of the drunken people in the room got it in their heads that his seizure had been a part of the show. They began applauding him. He sat up, glancing at Link who shook his head wearing a shit-eating grin on his own face.

"Nice." He mouthed.

"'least I didn't kick over your equipment." His muscles were quiet now. He reached up and pushed his hair behind his ears. Even his voice was barely slurred. His tongue seemed to have caught up with the commands he gave his mouth.

"If you had, it would have been *your* equipment." Link quickly lowered the volume and began yelling into the mike. "WHEELS OF STEEL, everybody! I'm

Link, that's Top and then we have Tramp-stamp and Peppermint Patty on post-production. Thank you!"

Jason had barely wheeled himself from behind the table before the crowd converged on him now, slapping his back and telling him how much they liked the music.

"Man, you guys are sick! You ought to be mixing for real groups!"

"Thanks, man. That's the plan." He responded, amazed that people had so thoroughly disregarded the seizure. Did they really think he'd faked it?

He felt gentle hands on his shoulder and looked up. It was the watcher. She smiled at him. "Can you do other things as well as you can DJ?"

He grinned and then nodded.

CHAPTER 9

After returning Jason to his home, Robin couldn't get into her car fast enough and drive away from the bad experience. She was still so upset about the seizure that she was actually trembling. She didn't know why it bothered her so much, but she couldn't stop thinking about it. She couldn't do this. She just couldn't. Robin drove straight to Pinnacle even though she was dog-tired and needed a nap before work. The receptionist greeted her.

"Is Ben in?"

"Ben won't be in for several more hours, but Aaron is here." Aaron was the other manager.

"Well, I need to speak to him. Will you tell him that Robin Mathena is here?"

"Oh Robin, I made an appointment for you to take a course in seizure emergencies. I know you work two jobs, so I set it up for Saturday afternoon."

She grimaced. Saturday was the only day she had for herself; which didn't necessarily mean relaxing. It was the only day she had to clean her apartment, shop, and run errands as well as anything else that needed taking care of. Even Sunday was partially her mother's day because of church and their lunch date.

She was shaking her head at the woman and anxiously rubbing her hair where it was still confined into its tight ponytail. "I just need to talk to the manager." The woman, who Robin presumed was the same woman that Jason had spoken to earlier, got up and knocked on the office door before letting herself in. She was in there for a few moments, probably explaining that the jig was up and they'd have to find a new patsy.

"Come on in Robin." The woman ushered her into the office. A man in his fifties with dyed black hair and goatee so stark that he looked like the devil quickly rose from his chair and offered his hand. She noticed right away that he had a spray on tan from a can from the way that orange pigment gathered around his fingernails. She averted her eyes in embarrassment for him.

"Hello Robin. I'm Aaron Seiberling. We haven't met yet. Have a seat, please." He was polite in a rushed manner—the same way that Ben had been. She guessed hustlers had to be fast talkers.

"Mr. Seiberling-"

"Call me Aaron."

"Aaron, this job I'm on is not going to work for me." His eyes got momentarily big. She figured that would probably be the most honest expression she'd get from the man. He plastered on a concerned look.

"Ok, is there something that I can do?"

"Honestly, I'm not prepared to care for someone like him."

"Ok." He plastered on a concerned yet confused look. "What do you mean?"

"He has seizures; he needs me to stay with him while he's at school," she wanted to say that he was rude and crude and that she just didn't want to work with him, instead she took another tactic. "Besides, I've been working two jobs for several months. I think I'll take a break while Miss Lucille is in the hospital and then start back again."

Aaron began digging through some papers on his desk. "Miss Lucille Babbs..." he was reading something. "...won't be a client of Pinnacle any longer."

Robin felt her chest constrict. "What? Why? I-is she okay?"

"Her son is moving her to a nursing home when she's released." Her mouth stayed ajar. "Robin, we don't want to lose you at Pinnacle. You're a great asset, always on time, no complaints from the clients. The thing is, there's no other job that I can give you right now. If you're not working with Mr. Hamilton then we actually don't need you right now. If you can hang in there with your current client for a while longer, I can offer you the next job. How does that sound?"

Robin couldn't find words to respond. She wasn't ready to stop being with Miss Lucille.

Working with the older woman had become so much of her daily routine that the prospect of never enjoying her company again saddened her. Robin knew that the few extras that she did for the woman had made her dreary existence livable. The evidence was in her perky greeting each morning and their long conversations that now took the place of her pre-taped evangelist shows.

"Robin?" She dragged her eyes back to the dyed and tanned man before her.

"I—yes. Yes, of course I'll continue working with Mr. Hamilton."

Aaron rose again and offered her his hand. "I'm happy that we can keep you aboard. If you need anything just contact me or Ben. And don't forget your course in seizure management this Saturday from three to six. You'll have to pay the registration fee, but we'll refund it."

"What? How much is it?"

"Mary Louise will give you all of the information at the front desk." He gestured to the door with a friendly but rushed smile. She had been dismissed. She headed out the door and Mary Louise gave her an over-bright smile.

"So I wrote down the information about the class. It's this Saturday at three o'clock. It's downtown, on Broadway, room 525." She handed her a slip of paper.

"Aaron mentioned something about a registration fee?"

"Oh yes! It is one hundred twenty dollars, which Pinnacle will fully refund. We just need you to provide-"

Robin's eyes closed and when they opened they were narrowed in the direction of the receptionist. There was such a thing as going too far, and Pinnacle had just achieved it. "Mary Louise, you'll need to write a check for the one hundred twenty dollars right now." Mary Louise gave her a surprised look.

"Well, we can't do that. We have to go through appropriations for something like that. And we had to get this appointment out before that could happen and so, what I'm saying is that the cost for the class is not really approved yet."

Frustrated, tired and finally at her wits end with Pinnacle, Robin did something that was long overdue; she blew up.

"You expect me to literally pull one hundred twenty dollars out of my own pocket for a class that's going to be held in two days? Pinnacle presumes a lot; what if I don't have that money?! What if I had plans for Saturday?! And truthfully, that the funding for the class hasn't been approved yet doesn't make me feel at all comfortable. Let me just say it like this; if you want me to take the class then you will need to pay the full amount up front!"

Mary Louise just stared at her. Robin's brow went up. She turned and headed for the door considering the woman's lack of a response as an answer.

"Wait! I just need to talk to Aaron."

"No." She continued walking. "Not waiting."

"Okay, wait! I'll write you a check." Robin stopped, even more annoyed than before. Mary Louise knew that she could do this all along—freaking liars. She returned to the desk where the older woman pulled out one of the big check notebooks that she'd seen Ben using.

"I suppose that we can pull the amount from something else until it's approved." Mary Louise said, mostly for the benefit of Robin. Yet Robin knew that the money was just sitting there and they would have tried to find a way not to reimburse her. She had their number.

"Mary Louise, that check you're writing; if it's not for the full amount of the course and I have to come up with any out of pocket costs, then I'm walking away." Mary Louise looked at her. "There may be an additional fifty dollars to cover some state fees. I'll just make it out for one seventy-five, just in case."

Robin just stared at her without expression. Mary Louise handed her the check and Robin took a few moments to look it over. All of the I's were dotted and the T's crossed. "Thank you." She said and then left the office.

Once she left Pinnacle, instead of going home to nap as she needed to do, Robin drove over to University Hospital. She considered picking up a small bouquet of flowers but stopped at the snack bar and got a huge cinnamon roll instead. She had come to realize that the older woman had an affinity towards sweet treats and while she didn't want to give the woman a sugar rush, she enjoyed bringing her treats. Sometimes it was ambrosia salad, or yogurt parfait cups, sometimes muffins. But Miss Lucille always received them enthusiastically, praising her son for his thoughtfulness.

The elderly woman was awake and watching the television. When Robin stepped through the door, she gave her a big smile. "Robin!" She greeted her happily, though her voice was weak and she seemed short of breath. She still had an oxygen tube to her nose and monitors connected to her through lines that ran beneath her oversized hospital gown.

Robin momentarily froze at the entrance as déjà vu struck her. It was just like daddy. She plastered a smile on her face and quickly moved forward, taking the older woman's hand and squeezing it gently.

"Have a seat dear. You just missed my son and his children. They were here all morning. I really wanted you to meet him, but maybe next time." Robin wondered if their visit had just been a figment of the older woman's imagination — or maybe wishful thinking. She hoped that she wasn't wrong, and hoped that they had actually come to visit her. But she didn't believe they had.

"How are you feeling, Miss Lucille? You look good."

"Oh, I feel better. My own doctor gave me medicine to open up my lungs." She nodded her head. "I can breathe a little better now."

"That's good. Is there something I can do for you while I'm here?"

Miss Lucille was just happy to have someone to talk to and the two sat and chatted for a while, splitting the large cinnamon roll, nibbling from it as they talked. A man suddenly appeared at the door, pausing to look at Robin in surprise.

"Hello. Are you a nurse?" He was a rather nice looking man that appeared to be his late forties; tall and fit and dressed casually in jeans and a button down shirt.

"Oh, Bentley!" Miss Lucille held out her hand for the man. "Robin, this is my son Bentley. He's a doctor. Bentley this is my caregiver from Pinnacle, Robin."

Bentley came forward and took his mother's hands and then leaned forward and kissed her wrinkled cheek. He shook Robin's hand next, a slight frown creasing his brow. "You're from Pinnacle?"

"Yes."

"Well, I told them yesterday that we're not going to need them anymore."

"Oh, I'm not here on their behalf. I just came to visit your Mom."

Miss Lucille's eyes brightened. "I told you Robin is a good girl."

"Oh, Robin." His expression relaxed. "My mom talks about you all the time. Somehow I thought you'd have angel wings the way she goes on about you." Robin blushed and glanced at the elderly woman who was looking at the two of them as if they were the sun, moon and stars.

She stood. "Well, I'll get going and let you two spend time together."

"Don't rush off, I can't stay." He said quickly confirming her earlier belief that he and his children had not spent the morning with her. He turned to his mother whose happy smile vanished. "Mom, I just came by to let you know that your new home is all set for you. We had some of your personal items from the house brought over to make it comfortable."

Miss Lucille gripped her blankets and suddenly seemed flustered. "Oh, but I don't want to move, Bentley, I thought you said I could stay in the house."

"No Mom, that was before the hospital stay. I said that if you got ill we'd have to get you into a place where there are people who can take care of you."

She gave him a confused look. "Well, my house is a place where people can take care of me."

Bentley gave Robin an apologetic smile and Robin glanced at the door wishing for a polite way to make a getaway. Bentley took a deep breath and began again, as if he was talking to a toddler and had explained the same thing a million times.

"Mom, the place where you're moving will be very nice. There will be people that will prepare your meals, give you medicine, help you bathe and get to the toilet. They'll keep everything clean and neat for you. It won't be like those places you described, I promise. You'll have a bedroom, a living room and a kitchenette. It's really one of the nicer places."

"But it's not my own home," she said in a soft voice.

Robin felt nauseous. She didn't want to be here to witness this very personal conversation. "I'm sorry I need to go." She turned to Miss Lucille, a woman that she'd known for only a short time, but a person that she'd grown to care about. "When you get settled in, I'll visit you.

She gave her a hopeful look. "You will?"

"I will." She gave Bentley a pointed look and his eyes flitted away from hers. She was suddenly taking the old woman's hands in hers, and bending low enough to stare straight into her eyes. "You'll meet people there like the ladies from your bridge group. Maybe you can even start a new one. And maybe...maybe you can help keep some of them company — the ones who aren't as lucky as you are to receive visitors. Wouldn't that be nice to help keep people that are sad and lonely company? And I bet they will have good food, not just boiled eggs in the morning and a frozen meal at dinner." She didn't need to glance at Bentley to see that his back had stiffened.

"What's the name of the facility?" She directed to him without looking at him.

Sputtering slightly, he eventually managed to give her the name and she turned her attention back to the elderly woman, smiling gently. "You take care of yourself." She bent and kissed her cheek. Miss Lucille's smile returned and grateful tears sprouted in her eyes.

"Thank you for the cinnamon roll, and the butter and jam and all the other things." Robin stared into the woman's clear eyes. She had known what was going on all along, but sometimes pretending helped to get through.

"My pleasure."

Robin practically staggered home. She was emotionally and physically exhausted. Seeing Miss Lucille in the hospital had dug up old memories of her father's last days. Her chest felt tight and she found it hard to catch her breath; the inevitable hopelessness of losing someone was a feeling that she did not want to relive, but it was an emotion that she just couldn't shake.

She had no time to nap, only to bathe and make a quick sandwich for dinner. For about the hundredth time, she seriously contemplated quitting one of the jobs. She worked too hard. What was supposed to be just monitoring a sleeping patient had turned into actual work. She had one more year before the car would be paid off, but if she banked enough money perhaps she could have enough to float herself, or maybe she could even pay it off early.

All she knew is that it felt good not to have to turn to her mama to help her out financially.

And that thought was enough to send her off to work, tired and yawning but at least self-supported.

CHAPTER 10

"See," Link said with a grin as he pulled up to Jason's parking lot and deposited him safely to the sidewalk. "This was much nicer then digging for breaks."

He nodded happily. "I'm not complaining." What had begun as touch and go had turned out to be a great night. He'd made some great beats with his friend and had gotten a blowjob. The 'watcher' had taken him to one of the lower level bathrooms and had given him a blowjob as he sat sprawled out in his chair. Afterwards, he'd returned the favor when she climbed up onto the counter, positioning her legs on either side of his chair.

He'd never done that before and the only thing that could have made it better is if she would have let him kiss her. He'd never kissed anyone before.

"You know, you and I can make this a regular gig. There's good money in it." Jason turned his attention back to the other man. He hadn't actually seen Link get paid, but knew that it had probably been a paying gig. Link certainly hadn't offered him a cut, not that he would have taken it. Jason shrugged.

"It was fun. I'll think on it." He responded honestly.

"You are the most talented person I know." Link said thoughtfully. "And you do this for pleasure. Think about making this work for you, Jason. Wheels of Steel, it's ok. But we should be thinking bigger."

But DJ'ing wasn't his thing. He liked being behind the scene or mixing in private. Maybe if he didn't have CP it would be different, or the seizures. But he did have them and there was a lot more to consider when you had disabilities. First was the access, second was the way people viewed him, third was the transportation of himself and the gear. For the most part people understood that just because he moved and lurched and his head flopped and jerked, didn't mean that he was mentally disabled. His slurred speech was not indicative of slow thinking.

But then there were the others; he called them the 'head patters' and 'slow talkers'. Nothing much pissed him off more than these so-called 'well meaning' people. They got in your face and talked to you like you were mentally disabled; assuming that you were incapable of understanding.

He understood that he was luckier than some even though he was in a wheelchair. Others with CP couldn't even talk. They were people that could think and reason just like any capable person, but were trapped within a body whose muscles could not be controlled; looking to the rest of the world like a person with a mental disability instead of a person imprisoned within flesh and bone.

When people tried that 'head patting', 'slow talking' with him he let them have it. He had once caused an aide to fall down a flight of stairs when he was twelve years old. Every day, after his mother left for work, she'd call him retard. And one day he'd gotten so tired of it that for the first time in his life, he cursed. And once he started he couldn't stop. He'd kept advancing on her, spewing foreign sounding profanities; spit flying and green eyes in a rage. And she'd kept moving backwards until she was lying at the bottom of the stairs. He wanted to say, 'Now who's the stupid one?' when he'd been smart enough to stop and she hadn't.

She had been one of the worst ones, but there had been other bad ones in his life time, especially when he was little, before he knew that it was okay to fight back. He used to get sat in a corner for eight hours while his mom went to work, or tied to the bed. Once, an aide had slapped him in his face because he had spit up oatmeal that she'd been shoveling down his throat. His mother had seen the handprint when she returned home from work and had beaten the woman with the first things she'd picked up; a mug that said 'World's #1 Mom'.

Mostly his caregivers listlessly moved about their tasks, barely speaking or even considering him, but not neglecting or hurting him. And there were those very rare occasions when he'd met diamonds in the rough. One was a guy that had been old enough to be his grandfather, and who called him son and told him stories and talked to him like he was a friend and not just a client. Jason didn't have a relationship with his own father, so he enjoyed having him around. But he'd only stayed around for about six months and then had gotten a better job. He'd never seen or heard from him since.

Another time he had a therapist that had been with him since he was ten years old. She was fired when Jason was sixteen after his mother discovered that she'd recently been giving him 'happy endings' at the end of the massages. It was one of the things that he'd never forgiven his mother for. It always amazed him that people who had made huge impacts on his life could just arbitrarily walk out of it with no second thoughts, when they would be forever imprinted there in his mind. Over the years he'd learned to condition himself not to care. Aides never stayed around; the good ones found better jobs and the bad ones didn't have a job for longer than it took for him or his mother to discover that they were condescending, lazy, thieves, or cruel.

Jason tiredly dragged himself to bed for the night, but instead of sleeping he thought about the way he had felt DJ'ing with Link; he thought about the taste of a woman and how nice it had all been. The next day, even before he showered or used the toilet, he hurried to the computer and checked YouTube for the numbers on *More Love*, happy to see the numbers steadily rising and that there were more comments. He read them quickly. Surprised, he saw that someone had even commented on the party the night before. He couldn't believe how quickly word had spread.

"You guys looked good, wish I was there."

He frowned, not sure what that meant. How would she know if they looked good if she wasn't there? He next checked the messages on his homepage and was shocked at what he saw. Someone had posted a video of last night's performance taken from an iPhone. Anxiously he pressed play and the recording sounded pretty good, more than pretty good. It captured the crowd's reaction and he noted that he and Link looked oddly intriguing; sitting in wheelchairs and mixing and scratching music. It was almost like a gimmick; more so when the video showed him pushing his chair back and looking at Link as if waiting for some type of cue, and then the seizure.

Jason quickly pressed pause, his breath coming out in anxious gusts. He covered his face with his palms. Sweat had formed on his brow and he felt sick. He drew in a few shaky breaths and then when he felt calm again he pressed play and watched himself seizing. It was the first time he'd ever seen himself doing that. The guy videotaping it was repeatedly saying, 'Oh shit, Oh shit.' It didn't last long, and when it was over Jason watched himself begin to chuckle. The guy had somehow zoomed in to his face and there was peacefulness there in his expression.

Jason pressed stop and sat there silently. He didn't like it; that this very private moment was there on tape for everyone to see. It was yet another thing about his life that he couldn't control. Cursing quietly he took another deep breath and then went to the bathroom to shower and to get ready for school.

Maybe if his aide got here on time he'd make it to his first class, he thought this bitterly; bitter because yet again his life was being dictated by actions that he had no control over.

Robin was tired. She had messed up orders at work and gotten yelled at by a customer. Mama had called and instead of spending her break taking a power nap, she had spent it trying to thwart the whole vacation issue. True, she and mama had been getting along better, but that didn't necessarily mean that she wanted to spend a week with her.

And then, to make matters worse, after work, instead of driving straight home and doing a nose dive into her bed, she had realized that her tank was dangerously close to the big E mark and she needed to fuel up. She yawned as she filled the tank and by the time she got home it was after midnight. She needed to be out the door no later than five thirty if she hoped to be at Jason's by six. That meant the alarm would need to be set no later than four forty-five and she could snooze for about ten minutes. That was the plan.

That left her four hours sleep.

But instead of snoozing for ten minutes, she slipped back into a deep sleep only to jump up at a quarter after five. She showered quickly, cursing at herself and swearing that there was nothing that would make her late. With no time to tame her hair, she brushed it quickly and pulled on a ball cap. She slipped on an Adidas jogging suit because it was quick, though not all that complimentary to her shape, and then she hurried out the door at twenty minutes to six.

Traffic wasn't too bad and she pulled into a parking space in front of Jason's apartment with three minutes to spare. She rang his doorbell proud of herself even though it had been touch and go for a few moments.

The door swung open and Jason wheeled around and retreated without a word.

"Good morning to you, too," she said after a brief pause.

"I'm not a morning person." He grumbled. "First thing first; I'm going to show you how to use the coffee press." She followed him into the kitchen. The dishes from yesterday were still there. Yuck.

He instructed her to fill the teapot and set it to boil. Then he showed her where the coffee was located. He explained how much to put into the bottom of the glass carafe. She hadn't had time to get her own coffee, so when he showed her where he kept the mugs she retrieved two. By that time the water was simmering in the teapot and she poured it over the grounds.

"By the time you get the cream and sugar out it will be time to press it." She smiled. Well, that hadn't been as tough as it had looked. "Now if you wouldn't mind, I like heavy cream and sugar in mine, and I'm going to the restroom." He disappeared and Robin made up their coffee. He used a tall plastic traveler's mug and she made sure to put the lid on carefully. All she needed was for him to burn himself and get mad at her.

Then, while he was still in the restroom, she did the dishes hoping that he wouldn't get pissed or expect her to do them all of the time. The thing is, she felt that if he left dishes in the sink then one day she'd walk into the kitchen and there would be roaches, and that was something that she just couldn't tolerate.

In the bathroom, Jason was in front of the mirror, struggling with the hairbrush. His hair, dampened by his morning bath, was impossibly tangled. Some days he worked the knots out, some days he didn't. It was a chore to maintain his shoulder length curls, but he wouldn't cut it. He needed his hair long in order to show his mother that he was man enough to make his own decisions. She hated his hair long and therefore he wanted it this way.

He had a brush that had a Velcro strap that went around his fist so that he wouldn't constantly drop it, but he still managed to pull out more knots then he managed to work through. Eventually Robin made her way to the bathroom when he didn't return to the kitchen and the clock was ticking. She stood in the open doorway and watched him struggle.

Fatigue took away much of her inhibitions. "Let me have that brush." He gave her a mean look but when she didn't retreat, he handed it to her and grumbled under his breath. She realized that much of his annoyance wasn't directed at anyone in particular; he was just a grumbler. She gripped a handful of damp curls and quickly brushed them smooth. When she had the ends tangle free, she gently worked the brush from scalp to end. She had his hair smooth in about five minutes.

"You did that quickly." She met his eyes in the mirror and then she quickly swept off her cap. Her tight curls sprung out from beneath it. "Ah," he said in understanding. She had hair about as unruly as his. She handed him back the brush and then quickly pulled the cap back on her head. She looked over at the toilet.

"Did you already...?"

"Yep. All taken care of." He wheeled out of the bathroom. "I'm going to eat breakfast and then you can help me shave. After that we can hit the road." He ate Cheerios again and was equally as messy. Robin sat at the table sipping her coffee and watching him with steadily drooping eyes. He read the paper and ignored her. When he coughed she sat up straight and stared at him as if she had gotten caught with her hand in the cookie jar. If he noticed he didn't mention it.

Just so that she wouldn't feel the desire to continue to doze off she told him about the class. "Mary Louise set up my seizure emergency class for this Saturday." He peeked at her over his paper.

"Yeah. She left me a message." He folded his paper neatly. "I made you a schedule of my classes. Tomorrow is Friday and I only have two so you won't have to get here until eight." She almost wanted to drop to the floor and kiss his feet. "But I have massage therapy and I'll need you to get me there and back. Still, it will be a fairly short day."

"Okay." She wondered something. "Jason, you don't have an aide for the evening, do you?"

"Currently, no."

"Well, don't you need one?"

"At dinnertime and at bedtime, yes. But most times I just have a shake or soup so I don't have to worry about choking." He wasn't a hermit, so if people came over or he went out then he could risk heavier food. Bathing still required some effort; not the actual washing himself, but getting in and out of the tub without killing himself. And it would be much more efficient if he had an aide that could help him with the bathroom, but he already knew that Robin was too green for something like that. He could do it; it just took three times as long.

"So what do you do in the evenings if you have to run an errand?"

He gave her a long look. "I don't." He sipped his coffee and saw the look on her face. It was filled with pity, which he didn't like. "My mother helps me if I need to do things like shop. She comes over every Friday for that kind of stuff. And she takes me to doctor appointments. But I had a decision; either have an evening aide or a daytime aide. Obviously it was more important for me to have a person during the day." She knew that Pinnacle didn't have enough people; gee she wondered why.

She heard a faint sound of musical beats and he reached in his pocket for a cell phone. "Link," he said. "Yeah, I already saw it." His brow gathered and he looked peeved. "It's not cool. I don't give a shit, that wasn't cool to post that-that was…" He just shook his head a grimace appeared on his face. Robin got up and washed the remaining dishes while he talked.

"Dude!" Link was saying. "No one even thought the seizure was real, didn't you see that?! The guy filming it was tripping out at how you threw that in at the end! Fuck, Top, if we start teaming up I'll throw a seizure in at the end! They all love the fact that we're in wheel chairs and our logo with the wheelchair and it's like Daft Punk with the helmets! Top, man we gotta talk about expanding our horizons. Go check out the comments on that guy's page! People want to know where they can see us play!" Jason put the phone on speaker and wheeled into the living room.

"Hold on, I'm looking." He refreshed the desktop computer and went to YouTube. After a moment he was back at the video letting it play out as he read the three messages. "Link, you ass! There's only three messages and you left one of them!"

Link was laughing. "Yeah, well."

But the other two were asking about where they'd be playing next. And one even said that they had all of Wheels of Steel mixes; which only amounted to seven, though YouTube had some practice mixes that got lots of positive feedbacks.

Robin had washed up the last few dishes and the Portishead beat caught her attention. She went out to the living room, curious, and saw Jason at the computer. Then she heard someone begin scratching with the tune and it was really good. She walked up behind him to see what he was looking at. It blew her away when she saw the familiar red tangle of curls suspended behind headphones.

She looked at Jason in awe, pointing at the big computer monitor. "That's you?" Jason looked at her quickly and then pressed stop.

"Link, I gotta head out."

"Top-' But he disconnected the phone.

"You're a DJ?" She asked in admiration. Then she really took a close look at his equipment. And that's when she finally understood what the woman in the cafeteria had been talking about. And of course Top was his stage name. God she felt dense. Jason was shutting down the computer.

"Some friends and I mix music and make videos under the name of Wheels of Steel."

"Oh, that's so cool! And you're on YouTube?"

He wheeled himself to the closet. "Yep. Look, as much as I love talking about mixing and beats, we gotta head out, it's after seven. I need you to grab my backpack and laptop."

Robin jumped to her task even as she was still curious about the new information she'd learned about this strange young man.

He rubbed his cheek. "My mom's going to shit if she sees this." She hated facial hair. He didn't much care for it either, but now he was getting pretty shaggy and even though it was his thing to be the defiant son, the beard was just damn itchy. "You'll meet my mom tomorrow. Open the door."

She opened the door. "I'm going to meet your mom?" She didn't know why she needed to do that. If his Mom was going to be around then she didn't need to be here. She kept that thought to herself though. He wheeled down the walkway and to her car. She opened the door for him and he stood up and swung his legs out until he was in position to sit down in the passenger seat. Once again she wondered why he didn't use crutches or a walker. She loaded his things into the backseat and then quickly loaded the wheelchair into the trunk. Today she did it much faster.

He was already wearing his headphones and had tuned her out. She would have asked him about his music, but he obviously wasn't interested in talking to her. She slipped a CD into the player. He wasn't the only one who enjoyed music while driving. She put in Maxwell's *Black Summer's Night*. After a while she saw Jason smirk, or at least she thought it was a smirk. Sometimes it was hard to tell when his face tensed and relaxed under a power that wasn't his own. The only things that were exceedingly clear were when he smiled or when he scowled—the latter done with more frequency.

"What?" She had thought about ignoring the look but was curious. "You don't like Maxwell?"

"It's not that. Let me just guess, you have C.D's with Erykah Badu, Trey Songz," he stared at her, "and Drake when you're walking on the wild side."

She glanced at him. "What's wrong with that?"

"I didn't say anything was wrong with it. I just had you pegged right." She listened to the same rehashed R & B and hip hop and probably thought that was all there was.

"I don't have any Drake. So there, you were wrong." Now it was her turn to scowl. "And it's no big leap to look at a black woman my age in Cincinnati and guess what kind of music I listen to. If I was in the south you would have guessed Ludacris, T.I., and Chamillionaire."

He was staring out the window when he said, "Oh I'm sorry Miss Jackson, did I forget OUTKAST? I apologize a trillion times." She cracked a smile. Well, he certainly knew his music.

He glanced at her. "So what do I listen to?"

"Everything," she said. "You're a D.J."

Jason looked at her; really looked at her for the first time.

CHAPTER 11

At school she got him out of the car and into the building quite efficiently, not giving him the opportunity to complain about anything she did. His first class was some type of math. She could tell by the equations written on the dry erase board. They were early enough that people were still filing in. Jason pointed out where he wanted the laptop set up and then he wheeled up to the professor. They talked in hushed tones. The professor seemed to be considering something and he glanced at her then he nodded his head.

He wheeled back to where he had her set up but didn't bother to explain what he and the Professor had been talking about. "I wish you would have remembered to grab my coffee," he said. Then he opened his laptop and powered up. She ignored him, wanting to say that she was an aide, not a psychic. But she wasn't interested in starting an argument. He slipped on headphones and she saw him navigate to YouTube. Damn, is that all he did, just listen to music? She liked YouTube too, but she did do other things.

He was plugged into a playlist, which he minimized and then he pulled up another page. It looked like hieroglyphs. He then opened up the book bag that she had set out for him and withdrew a calculus book. She knew it. Some type of math.

He stared at her. "Okay, Robin. I use graphing software for calculus because my handwriting is pretty bad. The program I use is MathEQ, but sometimes I need hands. So I'm going to ask you to write some things out for me-"

She sucked in a nervous breath. "Jason, I don't know anything about calculus."

"You don't need to. I'm going to show you what to write, ok?"

"Ok." She did not want to do this, but as long as all she had to do was copy what he told her then she'd do it.

"Ok, on the board is the problem. Write it on the paper. Write the word PROBLEM first and then the figures.

Oh my God. She wrote the strange figures down. He pulled up an online calculator and began putting in figures. It seemed to take him a long time of putting in figures, concentrating on what he was doing, but after a few minutes he turned to her again.

"Write the word; LIM." She did it. "Write an equal sign next to it. Now draw a horizontal line...longer. Good. Now on the top line write a number three..." And on and on he went telling her to write numbers and X's and minuses and parenthesis and then a new row of numbers and symbols and then finally the last which was the answer. "Robin, write Solution. Write my name on it and hand it to the Professor."

She got up and went to the Professor's desk. He appeared to be doing some grading. He glanced up at her and she handed him the paper. When she turned to go back to her seat he stopped her.

"Just a minute. This will only take me a moment." She waited while he placed various checkmarks on the paper. He handed it back to her with a giant C circled. Then he went back to his other problem.

She took it back to Jason who grabbed it out of her hand. He nodded his head and powered off the computer. "Come on. Let's get out of here."

"That's it?"

"That's it."

"One problem and you just walk out?"

"Well, if I know how to solve the problem I don't need him, right?" She grinned. If only high school had been like that! "I have a syllabus." He continued. "I do five problems for homework each night and then email them to him and he lectures on Mondays."

"So what do we do now?" She asked as she rolled him out of the class.

"Anything we want. I have forty-five minutes before my next class."

"Good, because I have to use the bathroom."

While they headed to the ladies room, he was greeted by several people that high fived him or asked about a CD. He finally just directed her to the restroom while he talked. She rushed off, close to being at a critical stage. When she returned, he was with another guy who was also in a wheelchair. She recognized him from lunch yesterday.

The guy looked at her and then smiled. "Hi. I see you returned. Most of them don't," he joked. Jason shook his head as if the guy was no more than a pesky child.

"This is Link. He's one of my DJ partners." Link reached out and shook her hand. He had short cropped blonde hair, blue eyes and a tan that suggested that he got out every so often. He was handsome and wore an easy smile with a big upper body, though Jason had a big upper body, too. It must be a wheelchair thing.

"Nice to meet you," she said, thinking this is something that Jason should have done yesterday. "I'm Robin Mathena."

"So this is your first job as an aide?" She nodded wondering how much Jason had told about her; he'd probably described in detail every mistake she'd made.

"They're not all as bad as him." He winked at her and Jason managed to give him the finger. "Look," he became serious again, turning his attention back to Jason. "I need to make more CD's. *More Love* is selling like crazy." He reached into his pocket and withdrew a thick wad of money. He counted out several hundred dollars. "That's your cut minus the cost for the CD's." Jason counted out the bills and pocketed them.

"How many do you want to make?"

"About two fifty each."

"Fuck! Are you serious?"

"Yeah, that's what I'm saying Top, we need to be thinking on a bigger scale." Robin followed quietly as they wheeled themselves out of the building and to the parking lot.

"Well fuck that, we're not burning five hundred CDs. We need to talk to Amberly and Patty about this."

"It'll cost money if we don't do it ourselves."

"So. It takes money to make money." They reached a van and Link wheeled around to the back and unlocked it. Inside was a box half filled with CDs. He went around behind Jason and grabbed the younger man's book bag and placed about ten of them inside.

Link suddenly looked at her. "Did you give her one yet?" Jason didn't answer. "You are one tight mother-fucker." Then he smiled sweetly at Robin. This all made her a little uncomfortable; boys cursing and giving each other the fingers. Boy's just naturally had bad behaviors and she wanted to make sure that Jason understood that she wasn't going to be treated badly.

"Here, sweetheart. Hope you like it." Robin accepted the CD. On the cover was an upside down wheelchair over a drawing of a turntable. *More Love* was written across the top in fat white block letters.

"Thank you." She was very interested in listening to more of what Jason did; especially if it sounded as good as the mix she'd heard earlier. "Just one song?"

"One song is all you need when it's eighteen minutes long." Link responded while filling up his own book bag. "We sell these for ten bucks. Let your friends know. Great for parties." He sounded like a salesman. He turned his attention back to Jason. "We oughta record that one we did last night. Man that was so sick!"

"It was pretty sick." Jason agreed with a reluctant smile.

"Fuck, it made my balls explode!"

"Hey, there's a lady present." Jason said. She gave him a surprised look.

"Sorry." Link said, remembering her. "Alright guys, I'll see you at lunch. Gotta dash!"

"Bye." She said politely. She positioned herself behind him. "So, where to now?"

They moved to Western Philosophy. And while Jason interacted in the lively discussions, Robin was bored. Her eyes began to droop. She tried every tactic she could to stay awake but two jobs, four hours sleep and coming down from a coffee buzz was more then she could bear and before she knew it she was sound asleep.

Sensing movement around her Robin quickly came awake. People were getting up and leaving the auditorium. Jason was powering down his laptop. God, she'd messed up big time, she'd fallen asleep while she was supposed to watch him. She felt awful. She jumped out of her chair, heart pounding in her chest as she rushed over to unplug the laptop from the wall. She was reaching for it to place it back into the case when she felt his hand on her wrist. When she met his eyes it was to see a cold, angry look.

"Robin, I don't really care," he gulped down a breath voice sounding slurred in his anger. "…what you do when you're not here. But when you get here I expect you to be rested and drug free-"

Drugs? "No Jason, I was just-"

"*And* I expect you to take this job seriously enough not to fall asleep!" Some of the people exiting the room turned to look at them and Robin felt two inches high. Her hands began to sweat and shake.

"Ok." She said quickly. "I'm sorry." She murmured. She picked up his laptop and moved it into the case. Then she placed this and his book bag behind his chair. She followed behind his chair and felt that everyone was watching her. She wished that she could hide somewhere but all she could do was to look down at her feet and not meet any of the curious stares. Then she felt the tears of embarrassment stinging her eyes as the floor began to blur.

Oh God, not this. She spotted a restroom and cleared her throat. "I-I have to use the restroom." Then she quickly dashed through the doors of the lavatory. It was swarming with girls who were laughing and talking and felt at home here. Robin hurried into an empty stall and once the door was latched she felt the tears fall freely. And then her stomach did the one thing that she hoped would never happen while she was on duty with Jason; it began to cramp in an unmistakable attack of irritable bowel. She couldn't believe that everything was hitting her at once. She had just embarrassed herself in front of a client *and* in front of a college professor, a classroom of college students, and now her bowels were erupting. She never wanted to show her face again. Her body continued to shiver uncontrollably as her attack of nerves continued.

Robin knew that she was compounding it by being in the stall for so long, but this was something that would not be rushed. And when she was done, she was more anxious than ever. She pressed her fingers to her eyes and willed the tears to stop flowing, then she left the stall and splashed her face with cold water. She quickly dried her face and hurried out of the room. Jason watched her without speaking, but she was pretty sure that Pinnacle was going to receive a negative report about her. He turned and wordlessly wheeled to his business class.

Jason felt horrible. He knew that Robin was tired but he didn't think anymore about it until he turned to her in class and saw that she was not only asleep but leaning on her folded arm and snoring softly. He was going to wake her up then, but Professor Fox didn't particularly care for him and his 'disruptive' nature. That's what he'd written on his midterm report last year when he'd had him for Introductory. Jason had been so pissed about it that he had faked a seizure the very next day and ended up on the floor flopping around like a fish. It was obviously fake; but there was nothing Fox could do about it.

And besides, there was only twenty more minutes left to class and that was long enough for a power nap. Then maybe she'd loose the dark circles around her pretty eyes. Jason didn't know any woman that didn't wear a stitch of make-up and still looked pretty. She hadn't even put on lip gloss, and he was impressed that she'd pulled off her hat and allowed him to see her hat hair.

After class was over, all he had planned to do was just to tell her not to let it happen again. Besides the look of embarrassment she had on her face when she woke up was a lesson in itself. Yet for some reason he'd started out all wrong and it had sounded like a lecture; like the ones that his father used to give him before he finally packed up and left. And then he saw the tears pop into her eyes and something else; Robin seemed to cave in on herself. If it was possible for a person to become small and insignificant, then she had achieved it.

He hadn't meant to do that to her. Every time before, she'd give it right back to him and he hadn't expected her to do anything different this time. Jason was used to putting up angry barriers and fighting dirty when he had to. What he wasn't used to was causing the same pain that others had caused him. He wasn't sure what to do in the face of that.

He felt like shit knowing that she was probably in the restroom crying, and when she came out, her downcast eyes indicated that he had guessed correctly. He had no idea what to say, so he had just gone on to class. She wordlessly set up the equipment. He kept trying to see her eyes but she wouldn't look at him. And then when she finally sat down she moved her chair behind his, which was actually pretty ingenious.

After class she gathered up his things. Several students came up to talk to him and two people wanted to buy CDs. She was already behind his chair when he finished and automatically went right to the cafeteria. He waited for her to get a tray.

"I'm not hungry," she said.

"Are you sure?" She just nodded. He got his lunch, feeling the weight of his actions weighing heavily on his conscience and headed to the table with his friends. It was crowded with more people than usual. They good-naturedly catcalled him and thumped him on the back, all except Amberly and Patty who were both giving him the stink eye. He cursed under his breath and offered them weak smiles. Usually his smiles were killer and he got pretty much what he wanted when he flashed it, but they both just scowled at him. He glanced at Link who shrugged almost imperceptibly.

Several people made way for his wheelchair and he gestured for Robin to follow. Instead she pulled up a chair and placed it against the wall about six feet from him. He hid his displeasure. He supposed there was no reason for her to have to sit right next to him, but he wished she would.

"Wassup, Top?" Patty said solemnly. "Heard you and Link had a good show last night." Patty was tall, big, and maybe even fat, with the stereotypical lesbian haircut; shaved short on one side, longer on the other. She was the type of girl that could whip the average man's ass and most men knew it.

"Once again, Patty, it wasn't me and Top it was just me. Top was a guest." Link was talking as if he'd repeated the same thing twenty different times.

"I already looked at the YouTube vid." Amberly spoke. Jason hated when she got mad because her voice was not normally slurred by her CP, until she was upset. Right now she sounded like a drunk. "I heard you mention Wheels of Steel-"

"Then you heard me mention you and Patty." Link said.

"But I didn't see our cut!" People were catching on that the conversation between them wasn't as benign as it had first seemed.

"Let's not do this here." Jason appealed to his friends. Amberly turned her frosty eyes on him.

"You two already did it."

Jason's brow furrowed. How did this day turn so shitty so fast? He slipped his MP3 player from the pocket of his jeans. Nobody made him participate in a conversation that he wasn't interested in. He turned up Hendrix's *All Along the Watchtower* until it was loud enough for everyone at the table to hear and then he quietly ate his lunch.

Robin was silent but she watched everything, especially the way the two girls were angry. No, not angry, but hurt. Jason and Link had apparently got busted cutting them out. Eventually, the one they called Amberly stood up and left. The other girl stayed and just basically glared at Link who seemed to be trying his best to ignore her while trying to keep the attention of the people crowding around the table. Finally even she got tired of his showboating and got up to leave.

Jason finished his lunch, ignoring everybody and then he silently wheeled out of the room with her following close behind him. He went about the rest of his day in a quiet funk and she wasn't much different. Dark circles had begun to deepen beneath her eyes and she was as tired as she had ever been in her life, yet she didn't dare fall asleep; she didn't even so much as yawn.

At the car she robotically loaded his chair into the trunk and then slipped into the driver's seat trying to clear her head of the sleep haze that engulfed it. She saw Jason put his hand on the dashboard and lean forward. She thought it was strange; maybe he couldn't get his legs in a comfortable position. But then she saw that his teeth were clenched and his eyes squeezed shut. Suddenly his body lurched back and then forward.

Alarmed she saw that he was in danger of slamming his face into the dashboard. Whatever fatigue had been in her body instantly disappeared as she leapt towards him and quickly shoved him back against the seat. Her heart was suddenly in her throat as she used her strength to keep his seizing body from thrashing forward.

His body suddenly stretched and he grunted repeatedly as his fingers and feet began to tap. She didn't have to hold him down now that his body was so taut, but she placed her hand flat on his chest just to make sure he didn't lurch forward again. His breathing suddenly stopped and slowly his face began to turn red and then purple.

Robin began to sweat nervously as she watched his breathless body straining. Was he choking? Maybe he had swallowed his tongue. That's what people said could happen. What did you do when someone swallowed their tongue?

"Jason?!" He was turning blue. She put her hand on his neck. The tendons there stood out; bulging, his body rigid like a board. She was on the verge of dragging him out of the car and performing CPR on him, when suddenly he collapsed and his body fell back into the seat. She could hear his rapid intake of breath and she exhaled in relief.

"God," she said mostly to herself. Her heart was still pumping, practically slamming out of her chest. He'd scared her so bad that not only was she no longer sleepy, she didn't think she'd sleep for a week. As she closed her eyes and tried to calm down, she felt his hand on top of hers where it still rested on his chest. Robin's eyes popped open and Jason was watching her with a tired expression.

"I'm sorry," he said plainly.

"What?" She had heard him clearly; she just wasn't sure why he was apologizing.

"I'm sorry that I made you cry. I didn't mean it." She moved back away from him, sitting back in her own seat, stiffly.

"I-well...it won't happen again." She said in a clipped tone. She glanced at him without meeting his eyes. "Put your seatbelt on please." Then she started the engine and drove off.

The ride to Jason's apartment was uncomfortably quiet. For once he didn't put on his headphones and seemed to just listen to whatever played from the car's CD player. She saw him looking at her periodically, but he didn't say anything.

When she pulled up into a parking space Jason finally spoke as she opened her door.

"I need to leave my leg braces in your trunk."

"Why?" She frowned.

He opened his door and positioned his legs out of the car. "Because my mom is coming tomorrow and she'll find them." With a curious frown on her face, Robin went to the trunk and retrieved the wheel chair and unfolded it close to where Jason now stood.

"Why are you hiding your leg braces from your mother?"

"Because she doesn't want me to walk." He sat down carefully in his chair as Robin silently watched.

Then she quickly gathered his book bag and computer bag and followed him back to his apartment. Once inside, he moved down the same hall where the bathroom was located but instead of turning right he turned left into a neat bedroom. There was just a bed, a dresser with a lamp and nothing else but artwork on the walls.

Robin hesitated before entering. "Come in," he said. He reached down and unlaced his shoes then he locked the wheelchair and struggled to stand. Robin quickly moved into the position that he had taught her; directly in front of him. He placed his hands on her shoulders and she placed hers around his waist and using her legs, helped him to stand. Again she was amazed that he towered over her. He wobbled for a brief second and then moved one leg and then the other towards the bed.

She followed him, as he was still holding on to her shoulder. When he reached the bed he began undoing the button on his jeans.

"Uh, what are you doing?"

"Leg braces? I can't give them to you any other way." She wasn't sure if he was being sarcastic or honest. Once his jeans were undone, he pulled down the pants. He was wearing boxers and his legs seemed a bit scrawny in them, especially since the rest of his body was pretty muscular and toned. She supposed it was a wheelchair thing, but his upper body was impressive and his arms popped with muscles. He flopped down on the neatly made bed and began pulling the pants down his legs and past the braces.

Robin knelt down and helped him, hoping he wouldn't get pissed and say something childish about being able to do it himself. But the only thing he said was for her not to take them off completely. Then he quickly unstrapped the braces. They left angry red welts above and below his knees.

"How did you hide them before I came around?"

"At school." Which he hated doing because then he'd have to go the entire weekend without them. "Or sometimes with Link and he'd bring them to me after she left." Once he'd had to leave them out back and he was a nervous wreck that someone would steal them.

Robin was watching him in confusion. But, he thought, at least she was back to speaking to him.

"Why doesn't your mom want you to walk?" That seemed insane to her. Walking would give him so much more freedom.

He reached up and pushed back his hair. There were several scars along his forehead and hair line.

"I have more on my chin, but you can't see because of my beard." There were more scars on his chest and shoulders.

"What happened?" Jason noted that the concerned look had returned to her sleep deprived eyes. He liked looking into her eyes, especially when she wore that expression of concern—at the same time that he hated how the dark circles there were evidence of her exhaustion.

"I fell into a glass table. It broke and so did I."

"Oh, God," she murmured still staring at him. He hid his surprise at her reaction. Most people just said, 'Damn, that's fucked up' and then went on. He was beginning to realize that she wasn't most people.

"Then I fell again. Not as bad, just a concussion, but my mom was like, 'No more.'" He made a face.

"But," her brow was still furrowed. "If you walk more and your legs become stronger, won't you fall less?" Then her face instantly warmed at how personal she was getting.

"But I'll always have seizures. And the alternative is to wear a helmet, which I'm not doing."

"So, you sneak and walk?"

"I guess."

Wow. She helped him back to his chair; he mostly pulled himself into it. She wondered how he did other things, like getting in and out of bed, in and out of the tub, onto the toilet. No wonder his arms were so impressive. He probably had to drag himself whenever he needed in and out of the chair. She was beginning to wonder a lot about him.

"I better go." Somehow it seemed wrong to leave him without the braces, and it seemed rather sad that he had to sneak and walk. And she felt worse about falling asleep and then becoming pissed at him for yelling at her. She once again remembered that this was just a job to her, but to him this was his life. With a sigh, she headed to the door.

"See you tomorrow." He wheeled to the door with her. "Get some rest."

She looked back at him, pausing momentarily. "I'm sorry about falling asleep. I won't do that again. When I'm here, I want you to know that you can trust me." Then she turned and disappeared into her car. Jason sat there for a moment and then he smiled. He kinda liked her.

Like an addict, Jason went straight to his computer, doing his usual; listening to music, checking the numbers. But his mind was elsewhere and didn't get the same satisfaction from it that he always had before. He began playing around with a new beat, thinking about the party last night—not the music, but the girl in the bathroom.

Replaying it all in his mind he felt a desire that caused him to harden rapidly. It wasn't necessarily the desire for sex—more a need to be one with someone. He replayed the events in his mind, the sensations, the sounds she had made; earthy, guttural; the sounds of pleasure.

Jason pulled up X-tube and listened to the female sounds of pleasure until he found one that reminded him of her; the watcher. Then he created a beat that reflected his mood and he chopped the vocal moans into it, slowing it down or speeding it up, almost making it sound as if she was climaxing to the beat. He liked it. He had translated his thoughts and desires into music so he called it *Jason's Mind* and after listening to it several times, he posted it to YouTube under his own name and not the name Wheels of Steel.

Wheels of Steel book 1

CHAPTER 12

Robin went home, climbed into bed and slept until three in the morning. She never heard the phone ringing; she hadn't even pulled off her shoes before flopping down onto her bed. But at just after three a.m. her eyes popped open and she reached for the alarm clock in a panic. Oh no. She'd completely missed her entire shift at the restaurant.

She had never missed work before. She had never even called in sick. Robin was a person that was so afraid of disappointing people that she would work while having a case of the flu or she'd cover someone else's hours even if it was an inconvenience to her. Realizing what she had done was almost more than her nerves could bear.

She hurried to the living room and played back her messages. There were three; all from the restaurant. She cursed to herself as she listened. The first one was filled with concern, 'Hey Robin, you're never late, wondering if everything is ok?' Then the second an hour later; probably right at dinner rush. 'Robin where are you? We're pretty backed up...Give me a call when you get this.' And then the final message; 'Well, I hope everything is ok, because when you didn't show up it really left us in a lurch. Look, we know you have a second job. And lately you've been coming in doing less than acceptable work; mixing up orders, slowness. You're going to have to make a decision on which job you want to keep because this isn't working for us.' And then a dead line. Wow.

She slowly slumped into her armchair and covered her face in shame. She wasn't doing a good job in either position. And yes, her boss was right; it was time to make a decision. She'd just slept 12 hours straight; of course she couldn't keep going like this.

With a sigh, she stood. Pinnacle sucked as employers and they were a pack of liars, but she already knew that she couldn't make ends meet at the restaurant. Maybe she could do better if she got extra hours as an aide. They needed more people and she needed more hours. But not now; now she needed to rest.

With that settled she felt marginally better—not that she could ever show her face back at the restaurant, not even to pick up her last check and certainly not to give two weeks' notice. Maybe she could call and quit over the phone and then have them mail her final check. She didn't relish doing that, but it was for the best; for her and for the restaurant.

Feeling a little better now that she'd made a decision, Robin prepared for work. She hadn't done much to make herself look presentable over the last week so she dressed in nice grey slacks, a red chemise with a nice white sweater. And because she had no food in the house as she had gotten behind on her own personal chores, Robin drove to The Waffle

House and had a huge breakfast, reading her book and not feeling rushed for the first time in days, maybe weeks. The stress of working two jobs was finally behind her.

Back at her car, Robin dug into her purse for the CD that Link had given her the day before. She slipped it into her car's disc player as she headed for Jason's. *More Love* began to flow from her speakers and Robin was surprised to hear that the backbeat was *Moments in Love* by The Art of Noise. It was one of her all-time favorite songs. She turned up the volume as she drove. The mellow groove surprised her. It was one thing to mix hip-hop beats because it was popular and what people danced to. But to make something this cool was not what she had expected from the angry young man.

She arrived at Jason's before the entire song had time to play out and reluctantly she returned it to her purse. No wonder it had gotten so many hits; the song was really good.

She climbed out of the car and thought, 'damn, wasn't I just here?!' She still had ten minutes but Jason would probably love that she was early instead of late. She rang the bell, prepared to start the day on a good note and to be pleasant despite the fact that Jason would fight her tooth and nail.

It wasn't Jason that answered the door, but a tall thin woman with graying red hair and cold green eyes. It couldn't be anyone other than Jason's mother.

Jason's mother looked her up and down before turning away. She didn't even say hi, bye or kiss my ass. Robin stepped inside assuming that since the woman hadn't shut it in her face that she was welcome to come in.

"Okay, so the contractor doesn't even look up in the attic." She said as she headed for the kitchen. So that's where Jason got it from; his rudeness. Robin followed at a slight distance. "He's going to give me an estimate when he doesn't even know what's going on up there?"

Jason was sitting at the table. His eyes flitted to hers briefly before returning to his mother. He was sitting at the table drinking coffee and eating scrambled eggs and bacon. Oh, so he could eat something other than Cheerios at breakfast. She noted that his normally untamed red curls were neatly combed and brushed into flowing, silky tendrils that reached his shoulders.

Even though she was shy about such things she decided to speak up. "Good morning Jason. Is there anything I can do for you right now?"

"No," he said, voice uncharacteristically pleasant. "My mom already helped me this morning. I guess I could have had you come later." She wondered what she would do for the next hour. Jason's mother leaned against the counter, drinking her coffee and watching Robin curiously.

"You're the new assistant." She stated. "Have you ever worked with anyone with CP before?"

"No ma'am."

"I see. You seem awfully young. How long have you been doing this type of work?"

"Not very long," she admitted.

"How long is 'not very long'?"

"Mom," Jason spoke. He picked up his plate of half eaten breakfast and scraped the remainder into the trash. "Robin is pretty good. And she's taking a seizure emergency class." He turned to her suddenly. "Can you load up my book bag and laptop?"

"Sure." She was happy to leave the room and sensed that Jason had created a task for her just to get her out of the line of fire. They still had a long time before they would have to leave for school so after putting his bags into the backseat, she decided to linger in her car and listen to the CD, but then got nervous that they might want her for something so after twenty minutes or so she returned to the apartment, not bothering to knock. They were no longer in the kitchen, so she went down the hall. Jason was sitting at the mirror with a towel across his shoulders and his mother had slathered shaving cream over his face and was in the process of shaving him.

"You can't let it get this thick." She was saying as she concentrated on the task at hand. "It's so much harder if you let it grow out. I know you don't like shaving, but you have a daytime assistant now." His mother glanced at her.

"You know how to do this, right?" Robin had shaved her dad once when she was little, not that she could gage how good of a job she had done since she had only been six. But really, how hard could it be? Jason's mother was using a safety razor, not one of the ones her dad used, where you had to place a blade into it. Thinking about her dad made her feel momentarily lost. She looked at what the mother was doing and the way she scraped down instead of up.

"Yes, ma'am."

"Come here and take over. I want to start the laundry." She waited for her to leave since three people would be a crowd in the small bathroom, then she sat down on the lowered toilet lid where the mother had been sitting and looked at the area of Jason's face that was now free of hair. She lightly touched his chin indicating that he should look up and then using a downward stroke of the razor blade began shaving him. The hair was definitely catching in the blade so she had to dip it into the sink of water pretty often. He flinched a lot.

"My dad had the other type of razor."

He was staring at her eyes. "The other type of razor? A straight edge?"

"No, the kind that you have to put a razor blade into."

"Oh, well I've never used that kind. I think my mom was afraid that I'd cut off my fingertips trying to replace the blade."

She wasn't sure if he was joking, so she didn't crack a smile.

Jason couldn't stop staring into her eyes as she shaved him. Where did those eyes come from? Was there some Irish guy lurking in her history? She was a dark nutty brown, so he didn't guess her for multiracial. And her hair was an unprocessed wild thing that she tamed only by pulling it back. He thought that she looked nice dressed like a preppy girl. Was she trying to impress his mother by dressing like that, or maybe trying to fit in at college? None of the girls he knew dressed in nice slacks and blouses; they just wore jeans and jean skirts or shorts. Maybe she wanted to look nice for him. It didn't matter why, he liked it.

"Okay, I think I'm done." She wiped his face with the towel and he looked at the mirror. He smiled.

"Good job." Robin watched him. He should smile more often. He had an amazing smile. It lit up his entire face and transformed him. He rubbed his cheek and Robin glanced at his freshly brushed hair. His mom had certainly done that.

Jason sighed and gave her a reluctant look. He didn't want to do this, but it was her own fault for having come back. He would not have predicted that she would be one to stick with the job considering their rocky start. "You can help me go to the bathroom, I guess."

"Oh?" She said in surprise. "Your mom didn't help you with that?"

"No. She was going to do that after I shaved. Help me stand, Robin." He leaned forward in the chair and she got into position, hands around his waist. "This is going to be harder since I don't have the braces." He whispered into her ear, presumably so that his mother wouldn't hear. Robin shivered slightly as the soft wisps of his breath tickled her ear and neck.

"Okay. Are you standing up or sitting down?" Translation: peeing or pooping?

"Standing is fine."

"Um…when do you…"

"Take a crap?"

She blushed. "Yeah."

He gave her a bemused smile as she got him standing. "I can control it so that it's only once a day. Mostly in the evenings, then I evacuate everything I've eaten for that day." He gestured to the toilet with his head as his arms went firmly around her shoulders. He wobbled a lot. "Robin, how strong are you?"

"Why?"

"Because if my knees buckle, you're going to have to prop me up."

"I can do that." Jason gripped the counter that was next to the toilet with one hand, leaning on her with the other. She was nervous, he was wobbly and she wasn't sure if he wouldn't just take a nose dive into the porcelain toilet bowl.

"Ok. You're going to have to pee me." He avoided looking at her.

She chuckled. "You already got me once with that one."

"I'm not kidding this time. I can't pull out my penis if I'm holding on for dear life."

Robin froze momentarily. She didn't want him to know how totally unprepared she was to do something like this. But this is what it meant to be an aide. Like when she'd had to wash Miss Lucille after she didn't make it to the toilet in time.

"Um, the door is open. Your mom might come in—"

His breath came out in a frustrated puff. "You're just peeing me, not giving me a hand job. Plus my mom has done and seen this a million times." He gave her a chilly look. "Do you want me to call my mom for this?" He already knew that she was too inexperienced for this—had already tested her more than once and she'd failed both times by not offering to wipe his ass and by looking like a scared rabbit the first time he'd mentioned peeing him.

"No." She said shortly, not liking the look he gave her; like she was inept, just because she didn't want to touch his penis. "I can do it." She realized that there would come a time when she would have to do something like this for a male, but she had always figured it would be someone old—and less attractive.

She unzipped his pants. Then she reached into the opening and he snorted. She almost dropped him and ran.

"What?!"

"You're going to pull me through that little hole?" She unbuttoned his jeans. He nodded. "Reach down into my waist band." Nervous sweat beads dotted her brow, but she did what he said. If this was some type of trick then she was going to kill him and then quit; or go to jail, whichever happened first. Her hands moved slowly. "Keep going...keep going." He said playfully. "Almost there...got it! Now pull it out."

Ew, it was so gross. It was like a thick dead worm but bigger; lots bigger. Ew. She hid a grimace as she gripped his flaccid penis with her forefinger and thumb, withdrawing it from his boxers and his jeans that had begun falling down.

His mother suddenly appeared with a handful of fresh towels and washcloths. Robin's face turned into molten lava.

"What time are you going to be back tonight? I thought I'd make us dinner."

"We'll be coming right back after physical therapy. Probably before five."

Oh my God, oh my God. His mother was just talking to him as if it wasn't strange that she was holding his penis. Oh my God.

"Honey, you're going to make a mess that way. Point it into the toilet bowl." She said to Robin. "And next time lift the seat."

"Yes ma'am."

"Okay, spaghetti and meatballs. How does that sound?"

"Sounds good."

Suddenly his penis jerked and stiffened slightly and then urine began streaming from it. Again Robin almost dropped him. She had to use two fingers so that she could keep it aimed. She looked down at it;

her fingers on some guys penis and she almost fainted.

Jason and his mom continued talking for a few more moments and then she left to finish whatever she was doing. Robin felt like a frozen statue as she tried not to move until his peeing had ended. She tried to think about something else, maybe small talk but she was absolutely blank. Then the flow stopped.

"Wait," he said. Then it started back up again for a brief few seconds. "Okay. Good job, Robin." He knew that hadn't been easy for her because she was trembling like a leaf. He supposed it hadn't been as amusing to her as it had been for him, especially when his mom walked in. He thought she was going to bolt right out the door. His mother had planned that, he knew, just to see if she knew what she was doing. He knew that mom would be forming several sneak attacks on Robin.

"Shake it," he prompted her. "Two good shakes should do it." He wanted to tell her the old joke, 'more than two and I'll enjoy it too much!', but she might just believe that. And in actuality there was nothing sexual about pissing in front of a girl that was so scared and disgusted that she would rather quit then do this. And as a matter of fact, there was nothing amusing about it either. Jason hid a scowl.

Once that was over she replaced him in his shorts, not very smoothly; grazing him against the rough material, but not worth complaining about. Theoretically, she would only have to do this on Fridays but maybe he'd just sit and piss the next time.

He sat down in the chair and zipped and buttoned himself. "Thank you, Robin." He wanted to ask if she was okay but it sounded condescending so he wheeled out of the bathroom, leaving her to wash her hands and get herself together.

She washed her hands, happy that her first contact with a penis was over, and then she joined him in the living room where he was pulling on his shoes. His mother had been in the bedroom making up his bed, which she knew he could do himself since she'd just seen his bed neatly made.

"So, are we ready to go?"

"Yeah, just two classes today; so a pretty short day for you." Yeah, then she could take care of quitting her other job.

"Mom, I'm leaving." She came out and gave him a series of kisses to his cheek. He hugged her, and the way that he clung to his mother surprised her. He closed his eyes and really seemed to enjoy being in her arms. Most people hugged but didn't really like the touch, but it wasn't like that with him. He broke the hug and then wheeled out of the door.

"Bye." Robin said politely.

"Goodbye. Drive safe."

"I will."

"Jason?" She asked as they drove to school.

"Yep?"

"What does your mom do for you on Friday's?"

"She cleans. She'll clean the toilet, mop, and do the laundry. Then she does my shopping for me. Sometimes she'll cook food to put in the freezer. She only works part time, not that she needs the money. My dad always keeps up with his alimony and he still pays her child support. He said he'll do it until I'm out of college." He got quiet.

"Do you want to hear some music?" She asked sensing his change in mood.

"How about I play *you* some music?" He turned in his seat and reached in the backseat for his book bag. He retrieved MP3 car speakers and plugged them into her CD player. Then he plugged his MP3 player into it. Soon she was listening to a cool hip-hop beat.

"Wow. Are these your beats?"

"No, this is D.J. Krush; a definite influence on my music making. You like this?"

"Definitely."

He was pleased. He was also conscious that he knew virtually nothing about her. "Are you, do you have kids?"

She gave him a surprised look. "No! No." She said a bit calmer.

"Okay." He chuckled. "I don't see a ring, so I guess you're not married."

"Nah. I'm single." She addressed each of these questions as if surprised that he might even suggest she would be otherwise.

"Single." He stated.

"Yep." He didn't say anything more and they rode on silently listening to good music.

CHAPTER 13

Jason's first class of the day was music appreciation. It seemed that it would be the least complex class that she'd attended with him, until he informed her that first semester had been learning how to read music. Link was in his class and they sat together talking about nothing more benign then the lesson at hand. Link winked at her.

"Hiya, sweetie. Still a glutton for punishment, I see."

She grinned shyly. "It's not so bad. I listened to the CD, the *More Love*."

Link's eyes twinkled. "And...?"

"I loved it!" She gushed.

Jason turned back to his computer and fiddled around wishing that Link wouldn't always have to be Mr. Charm. It was rather sickening the way women ate it up. He suffered through Link's flirting until class was called to order.

After music, they parted ways and he and Robin went to his last class of the day. He watched her as she listened intently to the lesson. He could clearly see that most times she had no idea what was going on. Yet she continued to watch and learn. He also watched the way the other guys seemed to be watching her. He wondered about her being single.

She was attractive with a full voluptuous body, but so shy that she barely met anyone's eyes. He saw several men trying to catch her attention, but she had no clue. Jason grinned.

After class, Jason sold some CDs while Robin danced from foot to foot until she told him that she had to go to the bathroom and rushed off in that direction. He saw Amberly and quickly wheeled to her.

"Amberly!" She turned and when she saw him continued walking. He scowled and wheeled faster. He was a beast in a wheelchair and frankly she wasn't that fast on two feet. "Why didn't you stop?" He asked when he'd caught up to her. "You still pissed?"

She finally stopped abruptly and turned to him. "Fuck you, Jason—Top, whoever you want to be!" He gave her a surprised look.

"Amberly..." He had never ever heard her say anything like that in all of the years that they had been friends.

"No! You threw us under the bus! I would have expected something like that from Link, but not you."

"All I did was to go to a party with Link. He was going to DJ and I went to listen. How is that throwing you under the bus? Just 'cause we were on YouTube? We didn't play any Wheels of Steel-"

"No Jason, because the DJ gig was a Wheels of Steel gig! Patty talked to Darby from Omicron House who told her that they wanted Wheels of Steel specifically because of *More Love!* So don't play us for stupid! If you don't want Patty and me then you don't have to have us!"

Jason was speechless. His mouth actually hung open. "Amberly, I didn't know."

She made a face. "You're trying to sit there and say that you didn't know? Then you got played worse than we did! Because he got you up on that stage and you played that new beat and nobody was worried about *More Love!*" The look on Jason's face stopped her. "You really didn't know?"

He shook his head. Amberly's muscles were popping, her head practically rolling on her neck as her agitation grew. She could barely stand in one spot, while, in comparison Jason was calm and virtually not moving at all. He reached out and took her hand.

"I still want you. I promise I do. I'm not trying to get rid of you. And I would never throw you under the bus. Okay? You are my girl and you know that." He and Amberly were friends back when he was a seventeen year old kid attending his first Diversity Club meeting. She'd already been at the University for a year and had taken him under her wing. Had it not been for Amberly's friendship, he wouldn't have adjusted with his disability as well as he had. Certainly she had paved the way by preparing him for the way people would misunderstand his slurred speech and lurching muscles.

Amberly suddenly reached down and wrapped her arm around his neck. She felt better knowing that she had not totally misread their friendship. He held her; touch being so precious to him—closeness more meaningful than even words; but he did not feel better. He felt tons worse.

Robin paced several feet away from them, not sure how she should let her presence be known, or even if she should. They were having a personal moment, and why had she assumed that Jason was single? She had come out of the bathroom in time to hear him telling her how much he wanted her. Obviously their earlier fight had almost broken them up.

She now found herself intensely curious about the girl; Amberly. She moved a lot better than Jason. She was petite almost to the verge of being too thin; with small, almost non-existent breasts. She was the type of pale that others described as porcelain. Her hair was dark and fine; wispy strands that seemed slightly unruly. She had dark eyes that were almost black; she was pretty and fragile looking. They made a very lovely couple. And that thought made Robin slightly sad because she had never known anything like that for herself.

She finally made her presence known because watching them holding each other seemed voyeuristic. She cleared her throat and Amberly looked up.

"I gotta go." The girl said while standing up.

"I'll call you." He intended to have a good talk with Link.

"Okay."

Jason glanced at Robin as Amberly limped away. He sighed, a slight frown on his face. "Lunch," he said.

"Lunch," she repeated.

"We have over an hour before my physical therapy appointment. We can go eat off campus. No reason to hang around here."

"I'm game. What sounds good?" They headed out of the building together.

"I don't know. You're driving."

"Hmmm. Chinese?"

"Yuck." Rice tended to cause him to choke.

"Okay, how about pizza?"

"I have that all the time. Come on, Robin. Think. What do *you* like?"

"Me?" It was Friday. There was one place that black folks in Cincinnati went on Fridays. "Well, we could go to Alabama's?"

" Alabama's? What is that?"

Oh wow, she couldn't believe that there was a person from Cincinnati that didn't know about Alabama's. "Do you like fried fish?"

"Um, I can't do bones."

"Filets; there's no bones. It's battered, deep fried filets." And the best damn fish bar in the state. Her mama called it 'ghetto fish' but even being all bourgeoisie, her mom ate there often enough.

"That sounds good, actually." He didn't eat much fried fish unless it was a McDonald's filet-o-fish sandwich when he was out and about with his friends. The thought of his friends caused a grim expression to fall over his face again. But Robin's enthusiasm caused him to momentarily forget his angst.

"Alabama's is like the most popular fish bar in Cincinnati! I can't believe you've never heard of it."

"Well, I think we have a place for lunch," he said.

She stopped before opening the door to help him in. "One problem, there's no place to eat inside."

"Hmmm, we could take it back to my place but my mom-"

"Or we could go to the park," she interrupted. No offense, but his mother was the last person she wanted to be around.

"As long as it's wheelchair accessible, then I'm fine with that." It was the end of summer and he hadn't had much opportunity to spend time outdoors at a park.

While she waited for her order, Robin chastised herself for this stupid idea. How smart was it to leave a boy prone to seizures in a car alone--and in 'Over the Rhine' of all places? What if someone tried to carjack him? One of the many aggressive panhandlers could knock on the window and Jason would probably roll it down and get jacked.

She was a nervous wreck by the time she had the two brown paper sacks containing steaming hot fish filets and fries. She let out a relieved breath when she returned to the car and saw him bobbing his head and listening to his MP3 player.

"Mmm, that smells delicious." He said while taking the food from her as she climbed into the car. There were several parks in close proximity to the restaurant and she selected one that she remembered to be easily maneuverable for someone in a wheelchair. He allowed her to wheel him while he held the food and two cans of soda.

Jason people watched until they got to a picnic table. Most everyone he saw was black—not that he cared. He just had never been to an all-black park before. Robin sat down facing him instead of the table and removed her meal form the now greasy sack. He mimicked her. Her fish was laden with hot sauce and ketchup while his was plain. There was also a strange bundle nestled between the filets and he looked at it curiously.

"That's sautéed onions and peppers. It's really good, but kinda smelly." She took her plastic fork and unfolded her sodden, wax paper packet and dug into the spicy looking sautéed vegetables. Then she munched her fish with fervor. Her fish and fries were coated in spicy smelling hot sauce and ketchup, the tantalizing aroma of the condiments stinging his nose. He frowned. Why was his fish plain?

"Where's my hot sauce and ketchup?"

"Well, I didn't think you'd want it like this." Frankly her mom always made fun of her for covering the taste of the fish with condiment goop. 'How about a side of fish with your ketchup, Robin?' "I got you tartar sauce…"

He wrinkled his nose. "I want it the way you have it." Using her fork she picked up two of her oversized filets and placed them on his plate and then she took two of his plain ones. Now satisfied, he picked up a chunk of the fish with his fingers and placed most of it into his mouth, the part that didn't make it to his mouth found its way to his shirt.

"Mmm." He hummed. He picked up French fries and shoved them into his mouth, and again, some actually made it in. She popped the top from his can of soda and after he'd swallowed the items in his mouth, he reached for it carefully and drank.

"That's good fish." He had hot sauce and ketchup all over his mouth and chin, as well as crumbs on his shirt.

"Can I-?" She reached out with her napkin and brushed off his shirt and cleaned his lips. He didn't protest and tried to stay still while she did it. But soon he had grabbed more fish and was continuing the mess. He unwrapped the bundle of onions and peppers and tried them.

But they wouldn't go down his throat, caught there as his throat muscles froze. Before he knew it, he was choking up gobs of partially chewed fish, fries and slimy onions. Robin jumped up, her unfinished meal flipping onto the ground. She grabbed Jason by the shirt front and yanked him out of the chair. Unsure of how she had managed it, she had herself positioned behind him and was attempting to administer the Heimlich maneuver.

As she applied fist over his solar plexus she heard him trying to say something, yet the words were masked by the strong force of air being pushed from his body. His hands went to her wrist.

"Drink-"

Robin paused in her attempts to save his life. "What?!"

"Drink," he tried again.

She dropped him back into his wheelchair and quickly grabbed the can of soda from the picnic table. He snatched it from her hands and gulped it down, belching and gulping in air, but no longer choking. Like she would do to a kid that had just recovered from a choking spell, Robin rubbed his shoulder and watched his face turn from red to its usual freckled white.

She waited until he stopped clearing his throat before she asked if he was alright. He nodded and rubbed the wetness from his eyes. She reached for her purse and got tissues to hand to him and he wiped the remains of the ketchup and hot sauce from his fingertips and face. Then he looked at the ground where all of their delicious fish lay trampled in the grass.

"Damn," he pouted. "That was really good."

"Jason, you almost choked to death." She stared at him remembering to remove her hand from his shoulder, but still not getting how he just let things like this bounce off of him.

"Well, that happens all the time." He reached down nonchalantly, and began cleaning up as much of the mess as he could from the ground. Robin took it from him and deposited it until the trash. She noticed for the first time that the two of them were the center of attention. Not that it was surprising considering that she'd bodily lifted a man from a wheelchair in order to give him the Heimlich maneuver.

He was already wheeling back to the car. "My physical therapist is going to wonder why I stink of onions and fish." Once back in the car she sniffed. Yes—perhaps not a wise lunch choice right before a massage session. He gave her directions to a sports therapy center inside of a strip mall.

"So you get a massage once a week?"

"Well, depending on the weather. When it's summer I won't have to go as often."

"Why is that?" She asked while following him into the facility.

"The temperature helps to keep me limber. The massages help keep my joints from locking up. I'm really lucky to have a lot of mobility. But sometimes my hip joints hurt." He knew some people relegated to wheelchairs got frozen in one position due to lack of movement. "A massage will also ensure that my muscles don't cramp and that they stay loose." He signed in at the front desk and Robin looked around. This was not the average sports therapy facility; she didn't see anyone else in a wheelchair, but she did see people that looked like professional athletes. Jason evidently had money. He had his own apartment— and a nice one, physical therapy once a week and his own personal assistant.

"You're here early." The smiling receptionist said to him.

"Yeah. Lunch kinda fell..." he and Robin exchanged looks. "...on the ground." She tried not to smile but he laughed first and then she couldn't help but to join him. Again she was surprised at how much his face changed just by smiling. "I'm going to get in the hot tub since my aide is here."

"Ok. Enjoy."

He wheeled to the locker with Robin following. "Wait here. I'll be out after I change." She stopped short, chuckling to herself.

"Right."

Jason wasn't long in the locker room. When he wheeled himself out he was wearing athletic shorts and nothing else. Robin's brow rose. He had two tattoos; a band of barbed wire around his sizeable bicep and a tribal circle on his shoulder.

"Wow," she said.

"What?"

If she could have blushed she would have. "I...um, always wanted a tattoo," she lied. She'd actually been admiring his big biceps. He was buff. Damn, he really looked good.

"Why don't you get one?"

"Oh, no. My mom would drop dead; literally."

"Come on." He led her to the back room where there was a sauna and private Jacuzzis. She wondered again about money and how much it would cost to come to a place like this. They bypassed the one-man Jacuzzi because you'd have to step up into them. But there was one set into the floor meant for four people. It was currently empty.

He locked the wheels on his chair and then easily lowered himself out of it and to the floor. He turned and scooted himself to the edge of the Jacuzzi. Then he swiveled his hips until his legs were into the water. He lowered himself carefully into one of the seats and then moved over to the controls. After he'd gotten the jets the way he liked, he leaned his head back and sighed.

"Ah," he said softly, eyes closing. "This feels amazing." He looked at her. "You should come in with me." She just smiled. "Seriously." He responded to her dismissive expression.

"Do you see what I'm wearing?"

He grinned, eyes lingering on her shapely form. "Yeah, I noticed."

"So I'm not exactly dressed for the Jacuzzi." She looked behind her for his chair and then sat down in it.

"Okay, well your loss." He dunked his head underwater and when he reappeared he pushed his sopping wet hair back and then closed his eyes again.

"Don't fall asleep," she warned.

"That's why you're here; to make sure I stay alert." After about five minutes of quiet, her cell phone began to vibrate. She checked it and saw that it was the restaurant. Damn, she had hoped to put this off at least until her shift ended with Jason.

When her phone continued to vibrate loudly and unanswered, Jason peeked at her. "Did you need to get that?" He was a stickler, but he wasn't so hard not to allow her to answer her phone.

"Um...I better." She quickly moved to the far side of the room, her eyes resting on him as she talked in a low voice. With eyes still closed, he strained to listen.

Robin was happy that Jason wasn't looking at her because she was cringing. Mike, the daytime manager was reading her the riot act. "Robin, where have you been? You missed your entire shift; no call-"

"Yeah, I know-"

"Well, obviously you know." He snickered dryly. "We couldn't get anyone to cover your shift last night at such a late notice." He paused, providing her with the opportunity to apologize or beg for mercy.

"Well, that's what I want to talk to you about, finding someone to cover me...permanently." There was silence and Robin closed her eyes and wished that this part was over.

"You're quitting?" He seemed stunned.

"I think it would be for the best. The message that was left for me last night kind of told me to make a choice." So there, it's made.

"So you're saying that you're not even going to give us a few days in order to replace you?" Robin chewed her lip without responding. "Can you at least come in tonight?" He pleaded. She suddenly realized that Mike had not anticipated losing her as an employee. He got off on giving people shit, but the restaurant couldn't really afford to lose a valuable employee like her. And now his tone was completely different.

Somehow that made her feel...powerful. She stopped fidgeting. "Mike. I'll come in tonight and as long as my final check is ready and waiting for me for the hours that I did work, as well as the shift that I'm going to work tonight, then I'll go ahead and work. But Mike, I want you to understand this; I overslept and missed my shift and for that I apologize. But I never call off, I'm never late and I fill in at the drop of a dime. I think that under the circumstances the message that was left for me could have been a bit more understanding. Maybe some employees screw people—but I don't." She was amazed that her voice didn't quiver although the rest of her did. She'd never said anything like that to an employer. Then she thought, 'what the hell?! It's just Mike.' He needed her, she didn't need him.

And he seemed to know it as he replied with stilted words. "Ok. I'll have your check ready. You'll have to leave your uniform, and bring in the spare."

"Fine, I'll be there tonight." She hung up. Then she smiled. That hadn't been so bad after all.

Jason had been listening quietly. Robin had been working two jobs? He felt even worse about yelling at her now that he understood the reason she'd fallen asleep. Did that mean she was hurting for money? Duh. And he'd let her treat for lunch and not even offered to pay it back. Then the food had fallen on the ground and gotten trampled. She probably thought he was such an ass. He was an ass, so why did she keep this job and not the other?

"Sorry about that." She said when she was done with her conversation. "I would have stepped outside, but..."

"It's fine. Look, Robin, I'm sorry that, um, well that I dropped lunch. And I meant to tell you thanks for paying."

Robin suddenly looked embarrassed. "Don't worry about it; you always pay for my lunch at school. And it's not like I can't afford to skip a meal or two."

He didn't know what to say, nothing seemed safe on that topic, especially since he thought her rounded form was nice, so he closed his eyes and relaxed again.

Robin watched him. Cerebral palsy was a disorder that had so many different faces. Over the last week she'd seen him in uncontrolled muscle movements, she'd seen him stuttering with spit flying, she'd seen him laughing, and now this; relaxed. Each emotion created a different face, but this one, where his eyes were closed and he seemed calm, was her favorite. So she sat and watched him, marveling at the number of freckles that covered his light skin. There wasn't an inch of skin that wasn't dotted with brown spots. But it was his ginger colored lashes that took up most of her attention. Their length actually seemed to leave shadows on his cheek.

Jason had the thick stocky build of a wrestler, but there wasn't an ounce of fat on him. If he hadn't been born with this disorder then he probably would have been a football player or something. He was definitely over six feet tall.

The whole package appealed to her, including the crooked tilt of his mouth which was evidence of his cerebral palsy. It didn't repel her; it was just a different way for him to move.

She looked away guiltily when two people entered the room and headed for the sauna. Then reality like a splash of cold water hit her because she had been having 'thoughts' about a nineteen year old disabled boy who also happened to be her client. It was totally inappropriate. She didn't have to be a real doctor or nurse to know that.

Jason pulled himself out of the Jacuzzi a few minutes later. Robin folded a towel in his chair as he instructed and after he was seated in it, she handed him a second towel and he quickly dried himself. She helped him situate his legs. He obviously had very limited ability to move his legs and feet; which was obvious by their diminished size. She glanced up and saw that he was watching the way she stared at them and she ducked her head down. She then followed him to the physical therapist office, stopping short of entering.

"I need to...," she pointed in the direction of the ladies room.

He nodded in amusement. Her bladder must be the size of a nut. "Come in when you're done." He wheeled himself into the room where his physical therapist was watching Robin with open curiosity.

"So who's the cute girl; new assistant?" Raymond was not just his physical therapist, but also a good friend. He was big, muscular, with ebony skin and a shaved head. He had been working with Jason since he was sixteen—after his Mom had fired the woman that had given him the hand jobs. She figured Raymond would be a safer option as a therapist.

Though the older black man had not ever given him a hand job, Raymond wasn't the most innocuous of people. Still, he was another that Jason would characterize as a 'diamond in the rough.'

Jason's lip twisted as he sneered playfully. "Don't go there, Ray. You're old enough to be her father."

"How old do you think I am, Jason?"

"Forties?"

Raymond's laughter rumbled from the pit of his stomach. "Damn. I'm thirty-two." He worked his thumbs into Jason's instep. "You should put in a good word for me. I haven't been on a date in weeks."

"Well, I think she has a boyfriend," he lied and wasn't sure why. He liked Raymond but a guy that good looking shouldn't have any trouble pulling in his own dates.

"Damn, well she's a cutie. Nice big body the way I like 'em."

Jason cleared his throat. "So, how are my feet looking?"

"Pretty good. I can tell you've been walking; though." He and Raymond had an understanding. Like Vegas; what happened in physical therapy stayed in physical therapy. He knew that Raymond wouldn't tell his mom about his walking, or the bruises. Once, Raymond had found him black and blue because he'd had a seizure while in the tub. He'd cracked his head pretty hard, but evidently not too hard; he hadn't knocked himself out or anything. Raymond had never mentioned it to his mother.

The big man rubbed and flexed his feet, rolling his ankle joints, listening for them to pop. Then there was a brief knock on the door and Robin poked her head in.

"Hey, is it okay if I come in?" She asked shyly.

"Come on in. Pull up a chair and make yourself at home." Raymond spoke. His face broke into a broad grin just as Jason's mouth pulled down into a sour grimace. Raymond nudged him. "Are you going to introduce us? Damn Jay, where's your manners?"

Robin sat down in an empty chair. The guy rubbing Jason's feet seemed nice and he was handsome which always made her nervous; as if she shouldn't even bother to speak because a guy like that would have no interest in what she'd have to say.

Jason sounded bored when he said. "Robin, Raymond. Raymond, Robin."

"Robin. What a pretty name for a pretty lady."

"Oh my God," Jason said. "You didn't actually say that did you?"

"Hush," Raymond said. "Don't mess up my game."

Robin looked from one to the other, not sure if there was flirting or if the two of them were pulling her leg. "Um, nice to meet you, and thank you."

"Game," Jason mocked. Grrr, he hated the way girls always acted flustered around guys like Raymond.

Raymond reached for the baby oil and Jason noted the way her eyes followed his every movement. He began rubbing Jason's calves.

"Robin, you should never thank a man for honesty. But forgive me, I'm flirting mercilessly. I wouldn't want your boyfriend to be offended."

'Don't fall for it Robin', Jason thought. 'Don't fall for the obvious line.'

"I don't have a boyfriend," she spoke shyly.

'Oh, Robin!' Jason felt like giving her a lesson in 'Pickup lines 101.' Or a book entitled 'Pickup Lines for Dummies!'

Raymond just gave her a surprised look and then he glanced at Jason. His expression brightened as he offered the younger man a hidden wink.

"So, Robin. Have you had to give a massage yet to any of your patients?"

"No." She shook her head.

"Hmmm."

"Well I haven't had many patients. I'm kinda new to this."

"Well you'll probably have to at some point. Come here, bring your chair over." Robin and Jason both gave him a surprised look.

"Well," she hesitated. "I don't know-"

"Come on, it's ok. I mean, unless, you know, you're not comfortable with it."

Jason blushed. "Raymond, she doesn't want to-"

Oh gosh, they thought she didn't want to touch him. "No, I don't mind. I mean, if Jason doesn't mind?"

Jason didn't respond, but Raymond jumped up and brought her chair over to the massage table.

"Okay, I'm going to do one leg and you do the other, and I'll tell you what I'm doing, ok?"

She nodded as she sat down. She glanced at Jason, who didn't seem all that keen on this. Raymond picked up his oil slickened leg and began to stroke the calf muscle. Robin took hold of his other leg.

"Get some oil first."

"Oh, right." She grabbed some baby oil and rubbed it into her palm then she gently began rubbing his calf; mimicking the movements that Raymond made.

"That's good. You can be a bit firmer. The key with Jason is to stimulate his muscles. You and I, this might hurt, but it doesn't hurt him."

She looked up at him for affirmation. He nodded once. So she did as Raymond instructed, kneading his muscles firmly.

"Good Robin. Now flex his foot; gentle. Never pull or tug. You'll feel the tightness and you knead it in order to release it." She felt how stiff his muscles were when she gently pulled back on his foot while working his calves.

"Wow, you're tight." Jason's face remained expressionless and he did very little moving. Robin turned to Raymond. "How long does it take to loosen him up?"

"In Jason's case? He has no concept of how to loosen up." Raymond chuckled at his joke.

"Shut up." Jason mumbled.

"See?" Robin smiled. She liked Raymond. He was easy going and his attitude put her at ease. He continued to rub and knead his calves. He loaded up more baby oil on his hands and ran his thumb firmly along the top of Jason's upper thighs, his large hands gripping his leg almost completely.

Robin reached for the baby oil and rubbed her hands together again. She placed them around his other thigh, cupping him firmly and then ran her thumbs into his muscles. Jason jumped and grunted. She froze.

"Too hard?" His face was beet red. Raymond looked at him a question. Jason's eyes flitted to Raymond; a silent appeal there. Raymond glanced down, and then his eyes grew big, a smile tugging at his lips.

"Hey Robin, why don't you go to the ladies room and wash the oil off your hands? I don't want it to ruin your pretty blouse, and I'll finish up here. Okay?"

"Oh ok. Thanks Raymond, for showing me how to do this. I really appreciate it." Raymond was already out of his chair and showing her to the door.

"My pleasure." He grinned in a friendly way. "You're a good student." She backed out of the door smiling and he closed it softly. He turned slowly back to Jason and burst out laughing.

"Oh my freaking God!" He laughed. "You got a hard-on?!"

"Shut up before someone hears!" Jason's hands were buried in his lap shielding it.

Raymond calmed down, but only some. "I'm jealous, Red. You never got one of those for me." Then he burst out in laughter again.

Jason was just shaking his head. "You are so wrong for that." He adjusted himself. "But thank you." Then he grinned. "It was cool until, you know."

"Until shorty appeared?"

"Ain't nothing 'short' about him," Jason bragged.

Raymond reached for a towel and tossed it to him. "Well here. Go get dressed. And if some bio matter appears on that towel, just leave it on the bathroom floor."

"That's gross." He lowered himself easily into his wheelchair and with the towel balled in his lap, wheeled to the lockers. It was true that his body could withstand a hard massage, because his leg muscles were atrophied. But what people didn't understand is that his skin was just the opposite. His skin was ultra-sensitive to touch. The hint of a breath against his neck, or the feel of someone's hands pressed to his chest to keep him from falling out in a seizure—all of those things were magnified in intensity.

CHAPTER 14

Jason plugged his MP3 player into Robin's CD player as they drove back to his apartment. "Oh! Your braces! How am I going to give them to you if your mom's home?"

Jason made a face. "You'll just have to hold them until Monday. It's no biggie." Once they were parked she helped him into his chair and followed him to the apartment with his things. Her plan was just to dash in, drop of his things in the closet and leave. It had been a long day despite the fact that it had ended a few hours earlier than normal, she still needed to complete her last day at the restaurant.

But when she got inside, Jason's mom greeted them enthusiastically. "How was therapy?" She asked while placing a kiss on Jason's cheek.

"Good," he answered while returning her hug.

"And your feet?"

"Tight, but they move."

Robin closed the closet door and opened her mouth to say goodbye, but Jason's mother turned her sharp eyes on her.

"So Robin, how are you getting along with this job?"

"Fine." His mother seemed to be waiting for more. "There's a lot to learn."

"Oh?" His mom waited again.

"Well, about seizures."

"Ah, true." She wrinkled her nose. "What is that smell?" Jason and Robin exchanged looks. "It smells like feet and…fish."

Robin turned to the door on that note. "Well, I better go. It was nice meeting you ma'am. Bye Jason."

"See you Monday," he said.

When the door was closed his mother turned to him. "She smells funny." Jason wheeled into the kitchen.

"Mom, that was lunch you smelled. We had fish."

"Son, fish is a choking hazard. Does she even know what to do in the event that you choke? She doesn't seem too experienced."

"She's fine." He responded in a short manner. He could have mentioned that she'd handled it just fine, but then his mother would have harped on the point that he should never have been eating fish because even filets still had hidden bones and blah, blah, blah.

He opened the fridge and grabbed a bottle of soda. His mother came over and took it out of his hand, and then she unscrewed the top even though he was capable of doing it himself. He gave her an incredulous look which she ignored, or chose not to see. When she handed it to him he just wheeled away without drinking it. She drank it absently as if it had been her idea all along to get a soda.

"So, when is dinner going to be ready?" He wasn't hungry but knew that she wouldn't leave until after dinner had been eaten and the dishes washed and put away.

He was right. She stayed another two hours, not leaving until close to six p.m. Jason loved his mother, so it really bothered him that he hated being around her. When he was younger, his mother was everything in the world to him; she was God and Satan and the sun and the moon.

But then he grew up.

She hadn't been out the door half a minute before he picked up the phone and called Link. He'd been anxious to do this for hours. It was time for Link to face the music.

"Hey, Top. What's up?"

"What are you doing?" Jason asked.

"Not what I'm doing, but who I'm doing."

"Oh sorry, am I interrupting?"

"Hold on." The phone went mute for almost a full minute. When Link returned he sounded out of breath. "No, I'm cool. What's up, son?"

Jason's lips pursed together. "Amberly told me to go fuck myself."

"Damn. I didn't know Amberly knew the meaning of the word. Maybe she thought she was telling you good morning," he joked.

"She and Patty quit the group."

Link didn't respond.

"You there?"

"Yeah."

"Well, any reaction to that?" By this time it seemed that Link had figured out that this was not just a casual conversation.

"I mean, what's the point of having them? For the videos? Like, what I want to do is play the music. I don't care about the videos."

"People like the videos. It completes the music."

"Whatever dude. I'm happy they're out."

"Well, thanks to you there is no more Wheels of Steel. Are you happy about that?"

"What?! Thanks to me?"

"Dude, I know you've been taking gigs under Wheels of Steel. And you've been keeping all of the money for yourself!"

"What?!"

"Oh fuck, Link! Don't play me. Patty called down at Omicron and got the truth. Man, you're treacherous."

"What the fuck...Who told her that I was taking gigs under WOS? That's a damn lie! I told you, Jason, I'm trying to do my own music! I mean, Wheels of Steel, I love this group but I'm not trying to share my take with two people that ain't helped with the music! Fuck that!"

"Wait a minute-" he blinked and then squeezed his eyes closed.

"Call Mike Hall at Omicron, he's the one that got me the gig!"

Jason frowned and shook his head. "I-I-I c-c-can't-" He felt a seizure coming and rapidly began flexing his fists.

"Fuck, not now Jason! I'm on my way over. Don't bust your head open! You there? Fuck." Jason didn't hear the line go dead, because he was already seizing.

Link was at the door fifteen minutes later and Jason wheeled to it and let him in. Link had an evil look on his face to rival any that Jason had ever worn. Jason just blinked at him unsure.

"Did you call him?" Link demanded.

"No, I called Amberly and Patty. They're on their way over."

"Good, I'm happy them bitches are on their way."

"Aw, don't say that, man." Jason grimaced. He didn't like this kind of thing at all. They were friends and partners and he couldn't stand for their bond to be taking such a beating.

Link wheeled into the kitchen and got something to drink out of the refrigerator. Jason didn't follow, knowing that his friend was pissed and didn't want to talk to him.

Amberly and Patty arrived a few moments later. Amberly could drive; she was seizure free. And Patty, who didn't have her own car, had evidently ridden with her. He greeted them. Amberly responded warmly, but Patty just gave him a brief, cold hello. Link had wheeled in from the kitchen and just scowled at them. He took a swig of his soda and after belching he gestured to Jason.

"So Patty, I hear that you have been making calls and digging up shit that you know nothing about."

Patty stalked towards Link, looking every bit as masculine as a linebacker, stopping short a mere foot from his chair. "Peter, you can go to hell." Her eyes flashed fire even though her voice remained calm. "I always knew you were a prick. I just never knew that you were a back-stabbing one!"

"I already told you a million fucking times! I got my own gig, sheesh!"

"That's not what Darby said," Amberly spoke.

"Darby? Who the fuck--? He didn't hire me. Pick up the phone and call Mike Hall. That's the one that paid me. Darby don't know shit about the deal we had."

Patty snorted. "You think I won't, asshole?"

"Do it you big butch bitch." He said, eyes seeming to pierce through her. She dug into her pants pocket for her cell phone. Mike Hall wasn't at the house so someone had to get his cell number and after five minutes she was talking to him. The one way conversation was filled with a lot of yeahs, Okays, and Mmms...

She finally pressed end on her phone and slipped it back into her pocket. She stared at Link. "I oughta pick you up out of that chair and throttle you for calling me a butch bitch, but I'm sorry for accusing you. I was wrong."

Jason slumped in his chair. "Shit."

"Yes," Link said tightly. "Now all of you can kiss my *black ass*!" The angry blonde haired, blue-eyed, white young man wheeled quickly to the door.

"Link," Jason called. "Link!"

"Link, I'm sorry!" Amberly called out. He was out the door and wheeling down the walkway.

165

Amberly and Jason moved to follow, but Patty held up her hand.

"No. Let me go. I'm the one that started this." Patty headed out the door, shutting it after her. Jason and Amberly looked at each other.

"Damnit, Amberly," he said bitterly.

"I know. I'm so sorry Jason." Her big eyes were watery. Shit, he didn't want to see her crying. He offered her a twisted smile. She just slumped on the couch and covered her face. Jason cursed under his breath and wheeled over to her.

"Oh my God," she murmured. "Link must hate us…"

He placed his hand on her knee. "He doesn't, he's just pissed is all. He'll get over it. He always does." She wiped her eyes and looked up. "I'm sorry, Jason. Really."

He took her hand. "It's okay." She gave him a shaky smile. There was a sudden trilling of musical notes as Amberly's cell phone began ringing. He wheeled away but listened. It was Patty telling her that she and Link had gone off drinking.

"See." Jason responded when she replaced her phone. "I told you Link would be okay. We'll get together, make some music. I have some ideas for the next video."

Amberly was already shaking her head. "No."

"What?"

"I don't want to join back up with WOS."

"Amberly-"

"You heard Link. He doesn't want us. And frankly, I'm not pressed. People aren't cheering for me and Patty; it's you and him. So..."

He struggled for something to say. "I-I don't want to lose our friendship-"

She rose from the couch and limped over to him, reaching for his hand which he gave to her readily. "We were friends before Wheels of Steel; we'll be friends after." She absently brushed her dark hair back behind her ears.

"You promise?"

She sat on his lap and placed her hands around his neck, than she leaned her forehead to touch his. Jason's hands went comfortably around her narrow hips. "I promise," she whispered. They sat quietly like that for a while.

"Jason?"

"Hmmm?" He murmured comfortably. Touch was something he valued and didn't get as often as he liked. His mother touched him, his physical therapist, of course, but beyond that no one; except Amberly, because her cerebral palsy made her skin just as sensitive to touch as his. "What?" He asked.

"Am I ugly?"

"What?!" He straightened quickly. "Did someone call you ugly?" He would run them over with his chair, leaving skid marks on their back.

"No, I just wondered how others saw me."

He gave her a serious look. "Amberly, you're the one that taught me that I was normal and not some charity case." He reached up and placed his hand on her cheek. "You remind me of a poem I heard in a movie called Cooley High. It went like…" He wracked his mind until he had it all. It had touched him so deeply that he had rooted around on the internet until he had found it.

"'Were I Pygmalion or God, I would make you exactly as you are, in all dimensions; from your warm hair to your intimate toes, would you be wholly in your own image. I would change nothing; add or take away.' That's what I think of you Amberly, and that's the way I want people to think of me."

Amberly stared at him for a long time before her brow gathered and she quickly stood and walked away several steps. "Why do you think we never got together?"

Jason froze, surprised at the question, surprised at the thought. He rubbed his hands together, suddenly uncomfortable. Had she taken the poem and the show of affection in the wrong way? He wasn't trying to hit on her. He gave her a serious look, unsure of how to proceed without hurting her feelings.

"I guess I think of you as a sister. And plus, you're like, old." He laughed. She did too. She was a full two years older than him and so would know that he was only being playful.

"Do you think it's bad that I'm only attracted to 'normal' people?" She asked with a worried look.

"I don't think so." For some reason he thought fleetingly of Robin. "Attraction is subjective and no one should judge you based on that."

"Yeah," she said tightly. "That darned 'attraction'. The guys I like don't look twice at me! They are too busy with the girls that walk straight, talk like their voices have bells on their tongues-"

"Jesus, Amberly," he hated when this usually upbeat girl was anything but that.

"I don't want to be a virgin forever!" His eyes got wide. She chuckled. "Don't worry; I ain't trying to hit on you. I told you I like average guys." He relaxed and something came to mind.

"Amberly, do people try to touch you?"

"Touch me?"

He blushed. "Yeah. Well, seems like girls always want to touch my, you know; my junk. Do people try to touch you?"

"I wish." She said seriously. She sat on the couch again and had a thoughtful look on her face. "I made a play for my massage therapist once. He was like forty and he didn't look at me twice."

"Hmmm." Jason explained about his massage therapist back when he was a teen.

"Maybe she felt sorry for you?"

"I don't know." Then he explained as discreetly as he could about the party last week and the rendezvous in the bathroom.

"God, you're getting play. I'm not getting anything!" She said in frustration.

"But-" How did he explain that it was empty? Oh he liked it and all. But it was almost like masturbation. He decided to just keep that thought to himself.

"So you're still a virgin?" She asked surprised.

"Yeah. I've never even kissed a girl before."

"Wow. Jason, you're really attractive. Girls like you."

He cleared his throat and scratched. "Yeah well, they don't like me enough." He went to the kitchen and she followed. He got them both soda. He opened hers for her because her hands couldn't twist things as easily.

"So," she said after taking a drink. "You know what I think?"

"What?" He asked while taking a swig.

"I think you and I should do it."

He choked. He choked so bad that she had to actually thump his back and Coca Cola came spraying out of his mouth. He got a dish towel and cleaned up. He peeked at her and her mouth was pulled down sadly.

"Wow," he finally said. "Are you serious?"

"Never mind-" she walked away quickly.

"Wait! I didn't say no. I'm just making sure that you're serious." He took a few moments to wash his hands and gather his thoughts.

"It will just be sex. No big deal, right?" She spoke hesitantly.

"I think of you as my sister…"

"Never mind-"

"Will you stop saying never mind?" He patted his lap. "Sit here." She came over and sat on his lap. He placed his hands around her waist in the familiar way that he had done a hundred times before. But this time he looked deeply into her eyes.

"Kiss me," he said. Amberly took a deep breath. She leaned forward and placed her lips on his. Jason closed his eyes and thought about the movies when the superstars kissed passionately. He parted his lips and tentatively touched hers with his tongue. He was very away of her hands moving up to his hair and the way she sighed. He mimicked the way the actor's lips parted and the way their tongues seemed to dart in and out of the others' mouth. He kissed her passionately, tenderly and at last, brotherly.

She pulled back and looked at him closely. "It wasn't right, was it?"

He could have lied, but he didn't. "No. It didn't feel right. You're my best friend, Amberly. I don't think I can do that with you, not like this anyway." She moved to stand up but he held her in place. "But, maybe we can make a pact."

"A pact?"

"Yeah. If you haven't lost your virginity by this day next year, I'll make love to you." He smiled. "I may still be a virgin myself. But you're not going to die a virgin on my watch." She smiled slowly and reached out her hand for his to shake.

"You got a deal, Top."

CHAPTER 15

Robin felt like kicking herself for agreeing to work this last shift. She was dog tired when she dragged into the restaurant, dressed in her polyester uniform that had grown loose over the last few months. The spare was in a plastic grocery bag and she marched right into the manager's office and placed it on the neat desk.

Bailey, the night manager gave her a wide-eyed look. "Robin, I hear you're quitting." She nodded.

"Yeah, that's my uniform. I'll leave this one when the shift ends." She was wearing athletic shorts and a t-shirt beneath the uniform so that she could make a quick change.

Bailey sighed and her back straightened, hoping that this didn't turn into something ugly and confrontational. She was just too tired to cope with something like that.

"Robin. I wish you would reconsider," he said carefully. She was already shaking her head.

"I can't make it work, I've tried. This job doesn't pay me enough-"

"I've been authorized to offer you a raise."

Robin hesitated. "How much?"

"Fifty cents-"

Fifty-freaking-cents? "I'm sorry but the answer will have to be no." She resisted the urge to rub her hands together in anxiety.

Bailey stared at her. "Robin, you're perfect manager material. The head office is really interested in making you a manager."

She frowned. If that was true then why did he just offer her fifty cents on the hour to remain in her previous position before offering her the manager's position?

"Well, they should have offered me the opportunity back when they first found out that I had to find another job in order to make ends meet. Now, I need to get back out on the floor. Do you have a check for me?"

He gave her a surprised look. The Robin of a few months ago would have listened quietly and agreed with everything that was said. But she was frankly too tired to continue playing these games. If they really wanted her then they should have told her. Now it was too late.

"Check?"

Shit. They were trying to pull a Pinnacle on her.

"It's fine," she said with a slight smile. "I was frankly too tired to work tonight anyway." She turned to walk out the door. "I'll pick it up tomorrow when I return this uniform."

"Robin, wait!" He opened a drawer and suddenly located a check. "Ah, here it is." She went back to the desk and held out her hand for it. She examined it.

"This is short."

"What do you mean?"

"It's for four days not five."

"Well you missed yesterday, and you certainly don't expect us to cut you a check that includes wages for days that you haven't actually worked yet, do you?"

Robin pulled off the poofy polyester hat and tossed it on the table. She unzipped the pants and slid them down her legs stepping out of them. She draped them across the table as well. Lastly, she pulled off the shirt and placed it on top of the other items until she was standing in just shorts and a shirt.

"What are you doing?"

"Nice working with you. Have a nice day." She opened the door and walked out of the office. Bailey came scurrying along behind her.

"Robin!" She didn't even hesitate. "Look I can go back into the office and cut you a second check if that's the problem. Come on, we can do that now." She didn't say anything as she continued to walk. "Robin, look you said you'd work so we didn't get anybody to cover for you. You can't leave us hanging again! That's just really a terrible thing for you to do!"

She finally stopped, but her face remained passive. "I told Mike what it would take for me to work tonight. It's not my fault that you didn't follow through with your end. So, what you'll need to do is pull your ass out from behind that desk that you sit at all evening and get out there and cover my shift yourself." She turned and walked out the door with all eyes on her. Bailey just stood there too shocked to say another word.

Well, she guessed she wouldn't be getting a reference from them.

She got home and didn't know whether to climb into bed and sleep, whether to pick up one of the many books that she'd wanted to start, or whether to get on the computer. She stood there in her apartment, not believing that she actually had time that she could call her own. She laughed and ordered a pizza, and then grabbed her laptop and got caught up on her internet surfing.

She was munching on pizza when she finally navigated to YouTube. She typed in Wheels of Steel and was surprised to come with a full page of hits. The first video she pulled up was only about a minute long. It was a fast and funky techno beat that she listened to twice before moving on to the next song. Robin did this for the next two songs, before watching the popular *More Love* video. She was mesmerized by the images of two dancing figures that seemed to stream light and float through the universe. When it was over she realized that she had been watching and listening to it with large eyes.

It was so good that she was compelled to leave a comment. She'd never left a comment before on YouTube but wanted the group to know just how much she had been touched by both the music and the video.

~I know that a lot of people have commented and I almost didn't, but I just had to let you know that I like this

*song as much as I like Moments in Love. People say stuff
like that all of the time, but I mean it. And I really love the
Art of Noise, Kraftwerk, Daft Punk...I put your work right
up there with them. Sweetheart in HC~*

Robin continued listening to the mixes, deciding to
check out Jason's page next which was linked to WOS.
He didn't have any pictures and she was a bit
disappointed, but he did have several sample bits of
music; no videos, just a black screen with the word
TOP written across it. But she found that the mixes he
did were totally different from Wheels of Steel. It
wasn't quite hip hop or electronic. There were violins
and piano behind a funky beat.

The description that YouTube categorized the
music was Lounge/chill. She supposed that was
right.

She saw that he had just uploaded a new track,
and instead of *Top*, he had it posted under Jason.
Curious, she listened to it. It was short but it elicited a
certain emotion from her. It made her...yearn for
something. She listened to the short song repeatedly;
feeling very mellow at the soft moaning that created
the backdrop of the sultry song entitled *Jason's Mind*.

Robin kept trying to connect Jason; mean, sour
faced Jason with the person that had put together this
music. She wanted to see it, to actually watch him
mix. Sometimes his limbs stretched and his head
arched and his mouth pulled. Sometimes his
breathing stopped and he had to gulp the air into his
lungs. Sometimes he talked, his mind moving
forward while his lips and tongue fell behind.

Sometimes he seemed like a man that was fighting for control of his very own body. And yet he still created these beautiful beats; he made this fantastic music.

Feeling a bit like a voyeur, she hit each member of the Wheels of Steels group, starting with Amberly. She discovered that the two female members of the group were in charge of the beautiful videos. There was a childlike quality to the girl. She favored videos with anime images and Disney characters. There were videos of them making beats and she found herself rewinding them more than once in order to watch Jason, oblivious to the camera, as he and Link created the beautiful sounds.

Next she checked out Link's page and found that he favored techno and punk; that he was great at mixing music and creating beats. He was cute and had hundreds of friends, but that didn't surprise her at all.

She checked out Patty and found that she had a following of Goths and androgynous people. Then she went back to Wheels of Steel to favorite some of the selections and saw that there was a response to her comment.

~*Sweetheart, thank you for the kind words. I'm a big fan of the same music. Sweetheart in HC? What's that? TOP*~

Robin's mouth dropped. Oh my God, Jason had responded to her comment. Her screen name was Sweetheart in HC and he wanted to know what the HC meant. She covered her mouth unsure of what she should do. Should she say, 'Hey it's me Robin?'

She began typing.

~Thanks for acknowledging my comments! I'm Sweetheart in Hamilton County. Congratulations on reaching a hundred thousand hits. If I had talent like yours I'd be making beats all day and all night. Is that what you're doing now? Sweetheart in HC~

It took five minutes of waiting and then she received a response.

~Sweetheart, I am very psyched about the number of hits the song got! And making beats is all I want to do. Are you into music? And check your inbox. I sent you a message there. TOP~

Having never chatted on line before, Robin was excited to be sending messages back and forth. It was like opening the Cracker Jacks box for the secret toy surprise. She quickly went to her inbox and was excited when it said 1 New Message. This was the first message she'd ever received on YouTube, or anywhere.

~Hi Sweetheart. Hope you don't mind me private messaging you here. It's almost eleven and I've had a hectic day. I thought I'd come online and check out some music and chill. Other than Wheels of Steels music, what have you been listening to tonight? TOP~

~Nothing. I came on specifically to listen to Wheels of Steel. I just learned about you guys this past week. I heard More Love and was blown away. Have I told you just how much I like that song? LOL! I have it playing now on a second window. Anyways, I'm really interested in knowing what you are listening to now. Care to share? Sweetheart in HC~

~I'll share. I have a chill playlist. Accept my friend request and I'll send it to you. TOP~

Wow. Robin accepted the friend request, marveling at how nice he was online compared to how nasty he had been to her in person. Maybe it was just her that rubbed him the wrong way. He certainly acted less disdainfully towards others. Actually, today he had been fairly normal acting with her. It made her kind of sad that he might not like her, because the person that had just shared his playlist was someone that she liked talking to. Could he be like that in person?

Following his link that was entitled *Chill Music,* she played the first song while she scanned the rest of the titles. She wasn't familiar with this type of music. It felt like hip-hop elevator music. She chuckled. She liked it. She liked it a lot.

She went back to leave him a message thanking him, but there was already one there waiting for her.

~I like your playlist. TOP~

Oh my gosh, he was her friend now so could see her playlist. She felt her face burn because she had a few strange selections; *Afternoon Delight* by Starland Vocal Band and *Ode to Billy Joe* by Bobby Gentry. He must think she's a total dork. But these songs were ones that she remembered her father singing when she was a kid and they had stuck with her. It made her feel closer to him somehow by listening to these songs—knowing that they were still here even if he wasn't. She loved old stuff like The Commodores,

Earth Wind and Fire and Stevie Wonder, just as much as she liked Miguel and Bruno Mars.

Robin sent him a blushing smiley face emoticon as a response. His response was just 'LOL'. When she went to sleep that night, she had a smile on her face.

CHAPTER 16

The next day was Saturday, and Jason spent the morning digging for breaks and playing on the net. He checked to see if Sweetheart in HC was available, leaving her a link to a Curtis Mayfield Dubstep. He'd enjoyed meeting a new fan and looked forward to talking to her again. His phone rang and he cursed, figuring it was his mom making sure he hadn't choked sometime in the few hours since he'd last seen her.

But it was Link. "What are you doing?" He asked blandly.

"Just fooling around in the studio. What's up?"

"Let's go out to lunch. I'll be over in fifteen."

"Ai-ight then." He hung up, brushed his teeth and splashed his face. He didn't bother with combing his hair; he just pulled on a stretchy headband to hold it all back. By the time he was lacing up his Timberlands, Link was out front blowing the horn.

"Want help?" Link called as he sent down the lift.

Jason gave him the finger in response and the two friends smiled. Once he was securely buckled in, Link pulled off. "What do you want to eat?"

"I don't care," Jason replied. "How did drinking with Patty go?"

"Um…I fucked her."

Jason started coughing, practically choking on his tongue. Link glanced at him.

"Are you shitting me?" Jason finally asked.

"No. And surprisingly, it was nice."

Jason stared at him. "Patty?"

Link sighed. "We were drinking and talking-"

"But isn't Patty a lesbian?"

"I don't know. I mean, obviously not. Maybe she's bi, I don't know. I do know that she likes dick. She *loves* dick-"

Jason coughed. "Don't! I can't. I don't want to visualize it!"

Link shrugged.

But Jason couldn't stop poking at the subject, like a stiff dead cat in an alley. "Okay, how did you get to the point where you..?"

"Fucked her?"

"Sheesh! Yes."

"We went to Louie's. We were calling each other bitches along the way. We had a couple of drinks and she told me that I wasn't half bad. I told her that she wasn't half bad. Then I was fucking her. I don't know, dude! It just happened."

Link pulled into Perkins Restaurant. Jason just stared at him.

"And you liked it?"

Link nodded without hesitation. There was quiet until the two were in the restaurant and sitting at a table.

"Are you going to do it again?"

"I mean, I don't like her or anything. It was just-"

"Fucking," Jason stated.

"Right."

Jason swallowed and scratched his head anxiously. "I uh...kissed Amberly." The last was mumbled.

"Did you say that you kissed Amberly?"

Jason peeked at him and then nodded.

"Why'd you do that?"

"Well, I'm not quite sure. Things started happening—you're not going to tell anybody about this are you?!"

"Hell no! You're not going to tell anybody about me and Patty are you?"

"No, like who would I tell?"

"Amberly."

"Hell. You already know Patty is going to do that anyways." A waiter came over and took their order. Since Link was around, he decided on a club sandwich. Sometimes, if the bacon wasn't cooked just right it caused him to choke.

"So," Link said, almost too casually. "What was it like kissing Amberly?"

"Terrible. I mean, not because she wasn't a good kisser," Jason blushed. "To be honest, it was the first kiss for the both of us."

"Dude!" Link leaned forward and stared at him. "I know you've been getting play-"

Jason shushed him and looked around; knowing that two guys in wheelchairs already garnered plenty of attention, especially considering that one of them had involuntary muscle movement.

"I get play. It just stops short of fucking, and kissing."

"That's messed up. Is it the spit factor?"

"Most probably." He had problems swallowing, so at times he spit when he talked. Most girls didn't care for spit. Strangely, those same women weren't repelled by sucking his dick.

"So are you two...?"

"No! No." He thought about Amberly; kissing her. But it was the image of Robin's face that caused his breath to catch in his chest, and the remembered erection during his massage. He decided not to mention the pact that they he and Amberly had made and thought maybe it would be better if she and Link were the ones that had the deal. He was by far the one to go to if a mercy fuck was needed. The food came and they talked about stuff. And then Jason looked at his friend and tackled the hardest topic of all.

"What about Wheels of Steel?"

Link chewed his burger. "Well," he swallowed. "We can just refer to ourselves as Link from Wheels of Steel or Top of Wheels of Steel. We don't have to actually tell people that we're disbanded, you know? We could just not make any more music under the group. And as far as the CDs, I don't think we should make any more. And whatever money we've already collected we'll just split; maybe at lunch Monday, we'll get together and split what we've collected. I'll contact the girls and let them know."

Jason nodded slowly. He had hoped that Link would say that he didn't want to disband, but it was obvious that he was the only one that wanted to continue with it. He sighed, and of course had a short choking spell where he spit up partially chewed bread while Link thumped his back, threatening to lodge it more firmly in his throat.

By then the waiter was hovering over him in concern and asking him if he was alright, even when he was too busy coughing up his lung to answer. They left without having to pay their bill and then caught a movie filled with stunts, killing, and mystical powers.

It felt great to catch up on her sleep. Robin didn't get out of bed until nearly 10 a.m. Then she agonized over the seizure class that she would have to take later this afternoon. She finished up her chores quickly, showered and then left for the class.

It was held in a large room on the top floor of an old building. It smelled faintly of mothballs and appeared to have once been used as some type of dance studio. Large mirrors covered one entire wall and the hardwood floors, though old and worn, were still beautiful. There were several metal desks and chairs set up, and they reminded her of the old desks that used to be in her elementary class.

People were just entering the room and signing in at a large table where a woman sat, taking money. When she got to the head of the line she paid her fee and smiled inwardly that the fee was the exact amount that Mary Louise had given her. She received a nametag and found a seat near the back of the class and spent the next three hours learning about seizures. It scared her and relieved her. Halfway through the class, she moved to the front of the room.

Clonic-tonic seizures are what Jason suffered from; or what's more commonly known as a Grand Mal Seizure. Clonic is when he stiffened and that lasted just a few seconds. And then tonic is when he began to convulse. She had never seen him do that longer than a minute or so. Robin learned that it was normal to stop breathing, and she learned that people don't swallow their tongues. There was no pain associated with the seizure, and generally no memory of it. This was the information that relieved her the most. That no matter how horrible it was to see, he would have no memory of it.

They watched a movie, which showed several different forms of seizures. And when they got to the Clonic-tonic her eyes began to prickle and sting. It was so horrible; seeing these people's lives so controlled by these neurological mischarges in the brain.

After the movie, they were taught how to actually handle a seizure. It was very interesting and she became engrossed in the course. She knew to lay him on his side, not to put hands by his mouth, not to let him bump into anything that might injure him and most importantly, not to allow the seizure to last more than 5 minutes without getting help.

They learned CPR, how to take a pulse, how to prevent choking. And when it was over they received a certificate that would be filed with the state. Robin was more than happy that she'd taken the course and left there feeling that she knew what to expect from Jason. These were the things that caused her to understand him better and to be more tolerant of his angry moods.

After class, Robin did some much needed grocery shopping and decided to pick up tissues for when Jason made a mess at lunch; baby wipes and a small first aid kit, which all fit nicely in her purse.

When she got home later that evening she excitedly signed into YouTube and went straight to her inbox. There was a message from Top and her heart raced in anticipation.

~Hi Sweetheart. I saw you had a Curtis Mayfield vid and thought you might like this Dubstep. Take a listen and tell me what you think. TOP~

She couldn't stop smiling. She liked how he called her Sweetheart. She quickly played the song. Her brow gathered. It was like crazy Curtis Mayfield with a speedy drumbeat. It made her want to dance and she found herself bobbing her head as she listened. Dubstep, what the hell was Dubstep? She did a Wiki search on it and found that it was electronic dance music.

She sent him a quick message.

~Oh my God, that was CRAZEE, TOP! I never heard of Dubstep before. I wanted to get up and start dancing. Thanks for the education, now I'm off searching for more Dubstep! Sweetheart in HC~

~You never heard of Dubstep? It's been around for over ten years. There are some really good artists out there; Mt Eden, Enigma. Here take a link to this one. TOP~

They sent messages back and forth like that for a while. Robin suddenly felt bad for not revealing her real identity. She should have told him who she was yesterday, now it was just plain awkward. Should she just keep playing that she didn't know him? If she told him who she was now, he'd probably be mad at her. But she had a purely selfish motive for hiding her identity; she liked talking to him like this and when he talked to her as his aide, he wasn't very pleasant.

So who would it hurt if she just didn't ever tell him?

~Sweetheart, do you have a yahoo or MSN messenger that we can chat on? It would make it easier to send messages back and forth~

~I don't have anything like that. Hold on, I'll download Yahoo~

Robin had never chatted before. She did the download, following the prompts and ten minutes later sent Top a friend request, wondering if he hadn't bailed out and went off to do something else. But then he accepted it and Robin felt herself smiling broadly.

~So you have never done a chat on the net before? ~, he asked.

~No, never. There're little smiley faces all over~ She sent him ten emoticons.

~LOL, how old are you? ~ Robin blanched. What should she say? Should she tell him the truth?

~Why? ~

~You're either too old to be familiar with chatting, or too young~

~Good point. How about I'm just too out of touch? I'm older than 18 but younger than 30. How's that? ~

~Cool~ He sent her a thumbs up emoticon which caused her to smile again.

~So, why are you talking to me? Don't you have a million fans to chat with? ~

There wasn't a response for a long time. Robin hoped she didn't come off as self-deprecating; like I'm a loser and you're a star. She was just curious. Why talk to her when there were over a hundred thousand hits on his latest video and probably hundreds of people to chat with?

~You make it seem like talking to you is a waste of time. You're interesting~

She sent him a crooked smile emoticon.

CHAPTER 17

Jason spent the evening chatting on line. He liked talking to the girl and though he could have done things like asking her for her real name or what part of Hamilton County she lived in, Jason didn't. In some ways, her talking to him online meant that she wasn't constantly looking at his jerking muscles or struggling to understand his sometimes slurred speech.

Jason felt that he could be more himself then his cerebral palsy allowed people to see. So they talked about impersonal things like music. And as much music as he sent, she still asked for more. She couldn't believe that a nineteen-year old white guy knew more about hip hop then she did. He pulled up links to rap tunes like KRS-*One Boogie Down Productions*, or explained that he loved a beat from a Jazz musician by the name of Bob James and this tuned called *Nautilus*. Then she'd get so excited and say that her mother used to play that song when she was a kid. Sweetheart's enthusiasm kept him online chatting well into the night. And then she said, '*I gotta get up for church tomorrow so I better go.*' He said '*Goodnight Sweetheart*' and she sent him an emoticon kiss.

He felt very good when he signed off and went to bed. He dreamed that he and Sweetheart were sitting right next to each other listening to music, only Sweetheart looked a lot like Robin.

Robin dragged herself out of bed. She had talked to Jason until after midnight and now she was paying the price. Church started at eleven, but mama liked being there by 10:30, so she was forced to get up early enough to be presentable.

"Robin." Mama beamed when she opened the door. "You look gorgeous." She received a peck on the cheek even before she could step into the house. Robin grinned. She thought her mother was the one that was gorgeous and she loved when she was happy and upbeat. She was tall, with honey skin, and grey eyes—she was more fit then Robin ever had been. Her mother did everything that a person 'should do'; from exercising, eating right, and of course—going to college and getting an acceptable job.

She stepped into the comfortable house, her eyes automatically moving to the photographs of daddy. It didn't make her that sad anymore, but she missed him not one ounce less than she had on the very day that he had left them. After the service, they went to Perkins for brunch, and while they waited for their order Robin decided to tell Mama of her decision.

"Mom, when did you want to go to the Bahamas?"

"I was thinking right after Christmas." It was October now so that was more than two months. Her mother gave her a hopeful look.

Robin sighed. "I want to go with you."

Mama made a happy whooping sound. "Oh, Robin! Are you going to be able to get off work?"

"I don't think it's going to be a problem. I've never scheduled a day off in all of these months, so I'll make it my Christmas leave. Besides, I'm not working at the restaurant anymore, so it's just Pinnacle."

Mom's arched brow rose. "Oh?"

Robin cleared her throat. "It was too hard working two jobs." She peeked at her mother preparing for her to bring up, once more, that she wouldn't have to work two jobs if she had a college education. But mama just listened with interest.

"Working as an aide pays more?"

"Yeah, it does. And I can get more hours." She shrugged.

"How's that old lady?"

"She's not doing so well. She had to be placed in an Elder Care Facility. I'm working with someone else now."

"Oh? Who?"

"I'm working with a young man who has cerebral palsy."

"Oh, that's so sad."

"It is, but he can do most things himself." Robin began warming up to the conversation. In the past, they couldn't talk about her job without mama ruining it by bringing up something unpleasant. Robin told her about how talented Jason was and how he had created music that was very popular. But mama didn't understand YouTube, so didn't take the fact that he had over 100,000 views as the big accomplishment that it was.

"Well, how old is this boy?"

"Nineteen."

"Nineteen? That's a man. What do you do for him? You don't have to bathe him or anything, do you?"

Robin's mouth opened and she thought suddenly of touching his penis. Her cheeks felt warm. "No. I just make sure he doesn't have complications when he's having a seizure. And I help him around his college classes..." Her voice suddenly trailed off as mama flashed her a piercing look.

"You mean, this boy, with cerebral palsy goes to college?"

Robin looked at anything but her mama. "Cerebral palsy doesn't mean that he's mentally retarded. It just means that he can't control his muscle movements."

Mama twisted her lips, but didn't speak whatever was on her mind, which most obviously was why a boy with cerebral palsy knew to go to college while her own daughter didn't.

But her mother surprised her by just changing the subject all together. "I'm really happy you're going to the Bahamas. It's going to be so much fun! This can be like a new start to everything, you know?"

Robin gave her a wide-eyed look. "I think so, too, mama." She smiled and it was the most real smile that she'd given her mother in months.

When Robin got home that afternoon, she was excited at the prospect of chatting with Jason and listening to some good music. She changed into shorts and a t-shirt and carried the laptop to her bed, where she plumped her pillows and got comfortable.

She logged into Yahoo and saw the smiling icon that let her know that Jason was signed on.

~Hey, what's up? ~ She typed.

~Hey Sweetheart. How was church? ~ She couldn't stop grinning at the way he referred to her as Sweetheart.

~Good. Thanks. Are you working on music? ~

~Kinda. Just digging for breaks~

~What's 'digging for breaks'? ~

~Basically, I'm listening to music trying to find the right sound, beats etc. ~

~Ha-ha. We do that every day. Find anything interesting? ~ Immediately two links appeared. They were two old school rappers that she had never even heard of. And when she mentioned that, he was amazed and proceeded to 'school her' on the origins of rap, naming people that she was amazed he would even know; Like Big Daddy Kane and Slick Rick.

~Do you only listen to black music? ~

~Girl, you amaze me. Music doesn't have a color! ~ Robin chuckled.

~You know what I mean~

~*No, to the first question, yes to the second*~ He sent her another link and she immediately began playing it. It was opera.

~*What the-?* ~

~*Don't type. Listen*~ She did as he requested. She leaned back against her pillows and watched the video. The man's operatic voice was against a funky beat and she was amazed when she felt chills running up her spine. What the hell was this? It wasn't opera exactly. She tried to make out the name; Vitas-Lucia Di Lammermoor (il dolce suono).

~*What the hell was that, Top? It was awesome! I got chills!* ~

~*LOL. It's called Trip opera*~

~*YOU'RE MAKING THAT UP!!!*~

~*Lol. No I'm not*~

~*I'm going to find something that you've never heard before*~

~*That would be great! Go for it*~

They talked for several hours, about nothing more benign then music — until she begged off in order to go to bed.

~*Work tomorrow?* ~

She hesitated.

~*Yeah*~

~*What do you do?* ~

She didn't like this; she didn't like this at all. She had never lied to him during this entire time that she'd chatted with him. The only lie she'd told was the lie by omission. She obviously couldn't tell him the truth about what she did if she didn't want him to figure out who she was.

~*I work in the restaurant business...so talk to you tomorrow?* ~

~*Sure. I'll be on in the evening after I get home from school and take care of some things. Have a goodnight, Sweetheart*~

~*You, too, Top*~

Whenever he called her Sweetheart it made her smile. No, it made her more than smile; it made her heart flutter.

~***~

The next day Robin was excited to see Jason. It seemed that it had been forever since she'd last seen him when it had only been two days. She retrieved his braces from the trunk and hurried up the walkway. She rang the bell, trying to keep her face from lighting up when the door opened.

"Hi, Robin," he said as he wheeled away. He had barely looked at her.

She stood there on the stoop, quiet for a moment. "Good morning." She finally mumbled to herself. She shut the door behind her and followed him into the kitchen.

"Thanks for bringing those." He wheeled up to the table and continued eating his Cheerios. "Can you make some coffee, please?"

"Sure." She placed the braces on the table and began the process of boiling water in the kettle. "So, how was your weekend?" His eyes stayed glued to the newspaper.

"It was good."

"Oh," she measured out coffee into the press. "Did you make any music?"

He glanced at her. "No."

Disappointed at his bare minimum answers, she moved about the kitchen; collecting his travel mug, cream and sugar. When he didn't try to continue the conversation, she decided to just shut up. Why had he been so talkative on the internet? Because he was talking to someone other than her, that's why.

"Is there anything you want me to do for you?" She mumbled after she had his coffee made. He looked at her as if he was surprised that she was still there.

"No." He picked up the braces from the table where she'd placed them and wheeled out of the room. Her face dropped as soon as he was no longer present.

Well, what did I ever do to him? Then she became a little angry because she had at least tried to be friendly, and he hadn't. Well, screw it. She didn't need his friendship. She just did the dishes and thought about ending this day that had only just begun.

Jason was in his bedroom, struggling with the button on his pants and cursing the fact that his fingers wouldn't cooperate. He finally got them unbuttoned, slipping them down his legs to pool at his ankles. Then he strapped on his braces, making sure that they were firmly in position. He could hear Robin doing the dishes and he paused and listened for a moment. Why did she have to look so pretty this morning? It wasn't that she had done anything special. Her short curls were held back by a stretchy band and she was just wearing khaki pants and a white blouse. She wore not a stitch of makeup and yet she seemed so vibrant and full of life; starting the day with a happy good morning.

He would not allow himself to be affected by her, because a job like this was a dime a dozen to an aide. One day she'd move on to something else and he was not going to allow himself to care. He wheeled back into the kitchen and picked up his coffee mug, not seeing a second one for her.

"You didn't want any?" He took a careful sip of the hot liquid. She had screwed the lid on firmly so not even a drop dripped on his lip. Some aides were so stupid that they didn't even have it screwed on tight enough or threaded right and scalding liquid would go running down his chin. He'd learned the hard way to be careful.

She shrugged absently. "No thank you."

He watched the way she tried not to meet his eyes and how she stiffly moved about wiping off the table, even though she had evidently already cleaned it since there wasn't any of his Cheerios mess present.

"Robin." She kept wiping and didn't answer. He thought about how friendly she had been this morning and how cold his responses had been and felt guilty. "I don't mind if you make yourself a cup of coffee when you make me one, or even if you just want one when I don't." She moved to the counter and began wiping that down. "I mean, if you want Cheerios, help yourself. And my mom pretty much loaded me up with stuff when she went shopping so there's other stuff in the fridge-"

She finally stopped and looked at him. "I don't think that would be right. I work for you. I'm not supposed to use up your resources," she shrugged. "Thank you, though."

"You didn't seem to mind having my coffee last week."

"Sorry about that. It won't happen again." She turned away and left the room.

He didn't know what to say. He didn't like when she was like this-like he was just a job, which actually is all that he was. Okay, so he knew that he had just been in the bedroom thinking about how to keep a distance between them, but he already knew that he didn't want that. It only took thirty seconds of her treating him like a mere patient to show him how foolish he was being. If he had to waste the time that they spent together being cold to each other, then he would rather go without an aide all together.

He wheeled into the living room where Robin had retrieved his book bag and laptop. "We only have about fifteen more minutes before we should head out." She spoke while glancing at his unkempt hair and his unshaven face. "Are you sure there's not anything you want me to do for you?" He ran his hands through his unruly hair.

"Do I look that bad? Don't answer that. In my book bag is a headband. Can you hand it to me?" She searched for it and found it. He pulled it on over his head and then slid it back to hold his hair out of his face. "There." She didn't comment. Grrr.

"Okay, Robin, look I..." He sighed and knew that if he didn't pause, he'd be completely impossible to understand. He closed his eyes for a moment and relaxed. When he opened them she was watching him with a bit more interest then she had a moment before. "I always had aides, since I can remember. And I guess that's all I ever knew for a very long time. I didn't go to a real school until college. The teachers at 'normal' schools weren't equipped to deal with my seizures and my mom didn't want me going to 'special' schools, so I was home schooled.

"My only friends were my mother and my aides; I guess everything revolved around them. When I met a good aide, they were like a lifeline to normalcy. My only friends were the adults hired to take care of me." He gave her a crooked smile. "That was my life. And then the job would end and they would just leave. They would leave like I was nothing. To me their friendship was my life. So I had to begin to realize that just because my life revolved around them, it didn't mean their lives revolved around me." Her brow gathered and she watched him with sadness. What a sad way to grow up.

"It's very easy to become too deeply attached to a person that is with you so intimately." He thought fleetingly of those few people that had left their impression on his life and wondered if he had done the same with them.

"So you began to push people away?" Afraid that they would leave him, she assumed.

"No. Not people; *assistants*. I push *assistants* away."

Robin's face fell. "Gotcha." Link had alluded to that fact when he commented on her return after her first day of working with him. Jason hadn't expected her to actually stick in there; which is why he hadn't bothered to introduce her to anyone. How many times had he made introductions in the past before his friends just stopped caring what body sat in the chair next to him to monitor his choking and seizures? And wasn't that what Miss Lucille had done when she had waited three weeks before even asking her name. She was so naive.

He nervously rubbed the wheels of his chair. "I was stupid, Robin. I don't want to push my assistants away. I would like to be friends, because maybe assistants go, but friends don't."

She gave him a surprised look at all that he had revealed, and then nodded. She felt that it was only right that she explain about her nervousness. It was a good description; a simple nervous condition, not anxiety driven paranoia. There was such a thing as nerve pills but they didn't stop you from breaking out in a cold sweat and hiding somewhere when you found yourself in a tough spot.

"Okay. I..." The words froze in her throat as she suddenly clammed up.

"What?" He prompted patiently.

"I don't have any friends. I mean, I know people, but..." he nodded. "I get nervous easily." She whispered the last.

"Shy?"

"Maybe a little more than that."

He smiled. "It's fine." He didn't really think of her as the nervous type, though she did retreat easily. But having no friends? That seemed strange, considering how sweet and open she was. Yet, if she did have crippling shyness, he guessed that would be the result. "Should we go?" Robin nodded in relief. It had been a revealing but uncomfortable conversation.

The drive to school was surprisingly comfortable even though Robin was too shy to start up a conversation, despite the unease that had existed between them just a short while before. She sipped her coffee because she had hurried to the kitchen and made herself a travel cup before leaving. As they drove in comfortable silence, she wondered again how to deal with Sweetheart. Maybe she should just slowly disappear. Yes, that would probably be for the best.

Jason felt a weight fall of his shoulders. It was a new concept; to open up again and allow an assistant to get close, especially in her case, since he had to admit to himself that he was a bit attracted to her.

CHAPTER 18

During class, he watched Robin more then he listened to his lecture. Sometimes she caught him doing it and she'd smile and he'd blush furiously. He learned new things about her, like the fact that she leaned forward when she was interested in what the professor was talking about. And when she was confused, she would lean back in her chair and her hooded eyes would dart around the room to see if anyone else was as confused as she was. When she got bored, she would cross her arms over her chest and her chin would slowly begin to rest on her chest. She wasn't falling asleep, just tuning out.

Sometimes she'd glance at him to see how he was reacting. He wanted to teach her what she didn't understand; explaining it so that she wouldn't be confused. But he knew that was stupid. She wasn't here to learn, but to assist him.

Then as his business class was letting out, he had a seizure. She had just placed his laptop into its case and had asked him if he wanted to build web pages for hire. Then came the sensation that he needed to stretch and yawn. He turned to Robin who was preoccupied with zipping the case, and that was the last that Jason remembered.

When he opened his eyes again it was to the sound of his own laughter. He was stretched out, legs no longer resting on the footrest but on the floor and he was twisted half out of his seat. Robin's brown face had paled and her eyes were wide. One of her hands rested on his chest, the other on his neck. He closed his eyes, tired, yet the chuckles continued; not loud, never loud. When he finally felt able to think clearly, he pulled himself up and straightened himself in the chair, grimacing.

"That was not funny," he said solemnly. She sounded scared

"I know. It's involuntary."

"Are you serious? It's like laughing turrets or something?"

He nodded squirming a bit in his seat. He was pulling at his pants.

"What's wrong?" She asked frowning. "Did you bite your tongue?" His face was bright red beneath the brown of his freckles.

"No—OW!"

She looked down and saw that there was something big in his pocket and he was trying to move it—OMG! It wasn't in his pocket and she knew what it was.

"Um, are you okay?"

His face was beet red. "I'm sorry, I'm sorry, I'm sorry. But I need to adjust..." Robin was looking away discreetly. The room was empty as the seizure had begun at the end of class. Even the professor had left; most probably so that he wouldn't be called to assist.

"What are you doing?" Why was he fumbling down there?!

"My freaking hands won't cooperate." He was trying to unbutton his pants. "And I need to adjust."

Robin moved anxiously from one foot to the other, and then she looked down at his lap where his erect penis was straining against his pants. She quickly brushed his hands away and undid the button. Then she briskly unzipped him hoping nothing would pop out and no one would walk in.

"I swear, "he said solemnly. "This is not a part of your job description; releasing patients erection." Sweat beats had sprouted on her forehead, but when he said that she burst out laughing; an explosive stress reliever. But then she saw him quickly reach into is pants and her eyes darted away. However, not before she caught a brief glimpse of the swollen tip of his penis peeking out above the waistband of his boxers as he pulled his penis flush against his body. Her face turned red hot and she knew that her cheeks were bright red, even through the brown of her skin.

"Button me! Hurry!"

Robin jumped and reached out to close and button his pants. His penis wasn't visible, but the evidence of his erection was unmistakable as it tried to tent out his shorts. It was so big. How had it gone from that wormy piece of flesh that she had held with two fingers to this huge snake-thing that he had to press across his pelvis? Her hands moved at lightning speed to get him closed and zipped.

With that taken care of, Jason quickly righted himself in his seat. His face was still blazing. "Thanks," he mumbled. He was beyond embarrassed, and people were just beginning to come in.

"Sure," she said and quickly grabbed his things while he began wheeling out of the room. When she caught up with him he offered her a shaky smile.

"Sorry about that. When I have a seizure I get a har- um, an erection."

She glanced at the passing people and hoped they couldn't hear what they were talking about. "Yeah, I heard that sometimes happens. I took that seizure class, you know. They said sometimes you can lose your bladder or bowels, too." She wanted to say, 'so I brought baby wipes in case that happens.' But felt that would be grossly inappropriate at the moment.

"I don't really have to worry about that. I've learned to control my bowels long ago and I'm too hard to pee." Robin looked at the distant spaces so that she didn't have to look at him as he described this.

"Right."

They moved on to the cafeteria, again she grabbed the tray and he got a grilled chicken sandwich while she got a burger and fries. The Goth girl at the cash register gushed. Evidently there wasn't always the same person at the register because this was the girl she'd seen the first day.

"Dude! That video of you having that fake seizure, oh my God that was so cool! Are you going to put that mix on CD? I'd buy it Top!"

He passed her his student credit card. "That wasn't a fake seizure." She just stared at him in confusion as he wheeled away.

She watched him and the solemn look on his face.

"Are you planning to pay for my lunch every day?" She joked.

"Yep."

Her face straightened. "Are you serious?"

He was almost at the table with his friends. "Why not?" The state paid him. It wasn't any loss to him to add her food on. And besides, she probably could use the break.

"Well, I can't do that-"

"It ain't my money," he said, and then he was there with his friends, who greeted him with shouts and slapped hands and they talked over each other, joked and made witty observations about each other while she sat quietly next to him trying to be invisible as she ate her lunch.

Link wheeled away from his place at the table and moved over to her. "What's up?"

"Hi," she said, struggling to swallow.

"Why do you keep coming back?" He joked while winking at Jason. Jason was talking to someone but paying attention to every word they spoke.

Robin smiled and shrugged. "I guess so that I can get paid."

"Oh, darn, I was hoping it was because you wanted to see me."

She knew that he was only joking but she began to blush furiously, especially when the big blonde girl that looked sort of like a guy stared at her as if seeing her for the first time. She and Link exchanged brief looks and then he seemed intent on trying to ignore her.

"So what do you do for fun; when you're not babysitting whiny crybabies like Top?" Jason absently gave him the finger.

Link leaned in and spoke quietly. "I only say things like that so that he can exercise that middle finger. We need to keep those hands of his working. Even though he had surgery, his muscles can still tighten up in his hands."

Robin glanced over at Jason's hands and saw the thin pale lines at his wrist that indicated he'd either attempted suicide or had gotten surgery.

"He doesn't tell much about himself, huh? Well, hang with me and I'll tell all of his secrets."

Amberly stood and limped over to Top, barely interrupting his conversation as she suddenly sat on his lap and put her arms around his neck. Robin watched as his hand went easily around her waist as he continued talking. Amberly picked up his partially eaten chicken sandwich and took a small bite. She offered it to him and he took a bite. He paused and looked at her while he chewed.

"Thank you. Are you trying to get my attention?"

"Yes. Stop ignoring me," she said playfully.

"Ai-ight."

"What did you do this weekend?" She asked. And they started talking easily.

Robin looked away and saw that Link was watching her watch them.

"You never answered my question."

"Which one?"

His blue eyes remained steadily on her. "What do you do for fun?"

"Oh. I guess I don't have any hobbies or anything. I read a lot, well, when I have the time."

"Ah, do you have kids?"

She chuckled. "No."

"Boyfriend?"

Robin shook her head and then met his eyes defiantly. "Do you have any kids? A girlfriend? And what do you do for fun?"

"Wow you're nosey," he joked. The comment made her laugh. She glanced at Jason and saw that he was looking at her. She wondered briefly if she shouldn't be talking to people. Maybe she should just be watching him instead of talking.

"You should come out and watch me DJ sometime. I have a gig in a couple weeks and I'd love for your boy over there to come and join me."

Jason gave him a surprised look.

"It's a paying gig. We'll split it right down the middle."

Then everyone at the table began encouraging him and trying to find out when and where. Link told everyone that Omicron House was printing up flyers, though an exact date hadn't been set. A lot of people began coming over; almost thirty people were crowding around the table, nudging and invading Robin's personal space.

Robin felt her heart begin to pound. It almost felt like it was slamming in her chest. She had to keep telling herself that these people were not looking at her, they were looking at Jason and Link and the other members of Wheels of Steel. She was invisible and they weren't looking at her. And then her stomach began to flip and she worried that she would have an attack of irritable bowel.

A hand touched her wrist and she jumped.

Jason was looking at her. "Are you okay?" Amberly had moved back to her seat and was talking to the butch girl. Jason was leaned in her direction.

"I'm okay." She tried to give him a shaky smile but even she knew that it wasn't very believable. He looked around suddenly; seeing things the way she saw them and then back to the look of panic on her face.

"Why don't you go get some air? I'll meet you in ten minutes."

"But lunch isn't over-"

"I'm done eating. Go. I'll be in the hallway in front of the bathroom." She didn't say anything else, she would have just swallowed her unease, but if he was urging her to go, then she would leave. She moved out of her seat and to the door, leaving her tray behind without a backwards look. Now that she was up, the need to go to the restroom was urgent.

Jason stared at her as he tried to respond to his friends. Nervous. He thought he was beginning to understand just what she meant by that.

Robin headed straight for the restroom. Her watery bowels barely held. She wiped her sweating face, feeling the twisting and knotting of her stomach fade as she relieved herself. When she felt that her legs were strong enough to stand, she quickly flushed and washed her hands. Catching sight of herself in the mirror caused her to bend and splash cold water on her face. Why did she have to do this now?

How long had she been in here? Surely more than 10 minutes. She rushed to the hallway where Jason said he'd meet her, but he wasn't there. She ran back to the cafeteria, no longer noticing people watching her as she darted through the crowded halls. But Jason and his friends were gone.

Oh no! She chewed her lip and rubbed her hands together with its renewed sweat. She'd lost her patient. Shit, shit, shit.

She decided to head over to the last class of the day which was computers. But then she remembered that Jason went to the restroom after lunch. She knocked on the Men's restroom.

"Jason?"

"Robin?" She heard him call back. Oh God, she was so relieved. She should just collapse right there on the floor.

"Yeah, I'm here. Do you need any help?"

"No. I'm almost done."

When he came out of the bathroom he gave her a curious look. "What happened back there?"

"Oh." She took a deep breath and thought about how to explain it. "I get nervous when there are too many people around."

"Nervous…"

"Yeah."

"How did you work in a restaurant if you get nervous around crowds? Unless it's like the worst restaurant in Cincinnati."

"No, I worked the drive-thru window. One car load of people doesn't bother me." Not unless they were angry about a messed up order or something. But she made sure never to mess up orders so that she would never have confrontations like that. And for some reason, the window that stood between them helped.

But if she looked out front and saw a line of people in front of the registers and they were looking at her expectantly; like she should be taking their orders, that was pretty hard. That is how she had learned to ignore people—to not always see what was right in front of her. Sometimes she would hide in the kitchen until she got another drive-thru customer. The people she worked with somewhat understood that she was anxious and they made things easy for her.

"What else makes you nervous, Robin?"

"Well, I get anxious if people get mad at me. And crowds. It's hard for me to meet new people; I don't say much. Just things like that, I guess," she whispered.

He just stared at her.

"People looking at me makes me sort of uncomfortable."

He sighed and moved his attention away from her. After a moment he spoke. "We better get to class."

During computer class he couldn't stop thinking about how hard it had been for him to transition from home schooling to the bustle of college life. His mother had wanted him to go to college as much as he wanted to go forth and get a taste of the real world. So she had found a college club that dealt with diversity and disabilities. It's where he had met Amberly. She had taken him under her wing and had become the big sister that he'd never had. It still took him a long time not to look at people with suspicion. Then when Link returned to school after his accident, he'd come to the meeting with anger and remorse. It was Jason that had made him look at what he still had and not at what he had lost.

He glanced at Robin. Maybe that's what she needed; someone to show her the way.

Once class was over, he waited for her to quietly put away his laptop. She seemed a little down. "Robin, I'm going to do that DJ gig with Link. You should come."

She gave him a surprised look. "Really?" She'd never been to a college party before but didn't think she'd be comfortable, but she was pleased that he had thought to ask her.

"I can't. I'll be working."

She placed his book bag behind his chair and the laptop strap over her shoulder. Jason frowned.

"I thought you quit that second job?"

"I did. But I plan to add another shift after this one. Well, after I recuperate from my last attempt at working two jobs. And it's just going to be a half shift." She was quick to explain in case he thought she'd be irresponsible again.

"What hours will you want to work?"

"I'm hoping between seven and eleven." It would give her time to get home, eat, and freshen up before the next job. And she'd still be able to get home to sleep through the night.

"We'll see what happens," he said and then changed the subject not giving her an opportunity to say no. "I was going to ask you a question." She followed him out of the building. "About your eyes."

"My eyes?" She touched her face self-consciously. "What about them?"

"They're very unique. You don't see many black girls with eyes that color."

"Hazel eyes on black girls aren't all that uncommon."

"But yours aren't hazel. They're green and grey. There's no brown in them."

"Well, I guess. My mom has grey eyes."

"Is she white?"

"No. Both of my parents are black." She got to the car and unlocked it for him. He pulled himself up into a standing position all on his own and

214

maneuvered himself into the passenger seat while she folded his chair and placed it into the trunk.

When she was buckled in the driver's seat he continued the conversation. "Where did those green eyes come from then?"

"Vegetables."

He looked at her confused.

"Because I eat a lot of vegetables," she said grinning. "Remember what Erykah Badu said? My eyes are green, 'cause I eat a lot of vegetables. It don't have nothing to do with your new friend," she sang.

Jason froze. "Sing that again."

"What? No!" She laughed and pulled out of the parking space.

He could not believe how beautiful her voice had sounded. Robin could sing. Robin was a natural born singer and he could tell just from that one verse.

"Robin, please!" He said urgently.

"Jason, I don't sing. And plus, remember what I said about being nervous? Singing in front of people is the top on that list."

"My God," he said softly. He was staring at her intently. "Why do you do that?"

"What do you mean?" Her voice and expression became suddenly serious.

He just stared at her. "Why do you give other people so much power over you?"

She opened her mouth to respond; deny or get angry. But she couldn't say anything. What he said was true.

They rode in silence to his apartment. Once she had parked, she set up his wheelchair and he slid into it on his own. She retrieved his book bag and computer case and put them away. In the apartment, Jason moved directly to his computer and wordlessly powered it up.

"Come here a minute." Curious as to what he was doing, she walked over to his 'studio'. He handed her a mic. "Sing."

"What? You're crazy."

"Everything you're saying is being recorded right now. If you don't sing I'm going to loop what you just said over and over and put it behind a beat. Then I'm going to post it on YouTube, with your name on it. So sing."

She gave him a look of panic. She tried to hand him back the mic, but he wouldn't take it. He just gave her a severe look. She finally placed her hand over the mic and whispered.

"No. I don't want to sing and I definitely don't want you recording me!"

He turned to his computer. "Okay. See you tomorrow." He put on headphones. Then he began hitting keys on the computer.

"Jason? What are you doing?"

He turned to her. "I told you what I was going to do. So, leave me alone so I can get working on it. I want it on YouTube by tonight."

"No. No Jason. You can't be serious?" He did something on his computer and she suddenly heard her own voice saying 'What? You must be crazy.' Then he made it repeat over and over.

Oh God, oh my God. Her brain kept repeating that thought. She knew he would do it, too. Robin brought the mic close to her mouth and closed her eyes. She began to sing the second verse of *Green Eyes* by Erykah Badu.

When it was done she opened her eyes and placed the mic on the computer table. Then she turned and hurried out the door. When she got to her car her heart was beating a mile a minute.

CHAPTER 19

Jason was in the zone. The music was in him and around him; so much so that he became the music. His mind said, 'slow it down, that's it. Find the beat...that's not it. That's not it...THAT'S IT!' His phone rang and he ignored it. His homework needed to get done and he didn't care. He hadn't gone to the bathroom and he put it off. Jason edited, cut and looped like an old school master.

When he was done he pressed play and listened. When it ended, he was grinning. It was perfect. It was perfection.

He was working on homework, of course utilizing his computer, when he saw the message pop up from Sweetheart in HC. He opened the dialogue box and read the message.

~Hi TOP. Hope you had a better day than me~

~Hi Sweetheart. What's wrong, hon? Hard day? ~

~Yeah. How was your day? ~

~Eh...But I got a new tune. Still a work in progress though. I need to finish up some things. Are you going to be on tomorrow? ~

~Yes.~

~Talk to you then~

~Night TOP~

~Night Sweetheart~

Robin had a hard time sleeping. What music had Jason made? She wanted to keep jumping up and checking YouTube to see if he'd posted new music, but knew that was a part of her paranoia. Still she tossed and turned most of the night.

The next day she got to Jason's house fifteen minutes early, just because she was so anxious. He opened the door a bit surprised.

"'Morning. You're early." His hair was a bit damp and fell in auburn colored ringlets over his shoulders.

"I hope you don't mind."

"Not at all." He let her in. "I was just blow drying my hair."

"I can do that for you."

"Cool." He wheeled into the bathroom and she picked up the brush.

"Do you have a comb?"

"No." She dug into her purse for her wide tooth comb. Then while his hair was still wet, she worked out the knots. Jason watched her reflection through the mirror.

"About yesterday-"

"I wish you hadn't done that," she interrupted bitterly.

"I'm sorry."

"I don't know if I believe that."

He didn't respond. "Would you like to hear what I did with your voice?"

She worked at the knots for a full minute more before answering. "Yes." He began wheeling away before she was completely done. But she followed him back to the living room and his makeshift studio. He powered up and pressed a button. She heard strings; pianos joined it and then a person's voice, humming. Was that her? She hadn't made any sounds like that.

Robin felt chills running up her spine. The melody was so full and rich. This wasn't hip-hop, this was a soul jam. She looked at him in amazement as her voice hummed along to the melody. There was no hitch, no break. How had he done that? The music swelled and then there was a break and her voice singing 'You don't mean nothing to me'.

She gasped and looked at him in surprise. The music swelled again and her soft voice in the background repeating those words as she hummed to the tune.

"Oh my God," she said when it ended. "Oh my God..."

"Did you like it?"

"Oh my God." She looked at him, her face falling and rising and she nodded. "I loved it." She pointed to the computer. "That was my voice?"

"Yes." He smiled in relief.

"How did you make it sound so good?"

"I didn't have anything to do with that part of it. That was all you."

She was shaking her head in denial. "You-"

"I just chopped and screwed it."

"What?"

"Chopped and screwed? That's what it's called when you take a song and slow it down. I just did that to your voice. It made it deeper, a little more soulful, and I made sort of a jazzy back ground to it. So you liked it?"

"I can't believe it. I love it!" She gushed. "What are you calling it?"

"Well, I was thinking of calling it *Loves End*."

"Jason, that's beautiful. Can you play it again please?"

"I will if you'll make coffee while I do."

"Oh! Right, school!" She jumped and hurried to the kitchen. She heard the beautiful music playing and found herself humming to it as she went through the familiar routine. Jason poured himself a bowl of Cheerios, and of course some landed on the table and the floor. But while he fixed his breakfast, he listened to Robin humming and something dawned on him that caused him to come to a complete stop. He had created sounds from nothing more than ideas in his own head. And now, today, Robin was in his kitchen singing and humming along to it. That meant that she was now the music that he had created. It was a full circle. Jason looked at Robin and his heart swelled.

He finally understood why people wrote love songs. He blinked quickly and returned to his cereal.

Robin noticed that Jason fidgeted a lot throughout the day. He seemed restless or anxious. He was a little quiet, too. He didn't talk much during open discussions in class. It had even taken two attempts before he had gotten the calculus problem correct. He grumbled under his breath about it. And once she'd dropped Jason's ink pen and when she reached to pick it up a very attractive guy scooped it up and handed it to her.

Robin smiled and thanked him shyly. Then Jason had run over his foot. He'd apologized, but Robin knew that it hadn't been an accident; he'd gone out of his way to reach the guys foot and to avoid hers. She frowned at him and he just looked away.

When he had a seizure in the halls before lunch, Robin crouched down in front of him, ignoring the stares. She held her breath when he held his, and as usual, became scared when he began turning blue. She placed a gentle hand on his neck and murmured repeatedly. 'I'm here. It's okay. I'm here." When he had finally relaxed, his eyes stayed closed longer than normal while she kept stroking his neck and rubbing his shoulders.

At lunch, he kept interrupting every time Link tried to talk to her. When Amberly talked to him, he just gave her one word responses. Then Amberly gave up on engaging him in conversation and went to sit in Link's lap. Robin peeked at Jason to see if he would be jealous about his girlfriend sitting in another guy's lap. But he had just been staring at her. Maybe he was worried that she would get nervous again.

She leaned in to whisper to him. "I'm okay."

"What?" His mouth began to pull and his neck followed and then his head began flopping. She knew that when he got anxious or angry his muscles twitched and pulled. But what was he anxious or mad about? Unless it was because Amberly was lap hopping.

"You okay?"

"Yeah. Let's get out of here."

"Okay," she picked up their tray and dumped their trash. "What do you want to do? We still have half an hour before computer class."

"Let's go outside. We can sit in the commons."

"Okay." She moved behind him and began pushing his chair and he sat back and relaxed directing her on where to go. It was beautiful. She loved fall and the beautiful golden leaves on all of the trees. He instructed her to wheel them off the path and beneath a tree. Once the chair was locked he reached out.

"Help me."

She gave him a surprised look and then leaned forward and helped him to stand. She held him in place as he adjusted to standing. She looked up at him, so accustomed to looking down at him and again was amazed by his height. He kept his hands on her shoulders and by all outward appearances; they looked like two lovers in an embrace.

"You're standing."

"You always seem surprised when I do that. Help me to that tree and I can lean against it." She did as he asked and very carefully released her hold on him.

He leaned against the tree looking very casual. She placed her hands on her hips and gave him a look of admiration.

"Jason. You should do this more often. It's got to be good for your legs; keeping the muscles from atrophying." She reached out and in an uncharacteristic move she gripped his hand and turned his palm out so that she could see the scars from his surgery.

"Link said you had to get surgery to loosen your muscles?"

"I've had several." He watched her as she held his hand.

"Where else?" He was very conscious that she still hadn't released his hand.

"Achilles tendons and my hamstrings."

"Wow. Was it painful?"

"I guess."

Robin stared at him, so handsome with his millions of freckles and green eyes, thick muscular body and six feet or more of height. She became suddenly conscious that she was still holding his hand and suddenly released it.

"Um, did you get mad about Amberly sitting on Link's lap?"

"Why would I get mad about that?"

"Because she's your girlfriend."

"What?! I don't have a girlfriend. Amberly's like my sister!"

Robin felt two emotions; shock and relief.

"Oh, I thought…"

"I don't have a girlfriend," he repeated much quieter. He reached out and took her hand again. She gave him a surprised look. "Help me back to the chair."

"Oh." She blushed and placed her arm around his toned body. He put his arms around her shoulders. "Lean on me," she said when it felt that he tried not to give her too much of his weight. "I'm stronger then I look." He leaned in to her and she helped him slowly walk to his chair.

"We should do that more often," he said when he was situated in his seat.

"That would be cool."

She wheeled him back into the building and to computer class. Once his laptop was set up, instead of navigating to YouTube, he went into his computer files. He handed her his acoustic headphones. She looked at him in surprise and accepted them. He used his MP3 ear buds and double jacked into the computer.

Then he played the song. She leaned forward and Jason watched her face take on a beatific expression.

As the week moved forward, Jason found that Robin had infiltrated many areas of his life. Between classes, he took the time to explain the meaning of something that seemed to confuse her. He took pleasure in watching her confusion disappear, replaced by her enthusiasm to understand.

For the first time in a long time, music took a back seat. His days were spent with Robin and his evenings spent talking to Sweetheart. Link called every day, wanting to work on beats. But he would put it off because he was too busy with two girls; one outgoing and funny, the other reserved but enthusiastic. He couldn't figure out which he liked better.

Robin was going through a similar situation. Each day she hurried to work so that she could see Jason and at night she'd hurry home so that she could turn into Sweetheart and be that cool girl that talked to boys and was easy-going and fun.

Things even changed at the school. One day she was staring quietly, trying not to meet anyone's eyes. And then the girl that they called Patty spoke to her.

"Robin." That's all she said but then a door opened for Robin as she met the girl's eyes.

"Yes." Not a question, just a confirmation.

"How bad does this suck?" The girl's lip curled into a slight smile as her eyes quickly swept the group of loud obnoxious friends, friend's that weren't hers.

"Less than it did one minute ago." And then Patty smiled full out and Robin did as well.

Every day after that, Link flirted with her, Patty included her and Amberly ignored her. But best of all, Jason opened up to her.

Sometimes at lunch they headed outside for the commons instead of the lunchroom and that is what she enjoyed most. After paying for lunch, instead of wheeling for the table of friends, he would just wordlessly head outside.

Then she'd sit on the grass in front of him and they would talk about class, people, music, everything. He didn't bring up the party to her, but he did bring up the Jacuzzi.

"Are you going to get into the Jacuzzi with me, Friday?"

"No."

"Why?"

She didn't want to tell him that she didn't want to put on a bathing suit. Some girls had bodies made for bathing suits, but not when your thighs and butt were more thick than slim. "I don't have a bathing suit," she said honestly. "And it is not easy to find one this time of year."

"I bet I could find you a bathing suit online," he said with a shit-eating grin.

"Never mind. I'll find my own bathing suit. And when are you going to practice for that gig next week?" She changed the topic. He chuckled.

"Fine, change the subject. Um, I'll do that next week."

She nodded and he hid a pleased grin that she would even ask.

Things felt better for Robin this second week with Jason, though Friday loomed ahead of her and the misery of seeing his mother again. Maybe she would come around now that he had. Thursday after classes, she followed him into his apartment as he wheeled for the bedroom to remove his braces for her to take.

He moved to the bed easily and again fumbled with the fly of his pants. She was just about to move forward to assist him when the button came undone and he smiled to himself proudly at the achievement.

Seeing that smile made her happy that she'd waited patiently.

Then he easily swept down his pants and unstrapped one of the braces. Robin worked on the other for him, almost smiling at the cute boxers.

"So your mom will be here in the morning which means-"

"Well, you can come later; at eight because my mom can help me with whatever I need done." He gave her an intent look. "But I'll be honest with you. My mom is kind of putting you through the test." Robin gave him an *'ah ha'* look. "And the quicker you pass it the better it will be for all concerned."

She stood up holding the braces. "Do you think that I will past her tests?"

Jason waited a heartbeat before answering. "You passed mine and that's the important thing."

CHAPTER 20

Friday, Robin arrived at her normal time. What Jason said made sense. The quicker she dealt with this last obstacle the better. She rang the doorbell and plastered a happy smile on her face.

Jason answered the door this time. He returned the smile, which was the first time she'd seen him do that in the morning. As he had indicated previously, Jason was not a morning person.

"Hello, Mrs. Hamilton." Robin spoke. His mother was scrambling eggs and had just slid them from a skillet onto two waiting plates.

"Hi…Robin is it?"

"Yes."

"Grab the butter out of the fridge, please."

Robin did as she was asked as the two sat down to eat scrambled eggs, toast and sausage. The coffee already sat before them so no need for her to do that. How was she supposed to pass this test if she had nothing to do? Jason was watching her discreetly. When he caught her eye, he glanced at the sink of dishes.

Mrs. Hamilton continued talking about some event that she was going to hold while Robin ran dishwater and began washing the cooking utensils. The drone of her voice along with the backdrop of music that was ever present in Jason's home caused Robin to fall into a comfortable rhythm of cleaning. She left the water so that she could finish the breakfast dishes, but then went into the living room to gather his things to place in the car. When she returned, his mother was finishing up the dishes.

Robin studied his shaggy face. "Jason, do you want a shave?"

"Yes!" His mother answered for him.

Jason's eyes narrowed slightly. "Sure Robin."

She hadn't shaved him at all this week, so he was fairly shaggy. "If you like having a beard I can just trim it for you."

"My mom doesn't like facial hair."

So she slathered his face with shaving cream, realizing afterwards that the cream expanded a lot and she had a bit too much. He seemed amused, but didn't reprimand her. His eyes did close as she rubbed the lather onto his face, and he sighed in contentment.

Rinsing off her hands in the basin that was half filled with warm water, Robin brushed his curls back behind his ears so that they wouldn't get snagged by the lather. Then she concentrated on stroking his face gently with the razor.

Jason could barely keep himself from staring. Had he ever seen a girl as beautiful? Why hadn't he ever realized how perfect she was; had never taken note of the bridge of her nose and how it sloped upward meeting that round tip of hers? And her lips were full, some would say big, but so perfectly formed that they bowed. There was a blush of color there that had nothing to do with makeup. Her skin was creamy perfection.

As Robin shaved him, she thought that she had never seen a more masculine jawline. Her eyes caught sight of the pale scars there and she pictured the injury that had caused it. The blood must have been bad. She was so happy that she hadn't had to see it. She would have freaked out. Her eyes searched his face for the other scars, along his forehead, one on his lip, and she knew that there was some on his shoulder. She had a sudden urge to run her fingers along each scar and to place a slight kiss on them.

After the shave, Jason looked at himself in the mirror and gave her a nod. Then she used her comb to work on the tangles of his hair and once that was smooth she cleared her throat.

"Time to use the bathroom?" He nodded wordlessly. This time Robin didn't care what his mother thought; she went to the door and shut it. Then, before doing anything else, she lifted the toilet seat.

She helped him to stand, noting the smell of shampoo and shaving cream as well as Jason's own distinct masculine smell. It reminded her of fresh baked bread. She liked it. And when he leaned into her so that she could help him stand, she closed her eyes momentarily to savor it.

Once standing and seeming to have himself braced, Robin unzipped his pants. She had thought about this for several days and had come to a practical decision. This was part of her job and she had no need to be afraid. Jason was a gentleman, he never made her do what she didn't want to do and she was being very unprofessional in not offering to help him whenever he had a need of it. She decided that from now on she would be the aide that he needed. That would include helping him with his toilet needs, as well as rubbing his legs the way Raymond had shown her.

As professionally as she could, she reached into his boxers and carefully removed his penis. She aimed it into the bowl and then watched Jason's face instead of the thing that she now held in her hand. He was looking down, either at the bowl or at his penis, she didn't know which, but immediately it jerked and a stream of urine hit the bowl.

Robin decided that if the bathroom door opened at that precise moment, then Jason's mother was a pervert. The door did not open. When he was done, she shook it as he had previously instructed and then she returned him to his shorts. She got him buttoned and back into his wheelchair.

"Thanks." He said as he wheeled out of the bathroom.

"You're welcome." She flushed and got everything cleaned up and then followed him into the living room. Mrs. Hamilton was sitting in the one armchair smoking a cigarette.

"Have a seat, Robin." Robin sat down primly on the couch. Jason was behind his computer and he glanced up curiously.

"Mom, I want you to hear a song."

"Play it son." She turned her attention back to Robin. "So what do you think of being a caregiver for a boy with cerebral palsy?"

"I...it's different then helping the elderly. They mostly sleep."

Love's End began to play. "Mom, Robin helped me with this song." Jason interrupted. His mother paused to listen and then gave Robin another look. "You mix music?"

"No, ma'am."

"You make the videos?"

"Robin sang that," Jason said enthusiastically. Robin felt herself blushing.

"Ah, a singer."

Robin was already shaking her head. "No, no I'm not a singer. I'm a caregiver."

"Are you a student?"

"No ma'am."

"Is this a profession that you intend to stick with?"

It had been a means to make money, but would this be her profession? She hadn't thought that far ahead. "I don't know. Maybe."

Mrs. Hamilton looked back and forth from Robin to her son. "I like that song. It's different then Wheels of Steel music. This is more my speed. You should do more of it."

Jason nodded in agreement. He wanted to do more, but hadn't had the courage to broach Robin again with his ideas. He'd already pissed her off once. She wouldn't be too anxious to do it again.

The two went on to school, and classes went smoothly with no seizure. At lunch they decided to give Alabama's Fish bar another shot and again went to the park to eat. This time Jason's fish came covered in condiment gook mimicking Robin's and he ate every delicious bite without choking.

At rehab, Jason asked if Robin was wearing a swimsuit beneath her clothing and when she told him no in a loud voice, he decided to bypass the Jacuzzi. Raymond greeted Robin with enthusiasm and Jason gave her a worried look. She seemed to like the man. He wanted to kick his friend when they went through their stretching exercises—he even tried to but it only amounted to a tap, which Raymond ignored.

After stretching his tight limbs, he got a full body massage. This time Raymond allowed him to lay on his stomach so that when Robin offered to rub his legs, she wouldn't see the effects that her touch had on him. He closed his eyes and concentrated on other things, but all he could see was her brown hand holding his paler dick from earlier, and how he had squirmed not to get hard. Now it was all too much and he lost the battle. He was just nineteen. He was at his sexual peak. Isn't that what people said? A stiff wind could make him erect, not to mention the touch of a woman that he found very attractive.

Robin had enjoyed her time just working one job. She had been able to get caught up on her rest and to pay another visit to Miss Lucille this week. She was getting healthier and would soon move to her new home at the eldercare facility. This they didn't speak of it during their visit. Miss Lucille didn't bring up her son the doctor, her grandkids, or the women's group. Miss Lucille spent the time asking questions about Robin's new client.

"How old is he?"

"Nineteen. He has cerebral palsy."

"The palsy. Poor thing."

"Yes ma'am, but he's very capable. He goes to college and has his own apartment."

Miss Lucille gave her a tired smile. "Is he nice?"

Robin found herself inexplicably blushing. "Yes."

Miss Lucille nodded as her eyes closed. "That's good, dear. Everyone needs a nice boy in their lives."

"Oh! But he's- well, he's not in my life or anything."

Miss Lucille's eyes opened. "He's your friend, right?"

Robin nodded. "Yes. He is my friend."

She closed them again. "I wish I had married a younger man. I loved my husband, bless his soul. I was 13 when I got married and my husband was 27. He died when he was 55 years old. I was a widow at 41." Robin knew all of this. Miss Lucille had mentioned it in passing as she told other stories. But she never talked about her husband directly, for some reason.

"He left me money and I was taken care of. And when he died I never remarried. Back in those days only a special kind of woman remarried. I fell into one of the cracks, and because of my position in the social circles, I didn't dally with men. You only dallied once you were married. People talked and it would destroy your standing if you did anything like being caught having an affair."

Robin watched her quietly. Miss Lucille seemed to be saying that she hadn't been with a man since she was 41, and she was surely in her late seventies.

She gave Robin another tired look. "Things were different back then. But I wish- I wish I hadn't cared so much about social standing. There was a man, he was a beautiful man. He was a black man and well, it would have been frowned on." Robin reached out and touched her hand. "My life, since then, has been filled with fantasy and dreams." Miss Lucille fell asleep and Robin had a hard time letting go of her hand to leave.

When she got home she called Pinnacle. "I'm ready to take on a part time client. But it has to be between the hours of seven and eleven p.m. I will not work even an hour after that." Mary Louise's response was enthusiastic.

"We'll let you know when there is something available!" Robin sighed. So many allowed others to create their happiness. She couldn't stop thinking about Lucille Babbs' sad life. She would make her own happiness, and that meant being Sweetheart in

Hamilton County for Jason. She went to the computer and logged in, seeking out Top's smiling icon.

~*Hey, Top. You have one minute to tell me what this song is,*" And then she began typing the lyrics of a song that she really liked.

~*That's Drops of Jupiter, Sweetheart. You'll have to try harder than that to stump me! Also, I could cheat by just cutting and pasting the lyrics into a Google search. Not that I would...Send me a link to a song that I've never heard.* ~

Robin chuckled and then carried the laptop to her bed where she folded herself cross-legged and settled down to wrack her brain for that elusive song that would surely impress Jason.

CHAPTER 21

Jason was being nosy and listening to Sweetheart in HC's playlist when she sent him a message. He was trying to find out more about her personality type. He'd already figured that she was more than likely African American. But her age was a tougher nut to crack since she had seventies soul jams as well as Paramore, Bruno Mars and Taylor Swift on her playlist. He was intrigued by her and wanted to know more about her. He planned to invite her to the gig Friday.

What would she look like? Should he ask for a picture? That seemed like bad manners. Tonight maybe he'd at least ask her for her name. Yeah. He definitely counted her into the friend's category. She should at least give him her name.

He actually dreamed of it that night in bed. He saw a pretty black girl watching him as he played at Omicron House and he knew that it would be her. In his dream he left the stage and Sweetheart in HC met him on the floor and then led him to the bathroom. Thoughts about his last visit to Omicron house instantly stiffened his dick. But then suddenly it was Robin there and he saw that he was standing in front of the toilet. As is the way with dreams, he couldn't remember if he was wearing his braces or not.

She reached around him and wordlessly unbuckled his pants. He gave her a surprised look and she didn't seem to realize it as she unzipped him. Then her hand reached into his shorts and she gripped his penis—not the way she had earlier that day; professionally. No, this time she gripped him gently in her entire fist. He looked down suddenly and saw her carefully withdraw him from his shorts.

He gasped. He was rock hard. He gave her a fearful look, but she didn't seem to know that anything was out of order. She aimed him toward the toilet bowl, but he couldn't pee. The dream Robin gave him a confused look and he was in a panic; one because her hand on his dick felt so good, and two, what if she thought he was a perv?

Suddenly, dream Robin gave his penis a quick squeeze. *Oh my god!* It felt so amazing. He looked down at his rock hard dick gripped in her brown hand and knew what was about to happen. He exhaled a strangled cry and then his buttocks clenched, his testes drew up, and then he came. His breath caught in his chest when her brown hand began to stroke him.

Jason's eyes popped open as he cried out. His back arched and he gripped the sheet in surprise as he ejaculated into his shorts. His hips pumped briefly before he relaxed back to the bed. Jason breathed heavily before cursing and sweeping away the covers. He pushed himself up in bed and stared down at the mess he had made.

He slid out of bed and into his chair and wheeled into the bathroom. He grabbed a wash cloth, slipped off his underwear and then cleaned himself. Pausing, he pictured Robin's hand gripping him and shivered. Damn, he could not let her pee him again. The results would definitely be embarrassing. He blushed as he imagined growing hard in her hand. She would freak out. Then he smiled softly as he thought about her.

Robin's phone rang while she was in church. Thankfully it was on vibrate, though mama could hear the vibration within her purse and gave her a curious look. Her response was just a shrug. No one called her. Robin did at least wait until services ended before heading outside to see who had called her. There was a message from Pinnacle. She quickly played it and could hear Ben's voice telling her about a job that they had lined up.

Ben described a job in Amberly Village which wasn't far from where she lived in Silverton. Her client would be a sixty-seven year old male that needed an evening aide to administer medicine, help him with his evening meal, and then help him prepare for bed. It would only be three to four hours a night and as soon as he was in bed she could leave, because he could spend the night alone. A daytime aide would arrive in the morning to assist him.

Robin could not see any hidden angles. Three to four hours a night from seven to eleven which is exactly what she had asked for. Once she brought Jason home between 4:15 and 4:30, she could go home, eat, and maybe even nap. Then the next client was less than 10 minutes away. Pinnacle couldn't trick her into added hours because she wouldn't have to wait for anyone to relieve her. Perfect. She called Ben back and told him that she could accept the job and he told her to report Monday.

Jason had been thinking about this all weekend and as he and Robin drove to school Monday morning he brought up the subject of *Love's End.*

"Robin, I want to post *Love's End* on YouTube. But I want to give you credit."

"You don't have to do that."

"But I want to." She gave him a curious side-ways glance, but didn't reply. He plunged onward. "Also, I was hoping that you'd do it again. I have so many ideas in which your voice would work so well." He held his breath and waited.

Robin licked her lips. "I'll think about it," she mumbled.

Well, she hadn't said no. He wanted to push, but didn't make that mistake again.

At lunch, Robin was the first to speak to both Link and Patty. She noticed that they seemed to be squaring off with each other silently, but both greeted her with enthusiasm.

"Did you have a good weekend?" Robin asked. Link acted as if that was a trick question as the smile on his face froze. But Patty smirked in response.

"It was eventful. What about yours, Robin?"

"I didn't do much."

Amberly sat down across from them and pulled a sheet of paper from her notebook. "I got one of the flyers for the gig Friday." Link snatched it and gave it cursory look before passing it to Top with a smile.

"'Omicron End of Summer Bash, featuring Link and Top of Wheels of Steel,'" Jason read aloud. Then he grinned and turned to Robin. "So are you going Friday?"

She shook her head apologetically and the smile slipped from Jason's face. "I can't. I just took on a second client. Today's going to be my first day working with him. After I leave you, of course," she added quickly, noting the look of disappointment on his face.

"Did you get the hours you wanted?" He asked.

"Yeah. Seven and I'll be out of there by eleven."

Jason grinned again and passed her the flyer. The doors don't open until eleven! So you can come." She studied the flyer. Wow, she would be ready to crawl into bed by then.

"Well," she passed it back to him. "I might be tired…" Her stomach was already flip flopping at the prospect of going to a party with people she barely knew. What was she expected to do while Jason was on stage? She wasn't a part of their group. They didn't have to include her.

"You might be, but you might not be. We'll see." He passed the sheet back to Amberly, who was watching the two of them with a steady gaze.

On the drive home, Robin rooted around in her CD case for music that would impress Jason. It seemed that is all she did, especially when she was Sweetheart. After hours, she had actually found an old one that he didn't know by Lee Oskar of the group WAR. He had been very impressed and had actually liked it enough to save some of the beats to his studio. She had felt very good.

"I wish we could listen to *Love's End* in the car. I can't get enough of that song." She had Jason play it several times each morning while she helped him prepare for school.

He chuckled. "Robin, it's half your song. I'll email it to you. When we get to the house write down your email address for me." She froze. Uh oh. Her email account was Sweetheart in HC. She would have to make him forget about the email thing until she could get home and create a new one real quick. "In the meantime," he continued while picking up her CD case and searching through her collection of music. "Let's listen to some Robin music."

She smirked playfully. "You already told me that 'Robin music' was going to be nothing but Trey Songz and Maxwell. Okay and there's a Drake CD in there, I lied." She laughed, but Jason became very quiet. "Did you find anything?"

"No." He said, practically slamming the CD case back into the console. "Let's just turn on the radio." His voice was flat and low.

She gave him a curious look. His smile had disappeared and he was staring out the window. He suddenly looked at her. His expression was impossible to read. But she suddenly didn't feel like smiling, either. He turned back to the window and stared out at the scenery and the rest of the ride home was quiet.

When she helped him out of his car he didn't bring up the email address, which was a relief to her.

"Well," she passed him his leg braces. "I'll see you tomorrow."

"Yep. Bye." He said curtly. She was surprised by the short response. She watched him as he wheeled into his apartment and then shut the door firmly. It was almost like day one again.

What was that about? She hadn't thought that she would see the cold side of Jason again. But he had returned. Could he be angry because she hadn't given him a firm yes about the party Friday? No, that couldn't be it because he was good up until the car ride home. She wracked her brain trying to figure out what she could have said to upset him. What in the hell was up with him? It hurt her feelings; as if making her feel bad was just a game for him. She drove away saddened.

Jason's lips were pursed in anger. He opened a can of soda and chugged it back, not caring when a good amount of it spilled down the front of his shirt, and then of course, he began to choke because he'd swilled it too fast.

"Damnit!" He cursed. He scowled and threw away the remainder of the soda. Then he wheeled into the living room and pulled up YouTube. He bypassed his own pages and went straight to Sweetheart in HC's page. He scanned her favorite music until he got to The Starland Vocal Band's *Afternoon Delight*.

"Fuck!" He yelled. Why did Sweetheart in HC and Robin Mathena both have Starland Vocal Band in their collection?

CHAPTER 22

Robin arrived at her client's house early, but had just sat in her car for fifteen minutes, listening to music and trying to mentally get into the right mood. The day had not been a good one. Jason had essentially flaked out on her for absolutely no reason and now she had a raging headache and her stomach hurt. Instead of resting, she'd been on and off the toilet with achy bowels. She just hoped she wouldn't have another onset irritable bowel while at this strange man's house.

She finally got out of the car and rang the bell to a small but neat house. She heard coughing that seemed to grow closer as someone evidently moved to answer. The door opened and a tall but stooped man was there. His watery grey eyes moved across her body before resting on her face. He smiled, but not to her, to himself. She almost felt like closing her sweater over her breast. She thought people called that look a leer.

"H-hello," she finally said. "I'm from Pinnacle."

"Yes. I was expecting you. Come in." He was wheeling an oxygen tank and a hose ran up to his nose. She remembered those hoses from when her daddy had been in the hospital. She stepped inside closing the door after her.

The man held out a shaky, thin hand. She shook it, noting that he had a strong grip.

"I'm Fred. Fred Baker."

"I'm Robin Mathena."

He was staring at her. "Such pretty eyes."

"Thank you." He was still staring at her, so she looked around his small living room. It was neat and everything seemed to have been recently cleaned.

"Let me show you to the kitchen." He walked very slow and got out of breath easily. Once in the kitchen, he sat down in a chair that had several worn cushions on it.

"I have a cart for when I have to go out." He caught his breath. "And I have a mask for when I get out of breath. Emphysema," he explained.

"Do you need me to get your mask?"

"No. I'll be okay. Just give me a minute."

"Okay." The kitchen was old but clean. The cabinets were metal and painted white. The appliances were sunburst gold. The counters were orange, but there was nothing out of place. After Fred caught his breath, he coughed and spit phlegm into a used tissue which he stuffed back into his pants pocket.

"Will you make dinner?"

"Of course. What should I make?"

"Just soup. There's a can of vegetable beef in the cabinet." He took a deep breath. "Then you can make me a cheese sandwich to go along with it."

"That's all you want?"

He took a deep breath. "Yes, I don't eat much."

247

Robin made the soup while he sat and watched her. It was really uncomfortable. She poured the hot soup into a bowl and went about preparing to make his sandwich. She searched the fridge for the cheese but it wasn't where he said it was.

He told her to check one more time behind the Tupperware dishes of left-overs and when she finally straightened and turned to him, she saw that he had been staring at her butt. She hid a suspicious look. Was that his game? Just to pretend to search in his fridge so that he could watch her butt? What a freaking pervert.

But now she was on guard. She had to feed him the soup because his hands shook too much. His skin was liver spotted and had strange moles on them, so she tried not to look at him closely; especially when she saw coarse black hair curling out of his nostrils.

After she fed him soup and made small talk, Robin did the dishes knowing that he watched her butt. She didn't even need to turn and catch him in the act. After the dishes were washed she led him to the living room so that he could watch TV for an hour before bed. She thought about Miss Lucille and her evangelist shows and missed the elderly lady. She should be comfortably in her new home at the facility. She would make a stop over there sometime this week so that the woman wouldn't feel alone.

Fred coughed and scratched and made small talk. He seemed nice enough, but she already knew that she wouldn't like him. His eyes were always on her breasts, or her butt. She gave him an insulin shot and his other medicine that had to be taken after his last meal of the night.

At ten o'clock, she asked him if he was ready for bed.

"You have to give me my bath first."

Robin sat there with a blank look on her face. Bath? Nobody had said anything about bathing him. She distinctly remembered the message stating, feed him, administer medicine, and help him to bed. Bathing him had not been included.

"Mr. - I mean Fred, um you want me to help you bathe?"

"Well you can just sponge bath me. That's what most people do." That leer was back in his eyes and Robin felt the sweat begin to form on her brow.

She jumped up out of her chair. "Um, can you hold a sec? I just have to make a phone call. I'll be right back." She darted out of the house with her cell phone in hand. She had Pinnacle's number on speed dial, which was an indication all itself that Pinnacle wasn't a place she could trust. Mary Louise answered.

"Mary Louise! This is Robin. I'm at the patient's house-"

"Is everything ok, Robin?"

"No, he's okay, but everything is not okay! He wants me to give him a bath."

"And? What's the problem?"

What's the problem?! "I know nothing about bathing a patient."

"Oh, don't worry about it. Just sponge bathe him. It only needs to be done every other day. He'll tell you how to do it. Now, if you run into any trouble just call us back. You'll be okay, Robin. You have a good night, hun." The phone went dead.

Shit. Oh shit, shit, shit. She did not want to do this. Calm down Robin, calm down.

She went back into the house. Fred smiled at her. "Ready?" He said as he stood.

She nodded feeling slightly sick.

Fred directed Robin to the pan that was used for his sponge bath while he went into the bedroom to undress. She ran warm water into the pan and picked up the bar of soap from the bathroom sink along with a clean wash cloth and towel.

When she returned to the bedroom, Fred was lying on the bed, and naked as a jaybird. Robin's eyes stayed glued to the older man's face, so while she knew that he wasn't dressed, she didn't quite see anything from the neck down. When she got to the full size bed, she quickly draped the towel across his pelvis and then she could think.

His breathing was so labored that she told him she'd get the oxygen mask.

"No. I'm okay."

"Do you want your hair washed?"

"No."

She sighed in relief. She dunked the wash cloth into the water, and then lathered it with soap. She wrung it out and gently wiped his face and neck, but when she got to his ears she almost lost it. Thick grey and black hair was sprouting from it like a primordial forest. She felt her stomach knot and she almost spewed her dinner. She had to look at something else as she dug into his ears with the soapy cloth.

When she wrung out the soap she saw that the white wash cloth was already dirty. She quickly wiped the soap from his face neck and was tempted to leave it in his ears, but gently swabbed them clean. She moved to his arms and hands and got those clean. Then she was forced to change the water. It was too dirty to continue working with. When she returned to the room with the fresh water, she noted that the towel now had a tent in it.

Her face burned. There was no way she was removing the towel. Fred just stared at her, breathing heavily as she washed his narrow torso. Ew, did all men have lots of hair surrounding their nipples? She helped him sit up so that she could wash his back and his chest touched hers. Fred sputtered and coughed and his body trembled as he tried to catch his breath. Robin quickly washed his back and got him lying down again.

He looked very tired, his eyes were only half opened and she figured it was past his bedtime. She was probably much slower at this than the others. She decided to do his legs next and saw that his towel was no longer tented. Thank God, no more erection to deal with. She quickly washed his birdlike legs and his dirty feet. The water was in dire need of another changing, but she just wanted to be done with it. So she slipped off his towel very quickly and without looking at his privates, she wiped at whatever the wash cloth came in contact with. By feel alone it felt like a sack filled with two withered plums and a water logged hotdog; half eaten.

She turned him onto his side and cleaned his bottom and by the time she finished, he was sound asleep and snoring. She went through his drawers and found pajama bottoms. She slipped these on him, happy that he was sort of clean — he still had a strange smell. When she was done, Robin went to the bathroom and scrubbed her hands.

At home, even though it was after eleven, she went straight for the computer. All she could think about was Jason's change of attitude and that maybe Sweetheart could discover what was wrong with him.

She signed in to Yahoo and saw that he was signed on as well.

~Hi TOP. Busy? ~

~Hello. No. I'm not busy~

~How did your day go??~

~Fine, just finishing up a song to get ready for YouTube~

~A new one or that same one? ~

~The same one. Would you like to hear it? It's called Love's End~

~I'd love to! ~ Robin received a link. She played it, saving it so that she could listen to it every day and every night without having to bother Jason about it anymore.

~Did you like it, Sweetheart? ~

~I loved it! ~

~Can I trust you? ~

~Trust me?   Yes. ~ She watched the screen in confusion. Why would he ask that?

~Because no one has seen this but you and me. We can't let it leak, you know. I never show my work before it's posted~

~No. I wouldn't do that~

~I know. I wouldn't have sent it to you if I didn't trust you~ Robin smiled.

~Sweetheart? ~

~Yeah TOP~

~Tell me about yourself~

Robin swallowed. ~What do you want to know? ~

~What's your real name? You know my name is Jason. What's yours? ~

Robin began to get nervous.   Name, name, name…*~Sharon~*

~Hi Sharon. Nice to meet you~

~Nice to meet you Jason~

~May I see a picture of you? ~

What???? ~A picture? ~

~Yes.~

~I don't have any on my computer~

~Oh? You should put some on just so you can share with people. Describe yourself to me~

Robin's stomach began to twist. She didn't like this. She didn't like this at all. She thought for a moment about how she should respond.

~I have medium brown skin. ~

~What color are your eyes? ~

~Brown~

~You're black, right? ~

~Yeah, why? ~

~I met a black girl recently with grey/green eyes. ~

~Oh? ~ She didn't know what to say. This seemed wrong.

~Yes. That song I sent you. I wrote it about her~

Robin's belly flipped again.

~Who is she? Your girlfriend? ~

~Hell no, ha-ha. She's my assistant~

~Oh. Why did you say Ha-ha? ~ Her face was burning.

~Because. I don't trust her~ Robin's mouth dropped. She felt her heart sink.

~Why do you have an assistant that you don't trust? ~

~I don't want an assistant that I don't trust~ Robin felt sick; she literally felt like she was going to throw up.

~You better get some sleep, it's getting late. Night~

Then his little Yahoo icon went to sleep, and Jason was gone.

~***~

The next morning, as she showered and dressed, Robin wrecked her brain for anything that she could have said or done to make him mistrustful. She had spent a very restless night of running back and forth to the bathroom. When she got to Jason's, she knew that she had dark circles under her eyes and she probably looked dumpy in sweatpants and a hoodie, but she couldn't seem to expend the effort to put together a halfway decent outfit.

She rang the bell and he answered with a good-natured greeting. "Good morning, Robin."

"Good morning." He wheeled out of her way so that she could come in. She hesitated and then headed to the kitchen to start the teapot going. He followed her, but didn't begin the process of making his bowl of Cheerios. He just watched her.

"Is there something you want me to do for you?" She asked.

He didn't answer. After a few moments of uncomfortable silence, he grabbed a bowl, spoon and the cereal from the cabinet. Wordlessly, he wheeled past her to the refrigerator and retrieved the milk. Then he made his cereal, picked up his newspaper and began to eat, ignoring her completely.

Robin fidgeted until it was time to make the coffee. She didn't try to make small talk. The two didn't speak one word and in the car Jason plugged in his earphones and shut her out further. It was like the very first day. With one exception. This time she wouldn't get sucked up into his anger. This time she would be professional and if he didn't trust her and couldn't tell her why, then the hell with Jason Hamilton. She was sick and tired of his games.

He had a seizure right before lunch, which caused them to be the last arrivals at the table. Her expression was uncharacteristically angry when they finally did arrive. Just as she always did, Robin placed her hand on his chest to prevent him from falling and when he came to, he rudely brushed her hand away from him and wheeled to the cafeteria without comment. Well, he didn't have to ever worry about her touching him again.

He paid for their lunch as normal and then at the table proceeded to ignore her. Even Link could tell that something was up. He gave Jason a questioning look, which was ignored. Then Link opened his mouth to speak to her and Robin held up a finger and opened her cell phone. She stared at Jason as she pretended to listen to a message. And a long time later, she pretended to text back and forth. She was watching him eat, so he couldn't complain. In that way, Robin allowed herself to slip out of the group that she had just become familiar with.

The ride home was quiet. Jason got into his chair, and angrily wheeled to his apartment while Robin angrily drove back to her apartment.

CHAPTER 23

Robin was in a foul mood when she reached her next job and she was happy that she didn't have to bathe Mr. Fred tonight. Despite that, he still creeped her out just as much. He actually touched her hand when she passed him a glass of water. And even though she had kept on the hoodie and loose sweat pants that she had worn earlier to Jason's, his eyes still stayed glued to her chest and butt. It was like he had x-ray vision. She even saw him licking his lips at the sight of her.

She fried him chop steak, made instant potatoes and opened a can of green beans. He kept asking her to eat with him, but she was too grossed out to have an appetite. She knew that she should not be having such negative thoughts and she tried hard not to let them show on her face. After about the sixth time of telling her that the food would go to waste, she practically snapped that it wouldn't go to waste since it was going to be leftovers for his dinner tomorrow.

After dinner, she gave him his medicine and then insisted that he brush his teeth; his breath was horrendous. But he just pulled out grimy false teeth and she had to clean them for him since he was too weak to do it himself.

He watched TV for a while and then said he was ready for his bath. Robin gave him a disgusted look.

"Tomorrow," she said.

He pouted but she stuck to her guns. He said he needed help putting on pajamas and she made him sleep in his underwear. When he was in bed she told him goodnight and practically ran out of the house.

She hadn't been in the mood to visit Miss Lucille, as she had planned. And she wasn't in the mood to pretend to be Sweetheart. She would be happy if she never spoke to Jason Hamilton again. And then she cried into her pillow until she fell asleep.

The next day was Robin's turn to be angry. When he opened the door for her, she didn't even wait for him to say good morning or go to hell. She walked past him and dropped her purse into the armchair, and headed for the kitchen.

He followed wordlessly and just like the day before, Jason waited in the entrance of the kitchen, watching her with accusing eyes.

She made the coffee and he still hadn't made his breakfast. "Do you want me to make your breakfast?" She finally asked.

Jason wheeled into the living room ignoring her. Robin waited a moment and then followed him. Her fist went to her hips.

"Did I do something wrong?" She finally asked.

"No." He said.

"Then why-?" She didn't know how to finish the question.

"Why, *what*, Robin?" His anger seemed to have disappeared, to be replaced by something much worse; hurt. He seemed to be truly disappointed by her.

"Why are you angry at me?" She knew that she was about to cry as her voice cracked. This was such bullshit. Why was she crying when he was the one being mean to her?

"I'm not angry." He stared at her. After a moment she made to turn away. He sighed in disgust.

"I can't believe-. You're not going to fess up, are you?"

"Fess up? Fess up to what?" She gave him a completely confused look.

"You would just keep going with this façade! You're Sweetheart in Hamilton County!!"

Robin's mouth dropped and her eyes bulged. She swallowed. "Jason..." She was speechless. How did he know? How could he have figured it out?

"Robin, what is wrong with you?! Are you playing some game? Why would you do something like that?! Are you trying to dig up something about me? You could have just asked me what you wanted to know!"

"I..."

"What?"

"I'm sorry." Her breath came out in a rush. "I wasn't trying to pretend to be someone else. I just commented on your YouTube is all." Her words were coming out in a rush. "Then when you commented back, I should have said who I was but I didn't. And when I didn't then, it seemed that too much time had passed. I mean, like it was kind of stupid to say 'It's me Robin', two days later. But I wasn't trying to play any games!" Her fingers began to twist and the sweat began sprouting on her forehead.

"I'm sorry. I'll leave." She spun on her heels. She was so embarrassed. The tears were already springing from her eyes. She wanted to run away and hide. She couldn't work for Pinnacle anymore. She had to quit that job. She would go home and bury her head under her pillows and stay there until she died.

"Robin." She couldn't stop walking. She had to keep walking until she was out the door. She couldn't bear anymore of his accusing looks. "Robin!"

She stopped and turned to him in shame.

"Why are you leaving?!"

"I...I need to go-"

"No you don't-"

The sweat was streaming down her back now. And she saw the spots before her eyes. She needed air. She couldn't breathe in here.

She blinked and he was suddenly there in his chair, right in front of her. How did that happen? "Come here, Robin. Give me your hand. Come on." He took her hand when she just stood there weaving on her feet. He pulled her hand, urging her down to him until she finally flopped listlessly into his lap. She was blacking out; she couldn't breathe, and she was blacking out.

"Put your head down." She didn't understand his words until she felt the gentle pressure on the back of her neck urging her head down so that it was almost between her legs. Then she felt Jason's fingers tracing small circles between her shoulder blades.

"It's okay, you're just hyperventilating. Relax." He was saying. "You're okay." He continued rubbing her back until the black dots dancing before her eyes disappeared. After a few more minutes, her breathing evened out and the tears stopped splashing from her eyes. She sat up and wiped her eyes with her hands and tried not to look at Jason or to think at all. He continued to rub her back with gentle fingertips.

She was sitting on Jason's lap. She was too embarrassed to meet his eyes, too embarrassed to even get up off his lap. She felt like a total idiot. Not only had she gotten busted in a big fat lie, but she had also had a panic attack right in front of him. She closed her eyes and covered her face.

"Robin, it's okay." She was shaking her head. "Yes it is. I'm not angry. Come here." He pulled her firmly against his chest until her head was buried against his neck. She didn't move, in complete shock that she was so close to him, but also feeling calmness take root. He put his arms around her and somehow that's exactly what she needed. She slowly stopped trembling and her tears stopped falling. She relaxed, breathing in the scent of his neck, his soap and shampoo.

It had taken a long time to calm her and when she did, she fell into an exhausted sleep on his lap where he continued to hold her in his arms. He was a little afraid. He'd never seen a panic attack before; what she called a nervous condition, he saw it for what it truly was. His anger had completely vanished in light of her explanation. It made perfect sense when she explained it. It was her shyness that had prevented her from coming forward.

What did it mean that Robin had continued to seek him out after work hours? Jason finally admitted to himself that he had feelings for her. He had known for a long time. But his own fear of rejection made it difficult to accept the idea that maybe—just maybe, Robin Mathena felt the same way for him that he felt for her.

He placed his lips against her forehead and then allowed her curls to brush his cheek as he carefully rested his head there. He yawned and locked his fingers together securely around her body. After a moment, he fell asleep himself.

Robin's head popped up and she looked around. Jason's hands tightened around her body and she looked at the sleeping man in alarm. His head was thrown back in the chair and he was snoring loudly. How she had ever slept through such a racket was testimony to how physically and mentally exhausted she was.

She tried to slip out of his grasp without waking him.

"Where are you going?"

She gave him a terrified look. "Uh, Jason! I think we're missing class."

He just chuckled; his hands remained locked around her body. "It's okay. I can just get on the computer for my lessons." She relaxed a little, but found it strange the way his hands were around her body; it was the way she'd seen him holding Amberly on his lap and he had said that she was like a sister, so it seemed okay. She relaxed a bit more.

"I'm really sorry about what happened-"

"I am so happy!" He interrupted.

"Happy?" She blinked at him.

"That I'm not the only one that apologizes. I'm always apologizing to you, Robin. Can we just, like, forget about it?"

She nodded quickly. She was good at putting unpleasant things behind her and just moving forward. And there wasn't anything that she wanted more, at this very moment, then to pretend that she had not just made a complete and total fool of herself in front of her client.

"I have to use the bathroom," she said shyly.

He wanted to laugh. Of course she did. "Wait." He unlocked his hands from her body and began wheeling them across the room. "I'll drive you."

She braced her hands on the arms of the chair even though he wasn't going fast. He stopped at the bathroom door and she stepped down and stood up. That had actually been fun, and she'd never sat in any man's lap; other than her Daddy's. So it had also been somewhat intimate. She liked being close to his big chest and feeling his long hair brushing against her face. And the feel of his strong arms around her body made her feel protected and loved. She looked at him and felt her chest tighten and her heart speed up. Did he really forgive her? Because she would never do anything like that again, just for no other reason than that she never wanted to see that look on his face again. She had learned her lesson.

"Thanks." She backed into the bathroom and softly closed the door. She put her hand on her chest and then touched her lips. Jason. The very word; his name, caused her to feel weak. 'I think I'm falling for Jason', she admitted to herself. And she had almost ruined it with a stupid lie. She smiled. He liked her, too.

Robin used the toilet and agonized over her appearance as she washed her hands. All she could do was scrub the tears from her face with soap and water and using wet hands, push back her springy curls. When she stepped from the bathroom, she could hear soft music playing. Jason was at the computer—big surprise—and he grinned at her when she entered the room. Thank God he wasn't scowling at her anymore. His big smile made her heartbeat quicken. How did people deal with feelings like this? Just looking at him sent her into near cardiac arrest.

"I pulled up a playlist; that one we listened to together on the computer the other night." She blushed at the memory of Sweetheart in HC. She never wanted to think of it again.

"Yeah."

He wheeled to her and took both of her hands. She tried not to look at him in surprise at the contact. "Hey, I liked Sweetheart. I still do. As a matter of fact, I was going to ask her to come to the party Friday."

She looked away uncomfortable. "Sweetheart didn't act as shy and awkward the way I do."

He didn't laugh at her. "Sweetheart is you, but that doesn't mean that you can't take on more of the characteristics that you associate with her. I mean, if you get nervous at things that Sweetheart doesn't, then maybe you should think of yourself as Sweetheart." He paused. "So, Sweetheart, will you come to the party with me?"

Was he asking her on a date? She smiled. "Well, I guess." And then she knew that there was nothing in the world that would cause her to miss seeing him make music. She nodded enthusiastically and was rewarded with another of his killer smiles.

"So how do I change Robin into Sweetheart?" What he said made sense about recreating herself to be more like her alter-ego. "I could have like, an accent; like maybe a Jamaican accent." She was only half joking, because she did like the idea of being someone else.

"God, no. I like your voice just the way it is."

She smiled shyly and looked away, gently pulling her hands from his grasp because she was getting too anxious with the contact.

"What would Sweetheart do that you wouldn't?"

"Sing!" Oops. Oh shit. She shouldn't have said that out loud. She didn't want to sing.

Jason grinned. "Do it Sweetheart. Sing me a song." Her heart leaped at the name. Mmm, she liked being called Sweetheart, and hearing the words come from his mouth instead of just reading it on the computer.

She swallowed and struggled to fight her shyness. "I'll sing, if you don't look at me." He immediately wheeled around until his back was to her. She checked to make sure he wasn't looking, and then she closed her eyes and began to sing a song by Ledisi called *Higher Than This*.

When she was done, Jason wheeled around. "Beautiful." His brow gathered. "Robin, when you sing Erykah Badu, you sound just like her. When you sing Ledisi you sound exactly like her. Can you sing Whitney Houston?"

She nodded. "I know that song from 'The Bodyguard.'" He nodded and wheeled around so as not to watch her. Robin closed her eyes and did an exact rendition of *I Will Always Love You* as sang by Whitney Houston. When it was over Jason spun around and leaned forward.

"Excellent! Robin, you have a very high octave range. You're a voice mimic."

She smiled. "My mother always wanted me to sing at church, but I was too shy. So what are we going to do for lunch? I'm getting hungry."

His eyes were popping out of his head. "Robin, Sweetheart, your voice is spectacular! I think you might have a six octave voice."

She smiled shyly. "Okay, thanks. Let's stop talking about it, though."

He gave her a curious look. He suddenly understood that she knew exactly the type of voice she had. And yet she still kept it to herself. She could be a professional; with that voice and those eyes, she could be a star. But then again, it wasn't a viable job for someone with crippling anxieties.

"Okay, enough about that. Lunch. We can order out."

Robin turned to the refrigerator and checked the contents, and then she checked the pantry and cabinets. "Well, there's a lot here. Your mom pretty much loaded you up." She turned to him. "I can make you something."

"Sure," he said happily.

"What do you want to eat?"

"Whatever you want to cook."

"Ah, you're an easy customer. Let's see. How about grilled ham and cheese?"

"And soup?" He added. She nodded. "Sounds like a plan!" He headed out of the kitchen. "I'm going to the restroom. I'll be back." As Jason wheeled himself to the bathroom, he paused and waited. And just like he knew she would, Robin began to sing softly to herself. He smiled and continued to the restroom; ears perked to her every sound.

Robin made the grilled ham and cheese and sliced them into strips. Jason dipped them into his tomato soup, but didn't make as much of a mess since he wasn't holding a spoon and trying to aim for his mouth.

"Are you at all nervous about the DJ gig Friday?"

"Not really. The only thing that would normally bother me is having a seizure, but that doesn't matter anymore. Everyone already thinks I'm faking."

"But aren't you afraid of being in front of all of those people?"

He shrugged. "No. That part doesn't bother me. People always look at me anyways. Might as well be up there showing them that I can do something cool." She guessed that was a good way of looking at things.

"So how was it working your second job?"

He remembered. She made a face. "I'm not sure." She got up and began cleaning up the dishes. She wondered something and since she and Jason were getting along well, and they'd already talked about the topic she wanted to broach, Robin decided to ask Jason the question that was on her mind. After all, he had used assistants all of his life; who would know better than him?

"Jason, I have a stupid question."

"Shoot." He said curiously.

"How- what's the right way to give a male patient a sponge bath?"

"What?!"

She chuckled and blushed. "I told you it was stupid. I have to give my patient a sponge bath and Pinnacle hasn't given me any training on this!"

"Well...ok." He wasn't exactly expecting this question from his own assistant. "Just get a basin of water and you should start from the top of the body and work your way down. Put a towel under him, right? And then only do one part of the body at a time like his arm. Then dry them."

"Okay."

"You can cover him with a blanket or put his shirt back on, or his pants, whatever. Do his genitals last." She was nodding. "So you'll have to wash them; front to back." He frowned. "So you've already bathed him once, right? How did that go?"

She made a face. "I don't think it went well." She didn't mention how gross it was, because it would make her appear very unprofessional.

"And what went wrong?"

She shrugged dismissively. "He was a pervert." She was drying the dishes and putting them away.

"Robin," he said in a smooth tone. "What do you mean by 'pervert'?"

She glanced back at him. His expression was calm, but curious. She ducked her head away. Why had she even brought this up?

"Well, when I was washing him he got an erection."

Jason sputtered. He found the idea of her washing some old guys erect dick very distasteful. Probably almost as distasteful as it had been for her to actually do it.

"He got an erection? At what point of the bathing did this happen?"

"I'm not sure, because I was only looking at him from the neck up. And I put a towel over his middle. When I came back from changing the basin of water, the towel had a point in it."

He sighed.

"But then it went away on his own," she added quickly.

"Oh my God Robin, he jazzed!"

Her normally heavily lidded eyes grew large. She was shaking her head, but she knew that he was absolutely right. *Oh my god!* She dropped the dishtowel and began pacing frantically. "Oh, that is so disgusting! I can't wash that man again! What if he does *that* while I'm touching it?!"

Jason's face was red and his lips were pale slashes in his angry face. "Don't go back there. Or better yet, do this; roll him on his stomach."

"Roll him on his stomach? What is that going to do? So I won't have to see it?"

It took him a moment before he could form a coherent sentence. All he could think of was white hot balls of heat. Finally, he spat out his words. "Wait until his dick his hard and then roll him onto his stomach!"

She gave him an alarmed look. "I...I can't do that."

"He deserves it. I guarantee you that the pervert doesn't need help washing. He's just using Pinnacle to supply him with people who will touch his dick so that he can get off! He's a pervert Robin. Trust me on this. If you don't roll him on his stomach, he will start getting worse. He'll be touching you accidentally, rubbing your ass or brushing against your boobs."

She crossed her arms around her chest, a stricken look on her face.

"Did he already start doing that? Oh my God...Robin, Sweetheart. Just do what I said."

"What if it hurts him and he has a heart attack?"

"I bet his heart is strong enough to-"

"*Okay I'll do it!*" She said loud enough to interrupt his next words. Jason stared at her, his face still pulled into a frown. "I'm going to finish the dishes," she said just to get away from his stare. Jason nodded and wheeled out of the room.

Robin's hands were shaking. Now that she understood what was up, it would take every bit of her nerves to face Fred Baker tonight.

Jason had wheeled into the bedroom. He had his cell phone in hand and was rapidly dialing, well as rapidly as his fingers could. Mary Louise from Pinnacle answered the phone.

"Hi, Mary Louise." His voice was more pleasant than his face indicated. "This is Jason Hamilton. Yes, I'm fine. Listen, Mary Louise, the reason I'm calling is to find out if you've found me a night time aide? I know, I understand. I know it was difficult to find an aide willing to follow me around school, but you did it. But I still need someone for the night and that person has to be trained in seizure emergencies, remember? Yeah. Well, if you don't have anyone then I'm going to have to accept the state's night time aide," he lied. "Well, they don't have any problem finding me someone for the evenings and that person is going to be able to work part of the day, so I will only need Pinnacle part-time." He knew that companies like Pinnacle moved fastest when they thought it would affect their wallets.

"I only really need someone to work four or five hours a night; seven to eleven is good. I mean, there's no need to pay someone to watch me sleep like the state wanted me to do, just so my night time aide could take me to school. Yeah, just seven to eleven." Jason smiled at Mary Louise's response. "You can? Wow, that's great Mary Louise. As soon as possible; tonight if it can be worked out. Ok. Thanks and have a good evening."

He pocketed the phone and wheeled back into the living room happily.

CHAPTER 24

By the time Robin, had finished the dishes Jason's mood had improved. He was waiting by the door.

"What?" She asked.

"Let's go for a walk."

She checked the time. "You got me for a few more hours. She grabbed her purse. "Where to?"

"Just outside. I live in a nice community; great for walking and there's a pond around back, with benches. I don't normally feed the ducks there, they start swarming around you like nasty little monstrosities. But if you want to, just grab the bread."

"Um, darn and you made it sound so compelling. But I think I'll pass."

Robin hadn't looked at much more than the walkway to Jason's house in all of her visits, so she had to agree with him that he lived in a beautiful little community. Kids rode on the bike trail and couples walked hand in hand. Jason wheeled while she walked along side of him. She thought back to the way he had stood so tall against the tree and felt a teeny spike in her belly.

"Jason?"

"Yep?"

"I know I keep asking about walking, but don't you want to?"

"Yeah," he responded earnestly. "But it's dangerous. I will fall. And no, I'm not wearing a helmet. That's not happening."

"Well, I can catch you." He gave her a surprised look. "What if you walk when I'm around?"

"I don't...I don't think that's a good idea. I could hurt you."

"I'm stronger than I look."

"I believe you, Sweetheart, I do. But I'm bigger and heavier than I look."

"Teach me the correct way to catch you then."

He seemed to be thinking about it, than he shook his head again. She stepped in front of his wheelchair and he gave her a surprised look.

"Tonic," she said. "You'll stretch and pull back. I need to be behind you when you fall. Then the Clonic; you'll seize and hold your breath. You kick and tap your hands and feet, but only for a few seconds, then you relax and you start breathing again. If I'm behind you, I lower you to the floor. That's it."

Jason licked his lips. He didn't know what to say. She knew his seizures like a science. "Did you learn that in class?"

"Class helped with the terms, but no, I learned that from you."

"I'm not a strong enough walker. I'm slow and it takes up all of my energy-"

"You just need to practice, then."

"Not by myself," he hinted.

She grinned and stepped out of the path of his wheelchair and they continued towards the small lake.

274

When they reached it she sat down on one of the benches. Jason locked his chair and easily moved himself onto the bench to sit beside her. She gave him a surprised look and he grinned at her in return.

They didn't speak for a while, just sat together, watching the ducks and the people passing by.

"Jason?"

"Yep?"

"What does it feel like? Does it hurt?" She swallowed and hoped he didn't mind her asking.

"My seizures? No, not at all. As a matter of fact, they feel..." He thought about it. "...the way a good stretch feels. When I feel one coming on, it's like I'm ready to yawn. Then I don't remember the actual seizure, but after I feel rejuvenated."

She stared at him; the way his eyes sparkled let her see the truth in his words.

"You stop breathing, though."

"Yeah, I know, but it doesn't hurt me."

"You turn blue. It scares me when you do that."

He slowly reached for her hand, gripping it lightly. "I don't even know it. I just feel a little tired afterward." Probably the lack of oxygen, but he didn't mention that. "And once I sit there for a while I'm good as new, better in fact. And it's really helped that...well, the way you touch me. That really helps."

She nodded. "Okay, I'll remember that."

They sat there holding hands without speaking for a long time. "Touch is really important to me, Robin. My skin is ultra-sensitive, so hugs feel really great; massages; even better—or just snuggling. My mom and Amberly are my connection to feeling normal. People don't really want to touch a person with a disability like mine." That made her feel sad. She wasn't very touchy; her family was more reserved. Yet she reached out and squeezed Jason's hand to let him know that she didn't have a problem with physical contact. He exhaled a shaky breath.

He suddenly released her hand and tried to push himself up. "Robin," he said. Then he threw his body back.

Robin's purse fell to the ground as she jumped up. Jason fell off the bench; his head went slamming onto the cement footer holding the bench to the ground. Robin pulled him roughly away from the bench before he started seizing.

"OMPH!" He grunted, limbs stretching. Several people came running over.

"He's having a seizure!" Someone yelled. "Put this belt in his mouth." A burley, older man began removing his belt.

"No!" She yelled. "Don't put anything in his mouth!" She cradled his head on her lap as his body strained and thrashed repeatedly. He didn't have violent seizures, but his feet did kick and his arms struck out.

Spit began to stream from his mouth, but his head was already turned to the side.

"Oh my God he's choking on his tongue..." A pregnant lady cried out. "Someone needs to call an ambulance!" Several more people began to gather around.

"Please, back up." Robin snapped. "I'm his caregiver, he'll be okay, just don't crowd him." She felt her own heart beginning to pound with all of the people surrounding them. Jason's grunting suddenly ended and his body slowly relaxed. After a few more leg and arm twitches he was quiet. "Hand me my purse." She commanded and someone quickly passed it to her. She dug inside for tissues and gently wiped his mouth. She stroked his hair and forehead repeatedly.

"It's okay, I'm here." Her heart was pounding. His head rested on her bent knee and his eyes finally fluttered opened. He gave her a groggy look. "Are you okay?" She asked.

"Fucking hit my head," he murmured. He sat up slowly and rubbed the back of his head.

"Let me see." She looked behind him at the back of his head, her hands gently probing his scalp. Damn, there was a lump forming there and it was pretty big. "We need to put some ice on that. Let me help you back in the chair."

"No. I can do it. Just wheel it to me." She hurried to the chair, most people had already left and gone about their business, some were still standing at a distance, staring and whispering. She tried to ignore them as she retrieved his chair, rolling it close to him. He pulled himself into it, and then he positioned his legs. Once he was settled in he gave Robin a tired look.

"You still think you want to help me learn to walk?" She crouched down until she was face to face with him.

"More than ever." He had a very sad look on his face.

She didn't know why she did it, but she leaned in and kissed his lips. He gave her a surprised look, but at least the look of sadness had disappeared.

The walk back to the house was quiet. Robin had no idea why she'd kissed him. He hadn't said anything about it, yet he didn't appear to have disliked it either. Still she was very self-conscious as she walked quietly alongside his wheelchair.

Once they got back to the apartment, she was happy to hurry to the kitchen just for something to do. She went to the freezer to make an impromptu ice pack, but found that he had several already there. She supposed a person prone to frequent seizures would have plenty of ice packs, bandages, and more.

He sat quietly and didn't make so much as a peep. But she noted that he was staring at her as she fussed with his head.

"I'm okay," he finally said, holding the pack to the back of his head. "Look it's getting close to the time for you to leave. You can go now if you want."

She looked at him a bit surprised. She was sort of enjoying their time together away from school. She would have hoped that he was enjoying it too. "What? Are you sure? I mean you just bashed your head in-"

He chuckled. "Hardly. Besides you'd be leaving in an hour anyways. You should get some rest for that night-time job. You're going to want to be alert."

She grimaced. "Don't remind me." He was probably right. "Thanks Jason." She gave him a sheepish smile. "And I'm sorry for all of that Sweetheart stuff."

He leaned forward. "Robin, help me stand." She moved in front of him and using the technique that he'd taught her, she crouched and gripped him around his body, while his arms went around her shoulders. Then she hoisted him up. He came up easily, his body taking a few moments to adjust and for his knees to lock into position with the aide of the braces.

When he seemed to have steadied himself, she smiled and looked up at him. But he had no smile on his face. His expression was completely serious; then he leaned forward and placed his lips on hers. Robin sucked in a surprised breath, her body instantly igniting. He kissed her again, lightly at first, giving her an opportunity to withdraw if she wanted to.

She didn't.

It was her first true kiss, not counting the one that she'd given him a few moments before, because that one had been out of the blue. No, this is one that Jason had calculated because she had consciously or unconsciously given him permission to bridge the gap from caregiver and patient to intimacy. And it scared her, but it also intrigued her.

Sensing that she wasn't going to back away, Jason leaned forward and pressed his lips to hers again, feeling her trembling response. He placed his hand lightly at the back of her neck and was rewarded when her lips tentatively parted. Jason had only shared his first kiss just a few weeks before, but the difference was total. Electrical currents ran through his body. His tongue brushed her lips as the kiss deepened. Robin parted her lips more, and then her tongue darted out quickly to touch his.

Jason groaned softly. How could pressing his mouth to another feel so incredible? He captured her bottom lip, slowly, sensually and ran his tongue over it. Robin's breath caught in her chest. Her tongue peeked out again and this time it slid against his. Jason's body began to tremble and Robin quickly clutched him, pulling him against her body, holding him in place. His kisses became impassioned and she accepted each one. Suddenly he pressed forward and sought her mouth; capturing the full bottom one again.

Jason's knees began to tremble. He was going to collapse if he didn't sit down. He pulled back slightly but she pushed forward, totally absorbed in the sensation of her first kiss. Jason lifted his head, breaking the kiss, but her lips moved to his chin and then his neck. His body felt like it was on fire. His nerve endings were inflamed and sensitized to the feel of her soft kisses.

"Oh…God," he moaned. "Sweetheart, I'm going to fall." He didn't want to stop, but he was still standing by sheer will alone. Robin suddenly blinked and she looked at him as if just now realizing that he was there.

"I'm sorry!" With an anguished groan she lowered him into his seat, but before she could right herself he pulled her down into his lap.

"Come here." She did, butterflies forming in her belly, at least until his lips found hers again; then vibrant electrical shocks spiraled from her belly to each of her limbs. His arms went around her, holding her; making her feel that everything was okay.

It was a long time later when they parted and that was only because they needed to catch their breaths. And even still, her forehead rested lightly against his, their breathing labored, hands still clutching and holding on to the other, their lips meeting periodically as they panted and blinked at each other.

"Jason…" His fingers travelled up and down her arms.

"Hmmm?"

"I liked that."

He chuckled. "Me too, Sweetheart."

She felt her mouth pull into a silly grin. "I like when you call me Sweetheart." She snuggled in his arms, head against his shoulders, the way it had earlier that day. He ran his hand up her arms and to her shoulder where he rubbed her there lightly.

"You are really sweet. You chose a good name. So it's okay if I call you that? It won't bring up bad memories?"

She smiled. "I would love it if you called me that." Her hand moved up his chest and rested there over his heart. His eyes closed.

"Mmm...that feels good." He opened his eyes and looked at her. "Can I ask you a question...kind of personal?" She sat up suddenly and watched him with trepidation, but he continued to smile while lacing his fingers around her body.

"Okay."

"Was that your first kiss?" He was beginning to form an idea in his mind; could Robin be a virgin? The questions she asked, the way she acted when she had to help him in the toilet.

Her brows rose, but she relaxed. "Was it that obvious?"

"No, God! You're a great kisser!"

"Really?"

He lowered his head to hers and kissed her gently. "Yes." She sighed and kissed him back. Suddenly she remembered the time, and sat up abruptly.

"Oh! I have to go!"

He grimaced slightly. He didn't want her to go, but she also bounced on his lap, making his dick ache. "I guess you're right. It is getting late."

She stood up and hurried to her purse while Jason quickly adjusted himself and pulled his sweatshirt down low, placing his hand on his lap. She turned to him and he smiled brightly.

"I guess I'll see you tomorrow."

"Okay. We can practice walking."

"Yes." She shyly went to the door. "Bye, Jason."

"Bye, Sweetheart." She seemed to blush and then she closed the door behind her and Jason immediately relaxed. His head fell back against his chair and his breathing was labored.

"Jesus...." He said. That had felt so incredible. It was nothing like that when he'd kissed Amberly, nothing. Jason brought his hand under his shirt and he stroked his nipple until his body shivered. He tugged at his erection and then forced his hands away from his body. He didn't want to jerk off, then his body would associate kissing her with the need to masturbate. He didn't want it to be like that.

Jason understood his body in ways that people with better muscle control quite possibly never would. He'd had to train himself to regulate his bathroom activity, as well as to help his erections to fade quickly. He knew that an erection would not fade as long as there was a stimulus. He knew that associating Robin with sex would mean that he'd constantly be erect whenever she was around. That couldn't happen or it would be incredibly embarrassing for him and her as well.

Fuck it, just this one time. He tugged the button on his pants and slipped his hands into them. He gripped his hard cock with a cry and stroked himself to release.

CHAPTER 25

Robin felt as if she were walking on a cloud as she got into her car. She couldn't wipe the stupid smile from her face.

She knew that she should probably go home and relax before meeting with Mr. Fred, but she felt very hyped and decided to get a well needed car wash and then an oil change. Then after that, she would finally pay a visit to Miss Lucille and see how she was doing in her new digs. She checked her cell phone while she sat waiting for her car detailing to be complete and saw that there was a message waiting from Pinnacle. It had been left hours ago and the high that she had been on since leaving Jason's apartment came crashing down. What could they want??

She replayed the message. It was from Ben.

~Robin, please call the office as soon as possible. Don't go to Mr. Baker's house before calling. Thanks. ~

She dialed Pinnacle, nervous about why they didn't want her to go to Mr. Bakers. She didn't care for the old man, but she hoped that nothing bad had happened to him. She felt guilty at the memory of her and Jason's earlier conversation and how bad she'd downgraded him. She couldn't believe that she had actually contemplated rolling him on his stomach and hurting his penis.

Maybe he had even called Pinnacle to complain about her not bathing him yesterday. As the phone rang, Robin began to agonize over all of the things that she could have possibly done wrong. When Mary Louise answered, it took all of her courage to sound confident.

"Hi, Mary Louise. This is Robin M-"

"Hi, Robin. I know your voice, hon." She responded pleasantly. "How are you today?"

"I'm fine."

"Good. Robin, I know that you said that you didn't want to stay with your current client, Jason Hamilton, but...well Robin, we have a proposition for you."

Robin felt sweat begin to bead on her forehead. They weren't going to make her leave Jason because of what she'd said that first day, were they? She listened politely, wanting to rush in and say that she'd made a mistake. She'd changed her mind. She wanted to continue working with him.

"Robin, Ben has authorized me to offer you a raise if you will continue to work with Mr. Hamilton."

Robin's mouth dropped. Huh?

"How would a dollar more on the hour sound?"

"A dollar?" A dollar sounded great.

"Well, there is a condition to that. We're going to ask you to take him on in the evenings as well. Instead of working with Mr. Baker, you would return to Mr. Hamilton from seven until eleven."

Robin's face felt hot in excitement. She would go back to Jason. She thought about their kiss and the tingling between her thighs returned.

"We understand that this is not something that you anticipated, Robin. And we do apologize, but Mr. Hamilton has been looking for a night time aide since becoming a client. We were lucky to have you work with him during the day and you have the training already."

Something occurred to Robin; they needed her. She cleared her throat.

"Make it one dollar and fifty cents an hour, and of course overtime and I'll do it."

"You have a deal." Mary Louise responded quickly, which told her that they probably would have offered her more had she kept her mouth shut. But it didn't matter. She wanted to see Jason; now she got to see him more and was getting paid to do it.

"When did you want me to start?"

"Tonight."

"Oh," she touched her face and wiped the crazy smile from her lips. "Okay."

"Thank you Robin. We appreciate it, and understand how difficult Mr. Hamilton can be."

"Well, it's understandable, I guess."

"Yes! Yes, of course!"

The two women hung up and when Robin's car was finished, she hurried home and headed straight for her computer to tell him.

His little Yahoo icon was wide awake. She quickly tapped out a message.

~Hi Top~

~Hi Sweetheart. ~ Came his quick response.

~Guess what? ~

~How many guesses do I get? ~

~None. I'm not going to have to go back to Mr. Baker's! ~

~Mr. Baker??? Pervert man? ~

~Aw. Mean. But yes! ~

~That's great. Did you tell Pinnacle that he's a perv? ~

~No…they assigned me a new client. Well not a new client; someone I know…~

~Is it me, I hope? I just got a message from Pinnacle saying that they found someone for me. It's you? ~

~Yes.~

A smiley emoticon was sent.

~I better go. I have a demanding patient and he will want me rested~

~Blush. Sorry about that…~

~Kiss~

A kiss emoticon with hearts floating around the head suddenly appeared.

Robin signed out, excitement causing her hands to sweat and her heart to pound. She'd never had feelings like these before; at least not ones that had been reciprocated. It was new and exciting. She took a long hot bath, listening to Wheels of Steel's music that ran from her laptop, which she had plugged into computer speakers that had been positioned on the bathroom counter. She closed her eyes and fantasized about Jason's lips and the way it felt being cradled in his big strong arms.

Jason called Amberly.

"Hey Tramp Stamp." She laughed.

"And where were you today?"

"Playing hooky."

"Bad boy."

"Well, I never call off. What are you doing?"

"Nothing. Why?"

"Can you bring me my crutches?"

There was a pause. "Jason, you're going to start walking again?!" Her excited voice became slurred. But Jason had no problem understanding her.

"I think so. I want to try." He had hidden his crutches with Amberly for the last year. She had been trying to give them back to him, but he wouldn't take them. There was no need for them when he couldn't use them anywhere but in the apartment. In addition, he'd just have to worry about hiding them once a week. So she'd been holding them for him.

"I'm on my way!" Jason went to his computer and navigated to the college bulletin board for each of his missed classes to get the assignments for the day. And while he waited for Amberly he saw Robin sign onto Yahoo. He perked up instantly. They chatted and he felt a bit sneaky that he didn't confide about his earlier conversation with Pinnacle. It wasn't important. The important thing was that she was away from that pervert.

Amberly arrived a short time later, carrying his crutches. She gave him a quick hug and he used the crutches to help brace himself as he pulled himself out of the chair and into a standing position. Amberly had to practically crane her neck to look at him since she was standing so close to him; presumably to catch him in case he fell, though if that happened Jason feared that he would crush her tiny body.

She took a few steps back so that he could walk. He leaned forward on the crutches, and then had to practically drag his lower body forward to catch up. He was greatly out of practice. This was not going to be easy. He could barely bring his legs beneath him to stand. He gave Amberly a doubtful look. The last time he'd walked, it was with the help of the Baclofen pump, but that had been removed and was never to return.

"You have to practice, Top. Call Raymond and let him know that you're going to start walking." He nodded. "And what brought this on? I've wanted you to do this for a year!"

He smiled. "I don't know. I want to stand without wobbling." She moved forward and placed her arms around his body and hugged him briefly.

"I'm proud of you, whatever the reason. I know it's not an easy decision. So, you want to go eat?" He glanced over at the computer to check for the time. It was five thirty and had plenty of time before seven, but he wanted to eat with Robin.

"Nah. Hey, you want to hear my latest?"

"Oh yeah!" She said excitedly. He moved back to his chair and sat down, tossing the crutches onto the nearby couch. Then he moved to the computer which was also his studio, and pulled up the song that he'd just recently created.

Amberly sat down on his lap and listened. She didn't have much rhythm when it came to bobbing her head to the slow beat, but she tried. When the song ended, she gave him a curious look.

"That was great, but different. Where'd you get the voice? It was so haunting; very beautiful."

"That was Sweetheart. A girl I met online. She's a pretty good singer."

"What do you call it?"

"Loves End."

"Can I make a vid of it?"

"Yeah, thanks."

Amberly relaxed in his arms. As it was the only seat in his 'studio', it was where she normally sat when listening to his music. His arms went around her comfortably and he considered how just a few short moments before, Robin had been sitting there and he'd been kissing and holding her.

"Top?" He looked at Amberly, his cheeks reddening.

"What?"

"I asked you if you knew what you were going to do when you and Link DJ Friday."

"Oh. Um, we're going to probably need to get together and jam. I'll talk to him about it tomorrow."

"You know what we should do? We should all meet over here Friday and jam out, listen to some music, watch Beat Street and party before the party!"

He smiled and then shrugged. They used to do that all of the time; meet here or at Link's and either watch old eighties rap movies or jam out making beats. Sometimes Patty would sing some crazy lyrics and Amberly would pull out her phone camera and videotape them acting crazy. It was why he hated for Wheels of Steel to end. He didn't want to lose that type of relationship with any of them.

"Yeah. Let's do it! Friday. You set it up with Patty and I'll set it up with Link."

She gave him a half smile. "Hey, did you know that they were doing it?"

His expression froze. "What do you mean?"

"Doing it..." She made the universal hand sign for 'doing it' which was one curled hand and then the forefinger of her other hand poking at the hole.

"I mean, I know what that is, but are you saying that they've done it more than once?"

"Yeah. I'm saying that. Patty told me that they just did it again yesterday after school and they did it all weekend."

"God, are they becoming a thing?"

"I don't know."

The two speculated about it and Jason checked the time once again. "I better get my homework done." She stood up.

"Alright. You gonna be at school tomorrow?"

"Yep." She limped to the door. "Bye, Top."

"Thanks for bringing those."

"You're welcome."

After she was gone Jason found himself laughing. He called his friend, Link.

"What's up?" He said trying to sound serious.

"I was going to call you later, thought you might've busted your head in the bath."

"Nah. Just needed a day."

"I hear you." Link responded.

"What are you doing?"

"Just finishing up with some homework. Getting ready to work on some beats."

"Cool. We need to jam. Amberly wants us all to get together Friday."

"Finally, dude! Yeah, I'm all for that!"

"Okay, well you let Patty know. Tell her 'hi' for me if she's there."

There was a pause and he knew that his guess had been right.

"What?" Came Link's stuttered response.

"Ha!" Jason laughed. "You and Patty are a thing, aren't you?!" Jason heard Link cover the phone. A moment later Link was speaking to him in a hushed voice.

"How'd you know?!"

"If you wanted to keep it a secret, you should have told Patty not to tell Amberly all about the fuck fest you two are engaged in." Jason wanted to fall on the floor laughing. It wasn't out of meanness. He loved both Patty and Link; they were like the two older brothers he never had.

"Jason, I don't get it! She's like, got a mojo on me!"

"Hmmm. Maybe you're tired of finding love in those vacant top-heavy bitches that you always screw. Maybe it's about being friends."

There was a long pause. "Shut the fuck up. I'm not in love! This is nothing about love! I just, she just likes my dick a whole lot. It's like it's not even connected to me."

"What about you? Why do you keep going back?"

"Because she likes my dick," he said as if that was reason enough. "I gotta go!" The phone went dead and Jason laughed, almost falling out of his chair. He checked the clock and saw that it was closing in on seven, so he went to the bathroom and brushed his teeth. He had already changed clothes, a necessity since he'd jerked off while sitting in his chair. Masturbation was best while in bed and with a jerk-off washcloth to catch everything.

Robin arrived promptly at seven and he was happy because he'd already stood up and was leaning on his crutches. He moved gracelessly to the door and opened it.

Her bright smile froze as her eyes met his. "Jason…" He knew she'd like it. Her reaction was well worth the sweat that was running down his face. Walking was hard when you could barely move your legs. He moved aside, trying not to look like he was ready to stroke out, so that she could come in.

"Hi, Sweetheart."

She smiled shyly. "Hi. Where did you get those?" She pointed to the crutches while closing the door.

"My crutches? Amberly had them at her place. Now kiss me quickly so I can sit down."

She had been waiting for this all evening. She moved in close to him and placed her lips lightly onto his." He smiled happily.

"Thank you."

"Okay, so let me see you walk," she asked excitedly.

"Okay." He walked slowly to the couch and when he reached it he collapsed onto it. Robin applauded like he'd just walked a tight rope at the circus. She came over quickly and sat next to him. She could tell that it had been hard, sometimes his legs did not come forward enough and he would keep straining forward until they were under him before he could move the crutches forward.

"I used to be pretty good at this."

"You'll be good again," she said honestly.

He stared at her, and then leaned in. She met him halfway, and they kissed. It seemed that everything that they had said and done since she had arrived was leading up to this; they had taken care of all of the niceties, and now it was time to just get to what they both wanted to do; kiss.

His hands moved to the back of her head where her springy, short curls were lose; being held back only by a band. He found his fingers exploring her thick mass of hair as his lips and tongue explored and tried to rediscover her mouth.

Robin took the cue and moved her hand up his chest. He shuddered involuntarily, but her hand continued upward to stroke his unruly locks of fiery red hair. They did this; kissing and running their hands through the others hair, until Robin finally pulled back.

"Are we going to kiss through my entire shift?"

"Well, I thought we'd stop to eat. But other than that...yeah."

Reluctantly, she untangled her limbs from his. Somehow one leg had made its way up onto Jason's lap and she stood with a sigh. She moved to get his chair, but he shook his head and picked up the crutches. He pulled himself up to his feet.

"Let's go check out what we have." She followed him into the kitchen. She wanted to walk behind him in case he fell. He pretty much dragged himself and looked fairly shaky. But he made it without incident. There were chicken breast fillets in the freezer.

"How about fried chicken?"

"Sounds good." She placed some of the fillets in a bowl of water to thaw. He went back out to the living room and sat in his chair. Then he wheeled to his computer to finish up his homework. "Robin? You want to listen to some music?"

"Sure." She yelled from the kitchen. She had found rice and was deciding on which vegetable to make. She heard Miles Davis. She knew Miles because her mom and dad used to spend hours listening to various forms of jazz. She smiled and after she had the water simmering for the rice she came out to stand alongside of him.

"Do you like jazz?" He asked while looking up from his studies.

"Yes I do! I was just listening to some Jazz a few weeks ago; Jazzmatazz-"

"By Guru; volumes 1, 2, 3 and 4," he added.

"Oh my God," she said in surprise. How did he know that? She hadn't even known about Jazzmatazz until she saw it on YouTube while searching for some old Bob James song. "How in the hell do you know that?! How do you know-?"

He chuckled. "I love Guru and he just died so I listened to all of his songs right after that happened." He pulled up YouTube. "Let me play you this. Volume 1 is the best in my opinion." He played *Loungin'*, then *Le Bien*. He continued with his homework while Robin moved back and forth from the kitchen to check the progress of the dinner that she was preparing, and to check on Jason. When she was in the kitchen she danced and hummed and then she returned to the living room appearing ultra-professional.

After listening to Jazzmatazz Volume 1, she asked him to play Volume 4's *State of Clarity*. "I like that one," he said and then proceeded to 'school' her in the ways of Guru. "First of all, let me just say that Guru is one of my all-time heroes. I have several, but he ranks high up there. Guru and Gangstarr helped form the foundation of Hip Hop. And then if you think about how we all go digging for beats; we're finding old jazz and turning that into hip hop. Well, Guru had the idea of actually recording with those Jazz greats;

Sanborn, Bob James, and creating a new type of fusion. I mean if you want to make music you want to listen to Guru." Jason went on excitedly talking about Guru and his brilliance.

"Wow. You really are a fan."

"Yeah, I am. But that's how I know about Jazzmatazz." She was still amazed. It seemed that she might really have a hard time finding something that this young man hadn't already discovered for himself. She finished up dinner and placed it on the table. She cut up his chicken breast. In addition to that and the rice was a can of green beans that she doctored up. Robin knew that she was a good cook, even if she seldom had a chance to do it. Even something as simple as fried chicken, rice and green beans was transformed into a feast.

"Come and eat," she called out from the kitchen. Jason felt all warm and fuzzy when he wheeled to the table and saw the meal. Robin was pouring juice into a sipper cup for him.

"This looks good, Robin."

"Thank you," she beamed. They sat down together eating the delicious meal with no conversation. Unfortunately, Jason and fried chicken did not go well together as he gagged several times. But he eventually got more down his throat then on his clothes. And he actually did enjoy it, although by all outward appearance he didn't.

"Is it too dry?" She asked worried.

"No. Fried food is just hard for me to swallow. But it's good." She placed that information into her memory banks. After dinner, before she could move to do dishes, he wheeled to the sink and began running dishwater. He washed while she dried and wiped off the counters. It was nine o'clock when he asked her if she wanted to go for a walk to the pond.

"Okay." Jason picked up the crutches. "Are you sure about this?" She asked.

"I'll need to practice to get better."

"True."

"Kiss me first." She did, relaxing a bit. While they walked, they talked about school and being a caregiver.

"So what made you want to be caregiver?" He was very curious about this.

"I...nothing. I didn't want to do this. I just needed the money."

He paused a moment to catch his breath and to look at her. "You don't have any kids, you're not married. Why do you work so many hours?"

She shrugged. He didn't have to work for a living, he was a student. She had to make ends meet. "Well, it's what I need to do to cover my expenses." He watched her curiously. What did she have; some type of drug addiction? She worked a lot of hours.

When the silence continued she looked away and crossed her arms over her chest. "My father bought me that car when I graduated from high school. The plan was for me to go to college; paid for by a nice college fund my parent's created for me; the one that they dangled over my head for fifteen years. Then I told them that I didn't want to go to college and they snatched it back. They were going to take my car too." It was a thirty-eight thousand, fully loaded Volvo and she absolutely loved it. She explained about her offer to take over the payments and how her parent's told her that she couldn't afford it. But she lived at home and had no expenses except the car, so they gave in.

She then explained about her daddy dying, and how he had been her buffer between mama's total control and her own sanity. And then she moved out and that's why she was in this predicament. She looked at Jason again.

"I worked two jobs to pay for a car that I can't afford. My car is my last connection to my dad and that's all there is to it." Jason didn't respond for a moment.

"When did your father die?"

"It'll be two years in October."

"I'm so sorry, Robin. It must be horrible losing a father. I- my dad is alive, but he isn't around. I can't quite say that I've lost anything, though."

"I'm sorry to hear that." She missed her dad so much that she couldn't understand choosing not to have a relationship with your own father.

"I don't care about him. When he was around, he thought I was stupid. I could never do anything right for him. Once, I heard him and mom arguing and he said 'Nobody in my family has bad genes. It's your fault! That's your son and it's your fault!'" A bitter look had crossed his face. Robin stopped walking and then he did as well.

"Jason, there is nothing stupid about you. You're the smartest person I know." He looked down. "Jason." He looked at her.

"I know I'm not stupid. It's him that doesn't know it. That's the problem."

She placed her hand on his shoulder.

It took an hour to get back to the apartment. Once they reached the lake, they sat for a while to rest, holding hands on the wooden bench and watching the reflection of the moon across the water. Back at the apartment, Jason collapsed onto the couch in exhaustion while Robin got them bottled water. Even though he was so tired that his legs muscles quivered, he felt a sense of accomplishment that he'd done it.

He took a deep breath and dived into what he needed to say. He didn't think it would be easy for her, but it had to be faced. "I have to go to the bathroom now."

Robin got his chair and wheeled it to the couch. He slid into it without standing and then looked at her. "I'm going to need help."

"Oh, ok." She wheeled him to the bathroom door. He stopped the chair before it could enter.

"I need to evacuate my bowels. That part I don't need help with. You can stay out here. What I'll do is flush; a courtesy flush, which will help carry away the flow of smell." He watched her, waiting for her to flush and turn red—maybe even to have a panic attack. But she just watched him blandly. She was doing a good job of masking her discomfort—or else she really wasn't all that uncomfortable with it. He continued, being as clinical as he could. "After I flush, you'll come in and I'll be leaning forward. I think you know what to do from there, right?"

She nodded and offered him a slight smile. "Right." He squinted at her. It seemed that she was trying to ease his own discomfort.

Jason wheeled into the bathroom, turned and shut the door. Robin hurried into the living room and picked up her purse. She rummaged around until she found the small, individual dispenser of baby wipes and then she hurried back to the hallway to wait for the sound of the flushing toilet.

After another moment, she heard the sound that she had been waiting for and she opened the door and Jason was indeed leaning forward, holding a freshly lit match. He immediately blew out the flame and placed the smoldering match on the counter.

Robin hid a grin. "Thanks for lighting a match."

"Well, it's the least I can do."

She grabbed toilet paper and cleaned his bottom. Then she used two of the wipes and swabbed him clean.

He gave her an appreciative look. "Nice touch; baby wipes."

She crouched down. "I use them myself. Put your arms around me and we'll get you standing." He liked the way she took control. And if wiping his ass had bothered her, she sure didn't show it. Though having to face cleaning the smegma from some old guy's dick probably made wiping his bum a minor inconvenience.

When he was standing, Robin reached down and pulled up his pants and shorts.

"Uh..." He began when his penis was in jeopardy of being grazed by the waistband of his shorts. But she gently and quickly tucked him in. She had his pants fastened and zipped before he knew it.

"Ready to sit down?" She asked.

"Okay." He watched her for any sign of fainting or even sweating. None. She gripped his body with strong arms and helped him to swivel around and then lowered him to the chair.

"I'm going to wash my hands now. You go ahead and wheel yourself out." Jason, once again, was surprised by her directness and control. He did as she requested and when she was finished in the bathroom she came out placed her hands on his shoulders.

"Did you finish your school work?"

"Yeah, I did. Okay, you didn't have any problem with what happened in there?"

"Cleaning you? Not really. I mean, I'd rather be eating cake, but- oh well. Jason, can you show me how you make a beat?"

After a moment of hesitation, he wheeled to his computer. Robin was not completely easy to understand. He just knew that he really liked her. She was hot, she was sweet, and she loved music. He was very lucky to have found her. He powered up.

"This, my dear Sweetheart, is an FL Studio. Back in the day we call it Fruity Loops Studio..."

CHAPTER 26

Robin stayed until eleven; which was her quitting time, but she could have stayed longer. Watching Jason explain beats and mixing was very interesting. But she was actually tired and once she was in her car, she found herself yawning all of the way home. She fell into bed and was asleep immediately.

The next day, she arrived at Jason's bright and early, feeling perky. She wasn't exactly sure what there was between the two of them, but she knew that she liked him a lot and enjoyed being around him. She looked forward to seeing his handsome, freckled face. She enjoyed his snarky wit. She liked that he was so smart and didn't let people push him around or intimidate him even though, with his disorder, he would have every reason in the world to give in to insecurity.

They lost about half an hour to kissing and had to rush in order to get to class on time. As Robin moved with him from class to class, she paid more attention to his reaction to the world around him instead of the way the world moved around him. He didn't try to fit in—he *did* fit in. He talked to the other students and they seemed to honestly like him. At lunch she 'learned' how people interacted and joked with each other, instead of trying to find a hiding place and go unnoticed. Jason's friends had a comfortable routine. And best of all, she stopped feeling like an unwanted intrusion, because no one really paid that much attention to her anyway.

After class, Robin carried his things into the apartment and put them away. Jason grabbed his crutches and when she turned back around, he was standing there waiting for her to notice him. They kissed for a time until she had to pull away, promising more kisses when she returned that evening.

She wanted to go shopping for something to wear Friday. Now that she had committed to going, she agonized about how to dress. She didn't want to go; the crowds alone would make her nervous. But if she was expected to interact with people that she didn't know, she wanted to make sure that she at least looked nice. So she bypassed her usual department store's juniors department and headed for the trendy stores that she always distantly admired. First of all, she was always too chunky for their skinny jeans and tight shirts. But she hoped to find something that would complement her more curvy body.

Everything she found looked really good on the mannequins, but when she tried them she looked like she was trying to be someone else. Finally, one of the young sales girls had mercy on her and they picked out an ensemble that was really smoking. There were black jeans, and a nylon shirt with a cool screen print design. It had a plunging neckline that was almost a deal breaker, but the clerk found a vibrant scarf to loop around her neck. With black boots that she already had at home, she knew that she was almost set.

It was just her hair that might need some work. She went into a walk-in hair salon at the mall, and walked out with a haircut. She pretty much kept her hair pulled back. It would be so much easier just to wear it short and natural. Plus she thought it really looked good on her more-roundish face. It had been ages since she'd gone shopping like this for herself, so she bought perfume and cute underwear; thinking fleetingly of Jason.

Jason was so cool. He didn't try to touch her. She could tell that he just enjoyed the kisses and snuggling. She had to admit that sometimes she got very heated and she knew that he did as well, but he always remained a gentleman. She just looked forward to him *not* being so gentlemanly.

By the time Robin got home that evening, she carried lots of bags and had put a sizeable dent in the money that had been accumulating in her account. But it was about time that she enjoyed the fruits of her labor. She didn't have time to do much more then freshen up, slip on some comfortable jeans and a nice blouse, before she had to head right back out the door to get to Jason's.

When he opened the door, his eyes got wide. "Robin, what happened to your pretty hair?" She touched it self-consciously.

"You don't like it?"

He paused and then smiled. "I love it. You look great with short hair."

"Are you sure?" She asked while touching the tapered back of her neck and walking slowly into the apartment.

"Yes!" He said honestly. "You look great." He reached out and stroked her hair and then her face and then slowly her neck. Robin shivered. He placed his lips on her temple. "It's beautiful," he whispered. He kissed his way across her ear. Her eyes fluttered close. "You're beautiful..." His lips met her neck. Robin's hands moved up his body and beneath his shirt. She felt him shudder and then move his legs so that he could lean forward, pressing her back against the wall. One of his arms went around her body and pulled her to him. She felt it glide down to cup her ass and a thrill shot through her. His mouth moved across her neck and then he urgently sought her lips.

It felt good; his hands on her butt. He'd never touched her like that before. Robin's body began a slow burn; the electrical shocks that she always experienced whenever Jason was near intensified and centered around her core. She felt herself pulsing between her thighs and her breath was coming in fast gasps.

Jason leaned his body against hers and she suddenly reached down and gripped his ass with both of her hands. She pulled him to her and could feel him hard and pushing against her belly. He stopped kissing her for a moment in order to catch his breath, his own hands continuing to clutch at her rounded ass. He groaned loudly and then took his other hand and braced it against the wall. His head suddenly dipped down to capture her neck again and to tease her with his tongue. His hand came up her side and lightly stroked her breast, cupping and covering it with his big palm.

Robin's body began to shake, electrical shocks threading between her thighs and causing her to groan along with him. He stopped abruptly, lowering his hand.

"I-I need to sit down."

"Are you having a seizure?" She asked in alarm.

"No, but my legs…"

"Okay." She hurried for his chair and his legs practically buckled beneath him as soon as she had it in position. His face was flushed and his hair was sticking to his wet forehead. She could see the evidence of his arousal and this time it was his green eyes that were heavily lidded as he watched her.

She crouched down in front of him, her own green/grey eyes just as heavily lidded. She placed her hands on both of his knees.

"Robin," he warned. His back arched suddenly and he gasped; she touched him and his body reacted without his control. Her hands glided sensually up his thighs and beneath his shirt. Jason's head fell back and he groaned loudly and bit his lip. Robin's fingers continued up his goose pimpled flesh until they reached the rounds of his flat aureoles with their miniscule bead of a nipple. His hands gripped her wrist, holding her in place. She didn't mind; her brain was now a heat seeking missile that seemed connected to the throbbing at her core. She leaned forward and placed her lips on his belly.

His body jerked and he cried out as if he were in pain. She was used to his body jerks and pulls but suddenly it was magnified. It wasn't a seizure; it was just his cerebral palsy going haywire. Robin understood that his skin was hyper sensitive and she knew that even something that felt good could be too much.

So she backed off. She closed her eyes and placed her head on his chest, still crouched their between his legs. She slipped her hands around his jerking body and held him for as long as it took for him to calm down; which was a few minutes. Eventually his hands were able to stroke her hair and back.

"I'm sorry." He said with a voice about as slurred as she'd ever heard it.

She looked up. "You're okay, Jason, really. I just like…" She stood up and rubbed her hands together nervously.

"Like what?" He asked, half sprawled in his chair.

"I just like being next to you."

Jason stared at her, he still wasn't completely free of the muscle jerks, but it was much better than it had been. "Will you sing something for me, Sweetheart? Something old and relaxing?" He was holding his hand out to her.

She nodded and then moved to take his hand. He lightly pulled her into his arms and onto his lap. She snuggled there, nestling her head against his shoulder and neck. He lightly stroked the back of her hand.

She began singing a song that was so low that it was practically a whisper, but he could hear every nuance of her lovely voice. It was an old Phoebe Snow song called *Poetry Man* that was older than her by twenty years. When she got to the end of it his muscles were calm again—at least as calm as he ever got. He was stroking her arm and his eyes were closed.

"I love you, Robin," he whispered.

She began to tremble. He gripped her and held her. Eventually she calmed. "I love you too," she whispered back. He reached up and traced the trail of tears on her cheeks.

CHAPTER 27

It was Friday; the day she had dreaded all week. She was torn between wanting to see Jason work his magic as a DJ, and not wanting to be at a party with people she didn't know. She'd gotten a taste of his DJ'ing skills as he practiced throughout the week between sharing kisses with her. Watching him actually pulling beats from other songs or creating his own — and then making it into a remarkable song, was still unbelievable to her.

Robin sat on the edge of her bed feeling in turmoil, and then suddenly, felt herself smiling as she thought about this man that she loved. How did love happen so quickly? She wanted to share it with someone, but didn't have any friends to talk to about it with. She wanted to talk to her mom and ask her questions about how she'd felt being in love with daddy. But at the same time she didn't want to share Jason with her, because then mom might do or say something to deflate her bubble and she didn't want that.

With a sigh, she dressed and prepared to leave. She slipped on jeans and a sweater. She would change when she returned in the evening. As she drove to Jason's she was anxious to see him but not so anxious to see his mother.

When she got to the door, it was Jason that answered and not Mrs. Hamilton. For the first time this week, he was sitting in his wheelchair instead of standing at the door for her. She had taken his braces and hidden them in her trunk from his mother.

She was about to make a comment about it when he suddenly reached out and gripped her hand, pulling her down to his lap. Once she was settled in her most favorite seat in the world, he kissed her sensually. Robin pulled back in alarm.

"Your mother!" She whispered. He just grinned.

"I told mom to come tomorrow instead of today."

"Ah." She relaxed in his arms.

"Yeah, I didn't want her to ruin our fun before the party." He absently stroked her thigh as he talked. "I hope this doesn't backfire on me. My mom originally used to come on Saturdays. But then she would spend the entire day." He chuckled. I'd be waiting for her to leave and she'd be there until dark. Don't get me wrong, I appreciate my mom, but I don't want to spend all day with her. So I devised an excuse for her to only come on Fridays, because even if she stayed until night, I didn't have to see her for half the day"

"I know the feeling, believe me. My mom- well she's all I have now-"

"You have me, Sweetheart."

"Mmm," she pressed her nose lightly to his. "Say that again…"

"You're mine and I'm yours."

Those simple words made her heart beat mercilessly. She stood up and his brow rose.

"Where are you going?"

"Out to the car to get your braces and crutches. I want you standing." She hurried outside to get the braces from the car. But when she returned to the apartment, she didn't see him. She went to the kitchen and then the bedroom where she saw that he'd pulled himself up onto his neatly made bed and was struggling to unfasten his pants.

"Aw. I'd have helped you." She hurried to the bed and unfastened the button on his pants.

"Damned hands!" He said in annoyance. He just lay there and stared at the ceiling.

"Are you okay?"

"I just want to use my fucking hands," he snapped. His eyes shifted to hers. "And I want my girlfriend to be able to touch me and I not get all *spazzed* out!" Her body warmed at the use of the word 'girlfriend'. It was the first time he'd used it; it was the first time *anyone* had used it in connection with her. It made her feel so good that she wanted to do the Snoopy dance and sing 'I'm his girlfriend' over and over.

But she didn't like seeing him upset about something that he couldn't control. Robin lay down next to him and placed her head on his shoulder, her arm snaked across his body. His hand slowly came up to rest on her shoulder, but he continued to stare at the ceiling, the look of misery still present on his handsome face. She hadn't known that he felt so deeply about it. If only he could understand how happy she was about everything.

"It makes me feel so wonderful that my touch and my hands on you sends you off. No one else does that to you, do they?"

He looked over at her. "No. No one."

"That makes me feel special." Her hand moved to his groin. "And if you can't do this, then I'll do it for you." Her fingers lightly grazed the denim material. She saw the sudden rise and fall of Jason's chest as she let her fingers grip the zipper and tug it down.

His eyes blinked slowly as he stared down at her hands, his lashes casting dusky shadows on his cheeks. She suddenly untangled herself from him and began to undo the buttons on her sweater.

"Robin! What are you doing?"

When her sweater was completely unbuttoned, she pushed the material open so that she lay naked from the waist up except for her bra. Jason sat up on his elbows and stared at the exposed flesh of her body.

"Touch me Top," she whispered.

Jason's mouth felt dry. He had, thus far, been content to hold Robin on his lap. To touch his lips with hers and to feel her responsive kiss was thrill in itself for him. And when she wrapped her arms around his neck and clung to him or placed her head on his chest so that they could snuggle, there didn't seem to be anything that could top the feeling of joy, peace and acceptance that he experienced. Certainly, the ensuing erection lent testimony that he desired more, but Jason was also content with what he had.

Yet for her to lay there with her clothes opened, with an invitation for him to explore her, sent him to a place that wasn't spastic at all, but calm as he considered what she offered him. Jason allowed his fingertips to gently stroke her belly.

Robin reflexively shivered at the soft touch. She closed her eyes and concentrated on the feeling that his touch was stirring up inside of her. She felt his hands move to the swell of her breast where he traced a gentle trail down her cleavage.

Jason saw her swallow. He watched her face and the way that her eyes were nervously closed. He could touch any part of her body that he wanted; the invitation was out there, but it was the line of her nose that he traced, down to the cleft beneath it, then over her full lips. She was so beautiful. His heart swelled with joy that she was his; that she had connected herself to him. He kissed her lips gently. And then he closed her sweater.

She opened her eyes and looked at him curiously.

"I will take you up on that invitation, but not now."

She nodded shyly and then quickly buttoned her sweater. Not knowing what else to say, she grabbed the braces.

"Okay, let's get these on you so that we can get you to the toilet." She sat up and maneuvered his pants down over his hips and down his legs. He sat up and watched her as she did this. "So, are you going to need help?"

"I can do it. With the crutches, I shouldn't fall."

She gave him a doubtful look. "You're still pretty wobbly on them. I'll just go in and make sure you don't fall."

He shrugged and walked himself into the bathroom. He used a crutch to lift the toilet seat and then he reached into his pants and pulled out his penis. Robin peeked. She couldn't help it. She was curious. Of course she knew what a penis looked like; she'd helped pee a man, and wash a man, but she didn't actually know what *his* looked like. So she peeked.

In Jason's fist was a big fat monster penis. He held it aimed at the toilet bowl, but nothing happened. He held his breath and then glanced at her. She fought not to retreat in fear and embarrassment and met his eyes. He glanced at his penis again, took a deep breath and held it again.

"Performance anxiety?" She offered, trying to keep her voice light so that she would sound cool, and not like a shaky virgin that was mesmerized by the sight of him.

"No. It's too hard." Instead of showing her ignorance of the subject matter, Robin decided to keep further questions to herself.

"Um, shall I run the water?"

"No." He shook his head. "Tell me something gross, something that will make it soft."

"Let's see. Well, this is kind of gross. Once I got bit by a Brown Recluse spider. The skin got all rotted around the bite; it hurt too. It swelled up like you wouldn't believe, and I got sick for about two weeks.

When I got better or when I thought I was better, I woke up one morning to find little baby spiders coming out of the swelling."

"Okay. That's gross, Robin." A stream of pee finally hit the toilet bowl.

When he was finished, she reached over and flushed the toilet. "I made that up."

"You're good." She watched him tuck his penis back into his shorts. It had shrunk a bit, but was still very impressive, indeed. She almost wanted to dig her hands into his shorts and-

"Okay, button me, Sweetheart."

She jumped to it, pulling herself from her fantasy. She could see evidence of his arousal and was just happy that he couldn't see evidence of hers.

Accompanying her *boyfriend* to classes was slightly different than accompanying her client. They stared at each other a lot and fantasized about kissing. He called her babe or Sweetheart and he was much, much gentler with her.

Since it was Friday, they decided to hit a restaurant for lunch before physical therapy. At The Waffle House, they both ordered T-bone steaks and eggs. Robin made sure to slice his steak paper thin.

"Gosh, babe. Do you want me to be able to see the slices?" He joked. He munched a sliver of meat. "So are you going to get in the Jacuzzi with me today?"

She stopped midway between forking eggs into her mouth. "No."

"Yes! I want to see you in a bathing suit."

She sighed. He was like a broken record. "Jason, I'm too fat for a bathing suit." She finally admitted.

"Fat? Is that the problem?!" His eyes bugged at her. "Robin, you're perfect." She was curvaceous; that's all he saw.

She blushed. "Yeah, well thanks, but I'm not wearing a bathing suit."

"I've already seen you in your bra, it's not that different." Two guys turned and looked at them in surprise. Robin ducked her head.

After lunch they headed to rehab. He didn't bring up the Jacuzzi anymore, and went to the locker to change into athletic shorts. When he returned, Robin's eyes scanned his broad freckled chest. She really wanted to run her hands over his muscles. It wouldn't be so bad to be in the Jacuzzi with him. She shouldn't be so shy about these things anymore. Jason was her boyfriend now and she trusted him. She promised herself that she'd Jacuzzi with him next week.

Once his chair was near the edge of the Jacuzzi and locked in place, he lowered himself to the floor and slipped into the warm water. He quickly positioned himself so that he was sitting facing her, and then dipped his head into the water. He fumbled with the jets and the controls while she took a deep breath, committing herself to her decision.

"Next week I'll bring a bathing suit and join you."

He grinned and moved over to where she was standing at the edge. "Roll up your pants leg and dip your legs in." She didn't have a problem with that and quickly did as he requested. Once her legs were in the warm water, she sighed in contentment. Jason touched her feet gently. He began rubbing her ankles, causing her to shiver. There was something very erotic about his simple touch. His hands slithered up her leg to massage her calf. He had a firm but gentle touch. Robin sighed; she'd never had anyone touch her like this before. She felt her nipples tighten and hoped Jason couldn't tell. She peeked at him, but he was staring at her shapely legs.

A man came into the room and entered the single Jacuzzi near them and Robin moved her feet and then splashed him playfully. He flashed her a grin.

"You shouldn't have done that!" And he threw a handful of water at her. She gasped and jumped up. It hit her right in the face and water streamed from her hair and down her sweater. He covered his mouth and tried to hold back his laughter.

"Jason!" She wiped the water out of her eyes and glared at him.

"Oops, sorry."

"You're in trouble." The guy from the other Jacuzzi said.

"Nah. She loves me."

She tried to keep a straight face, but couldn't.

Jason didn't stay in the Jacuzzi long. He pulled himself out and Robin helped him to dry himself.

Then they went to visit Raymond. The handsome black man flashed Robin a broad smile.

"Hi there, you two."

She returned his broad smile. "Hi, Raymond. How are you?"

"Great. Always a pleasure to be in the company of a beautiful woman."

Jason rolled his eyes. "Yes," he interrupted. "And by the way, I'm here, too. And I'm doing well."

"My man!" Raymond offered his fist and Jason hit it with his own. Then he reached out and possessively took Robin's hand in his. Raymond eyed their clasped hands with a knowing smile.

"So, you two...?"

"My girlfriend," Jason affirmed proudly. He hadn't told anyone else; it all had happened so fast. He wanted to tell his friends, but not with Robin around — strange maybe, but it was how he felt.

"Congratulations, you two. And you are a fast worker. So, is it okay for her to massage your legs now?"

He shook his head imperceptibly and Robin raised her brows. "What?" She asked.

Jason quickly changed the subject. "Robin, why don't you tell Ray what we've been doing all week."

Ray grinned in anticipation for a good sexy tale.

"Um, well, we've been walking."

"Walking?"

"With crutches."

"No freaking way! You got him on crutches, Robin?"

"Well, I encouraged him."

"Climb up on the table. I want to take a look at your legs." Ray kept flexing his feet and checking for swelling. He told him that he wanted to see him walking between the bars that were located in another room. Jason did, using more of his upper body then Raymond was happy with. He was instructed to continue walking, his legs were already strengthening. On their way out, Jason told Raymond about his DJ gig later tonight and Ray said he'd try to make it.

Back in the car, Jason reached out and placed his hand on her knee. A day like this was made into a vacation, just by having Robin along with him. Every day with her was made fun. She placed her hand

over his and they drove like that back to the apartment.

"No. I don't want the chair." He said when Robin popped the trunk. "Just roll it in. I'm going to walk." They headed to the apartment slowly. Jason moved a lot more smoothly now. He didn't have trouble getting his legs beneath his body anymore.

It was still early; just after three o'clock. Jason's mind was preoccupied with Robin's earlier actions and the idea of exploring her body. Now there was plenty of time to do it right. His friends wouldn't be showing up until after dinnertime. He felt himself hardening at the memory of her luscious curves as she lay across his bed. He followed her as she went into the kitchen for bottled water. He took a long drink, eyeing her.

"We can listen to some music and snuggle." He suggested.

"Okay."

"You choose the play list this time. Put on something nice, Sweetheart. And then, meet me in the bedroom." He turned and walked into the bedroom feeling more nervous than he sounded.

They snuggled every day; just a lot of kissing and hugging. It was the best part of her day. But she knew that this was something different; this would be more than just snuggling. She was anxious, but was ready to know what else lay beyond his kissing lips and his gentle touch. After she turned on his computer and found one of her Neo-Soul playlists that she knew he enjoyed, Robin went into the bedroom to see that Jason was sitting on the edge of the bed and pulling off his shoes. He tossed them into the corner and gave her an easy smile. He patted the bed next to him and she sat down, kicking off her shoes, too.

Jason pushed himself back to the head of the bed and plumped the pillows. Robin joined him, settling into his out stretched arms. They smiled and kissed; each knowing that this is what they both had been waiting for all day. They'd never done this on the bed before and Jason thought it was nice to stretch his body out against hers. He let his hand rest on her curvy hip while she cupped his stubbly cheek. He pulled back slightly, breaking the kiss.

"Robin," he said, watching her carefully. "Can we — do you mind if we take off our jeans?"

She smiled and quickly shimmied out of hers while lying on her back and then kicked them to the floor. Jason stared at her shapely brown legs and at the place where they joined, absorbing the sight of the faint impression of her vaginal lips against the thin black material.

He hadn't intended to touch her there first; so boldly, without working up to it. But his fingers had to know that faint crease and so he stroked her through her panties and felt her legs instantly come together, trapping his hand between her thighs. When he looked at her, he saw that she was watching him playfully.

"Can I have my hand back?" He asked.

"No. Keep it there." And he did just that. He leaned forward and kissed her again, his hand lightly stroking her mound as he did so until she began shaking uncontrollably. This time it was she that pulled back. She didn't think it could feel like this, like hundreds of teasing feathers; just stroking her outer lips. Certainly when she'd done this with her own hands, it hadn't felt so pleasurable.

"I thought you said *we* take off *our* pants, not just *me* take off *mine*." She reached down to quickly undo his pants and he fell onto his back and pushed them down. Robin sat up and carefully pulled them completely off. She stroked the flesh of his leg between the braces.

"Take them off or leave them on?"

"Off." He responded. She removed the braces and then rubbed the impression that they left in his freckled skin.

"Mmm," he sighed. "That feels good." She noted that his boxers were beginning to form a tent. She wanted to run her hands up his thighs, but wanted to also be careful of over stimulating him. She wondered what would happen if she touched his penis, if it would make him go over.

"You can," he said.

She looked at him sharply. Had he read her mind? "I can what?"

"Touch it; my penis."

"How...?"

"You're staring at my shorts." He chuckled. He hiked them down and his penis sprung out.

Jesus. It was huge, or maybe not. Maybe this is what a penis should look like; maybe everyone's was long and fat, but she only had her own vagina as a gage and she didn't think it would go easily into her, though women had babies so maybe.

She was a little afraid to touch it now; watching it standing up at attention. Her face felt too warm and the sensation of pleasure that she'd just experienced was disappearing in her fear of this unfamiliar body part. Jason sat up easily and cupped her face. He brought his mouth towards hers and she leaned forward, meeting his lips as he kissed her aggressively.

"I can stop. Do you want me to stop?" He asked breathlessly between kisses.

She just shook her head and his hand slid down into her sweater, where he cupped her breast through her bra. Robin quickly removed her sweater and he felt stupid with his underwear half down, so he quickly swept them off. Now he was completely naked and trying to figure out how this had happened. He wondered if he was moving too fast, but Robin was watching him in admiration.

He looked very sexy sitting there with his wild red hair and tattooed biceps and huge upper body — even while his big stiff penis pointed upward. Robin came up on her knees and then reached behind her and unhooked her bra. Her breasts fell from the cups heavily and she tossed the bra across the room to the floor. How could she ever be shy with this man when he looked at her with such awe, his need for her so evident in his eyes?

She lay down next to him again and waited.

"God Robin," he murmured. He reached out and allowed his fingers to glide across her breast and over her puckered nipple; which instantly swelled even more at his touch. Robin closed her eyes and tried not to squirm, but his fingers left electrical jolts of pleasure coursing through her body. She felt him gently grip her nipple and her breath froze in her chest before she released it slowly. His hair tickled her chest an instant before she felt his mouth covering her other nipple; his finger still gently tugging the first one.

He pulled her softly into his mouth and then she felt his tongue lightly exploring the swollen, sensitized flesh. Robin groaned and shuddered, bringing up her hands to clutch at his wild hair and hold him there, suckling her breast. Hearing her enthusiasm, he lapped and suckled urgently, yet gently, moving from one darkened nipple to the other.

She tasted good. Her breasts fit his mouth so perfectly; soft and full, not too big, not too small. He could feast there all day, just as he could kiss her succulent lips and hold her in his arms for hours; Jason felt that he would never get enough of exploring her breasts with his mouth, tongue and teeth. Every flick of his tongue brought a responsive reaction from her; a moan, a shudder, an exhalation of breath. Jason forgot that there was more, so much more — until he felt soft fingers wrapping around the length of his cock.

His body jerked and he forced himself to concentrate on Robin instead of on himself. Her warm hand slid slowly up his shaft and his breath was coming in short gulps. He released her breast and moved up to kiss her full succulent lips.

He felt harder then she had expected; like a steel rod covered in warm flesh. And the tip was wet and slick. He pulsed in her grip, especially when she gently ran her fist up and then down. They kissed passionately; Jason's lips nipping at her repeatedly, aggressively, as she stroked him. She suddenly felt his hands slipping into her panties and she spread her thighs to allow him to explore her.

She was very wet and slick, his fingers slipped over her clitoris which caused her to cry out and then jerk violently; a passion filled seizure. He watched her and did it again, softer this time, but repeatedly, as if he was strumming guitar strings.

She brought her knees up quickly and arched her back as she grunted, head thrown back and eyes tightly screwed shut. She bit her lips and then parted them, tongue peeking out enough to moisten them as she shuddered and cried out repeatedly with each stroke of his fingers. He watched her face, mesmerized at the show of pleasure that played across her varying expressions.

With a loud cry, he rolled onto her body and her eyes opened, hooded and cloudy and not quite alert. He knew that he was heavy on her body as he reached down to spread her thighs so that he could nuzzle between them. She rubbed her pelvis against him frantically; hot and cold shivers ran up and down his body.

He was trembling and straining against her body; no condom, it was in his wallet which was in his pants pocket—and that was crumpled somewhere on the floor at the foot of the bed. But he would pull out. He had to be in her, but he promised himself that he would pull out. They gyrated against each other for a few moments until he felt that he would explode, so he supported himself on one elbow while he reached between them and gripped himself with his other hand. His fingers were still slick with the juices of her pussy and he rubbed the head of his cock between the wet lips.

She cried out again when the tip grazed her clitoris. He pushed in a bit to test her boundary and felt a solid resistant. He looked at her, wanting to do it, but needing her to give her approval. Her pelvis thrust upward violently and that was the only invitation he needed. Jason pushed roughly into her, opening her up.

It had felt so good, his hands touching between her legs, his mouth on her nipples, his kisses. It was driving her crazy. There was an explosion building inside of her body; and not like the climax that came from her own fingers; but something much bigger. It was like something that would consume her entire body if she didn't find the release. He rolled onto her and she was never more ready. There was no fear. There was just need.

And then he thrust into her and everything changed. Robin felt the flesh in the most delicate part of her body give way and tear. Distantly, she remembered that this was supposed to be painful, and though she had realized that there would probably be discomfort, it seemed that it would be the type of discomfort that would still have pleasure mingled into it. Yet that wasn't the case. Jason's penis tore through her and she actually almost screamed. She swallowed it back, her eyes instantly watering and like a splash of cold water, she was intensely aware of his hips moving haltingly in and out of her and the excruciating pain it brought.

She didn't want to do it anymore. She wanted to stop, but he was still going, like it was something good instead of something horribly wrong. *This was horribly wrong.*

Jason looked at her, his eyes pleasure glazed. "Okay?"

Hell no. She wanted to scream; *hell no.* Instead, she nodded and let out a little squeak of pain.

"Do you want me to stop?" He said, slowing down.

Yes. *Yes.* She wanted to scream this, but she said in a rush of air that was now her voice, "Don't stop!"

He buried his head into her neck and she heard him whimper as his hips moved faster in and out of her. God, she wanted to beg him to hurry. It hurt so badly. First he rips her. Then he rubs his big dick against her ripped flesh like this was supposed to feel good. He was moaning and it was getting louder and his body was beginning to shudder. His hips moved faster and faster; which also translated to harder and harder. Harder equaled more pain.

And then, God forbid, the tears finally slipped down her face. Oh my God, I am the girl that cried when she lost her virginity. Don't let him see you cry; he's going to feel so bad. She closed her eyes and sighed and kissed the side of his face until he let out a loud guttural cry and he rolled off of her.

She would have loved to see him cumming, under normal circumstances, but it was the last thing she wanted to see right now; his 'thing' all covered with her blood and shooting off in pleasure. So she kept her eyes closed and tried not to grip her injured flesh. She did quickly swipe away the tear streaks from her temples and hairline as she listened to Jason panting beside her.

She felt him sit up in bed and move to the edge. She peeked at him then, because he was quickly putting on his braces. "Stay there. I'll be back." He said. He got up with the aid of his crutches and moved naked out of the room. Robin sighed in pain and tried not to whimper. She sat up slowly; it hurt still even though his big 'thing' was gone. And then when she looked down, she saw blood on the sheets and covering her inner thighs.

Was there supposed to be this much blood? This seemed excessive. She wanted nothing more than to go home and to soak in a soothing bath and forget about her loss of virginity. Jason came back with two towels and one was wet.

He sat on the edge of the bed and she reached for the towel but he wouldn't give it to her. "Lay back. I got you, baby." The grimace was still on her face. What was he doing? She wanted to do this herself. She didn't want him to have to touch her blood. But she did as he asked, lying back gingerly. Then she felt a cool wet towel on her pelvis as he gently dabbed the short curls at her pubis.

Gently, Jason cleaned her. He even brought her knee up so that he could get at the crease where her thighs met her body. She watched his expression, he was in deep concentration as he did this, but there didn't seem to be any disgust there. Soon there was no more trace of blood on her body, and then he concentrated on cleaning his dick. The towel was so blood stained that she feared it would need to be tossed away. Jason took the dry towel and placed it under her bottom.

Why was he doing that? She was going home to get a bath and maybe take a pain pill. When the task was done, the dirty towel on the floor, Jason leaned forward and placed a soft kiss on each inner thigh. She felt her clitoris twitch. How could she be doing that when she had been in the most horrible pain just a few minutes before?

Jason continued to place soft kisses on her thighs, moving slowly upward until he reached her mound. He nuzzled her like her pussy was a living creature, not attached to the rest of her body. She felt herself begin to ache; ache because she began to swell very slowly with pleasure.

Jason's fingers stroked at her crease, just the outside, gently, almost tickling her. She sighed and felt her legs relax, not realizing how tense she had allowed herself to become. She watched him, but his concentration was on her pussy and making sure that his fingers moved carefully and gently along her outer lips.

Robin slowly allowed her eyes to close as his repetitive strokes began to create a pulse deep inside of her belly that radiated outward; tingles that wrapped fingers around her clitoris and to cause her nipples to bead up once more. She felt Jason's curls on her thighs, which broadcast his intent seconds before she felt his lips gently kissing her nether lips.

Robin's breath came out in a surprised gasp. She wasn't sure what she wanted to do. She still hurt and wasn't sure if she wanted him down there, where there was just recently so much blood. But then his tongue parted her lips and slipped across her clitoris, which instantly elongated as if trying to stretch from its hood, only to bury itself into his awaiting mouth. He flicked and twirled his tongue around the bundle of nerve endings; circling it until Robin's pelvis began to roll against his face. A flush seemed to engulf her as the fire re-ignited within her. It had only needed stoking.

Jason gently lapped, amazed that her taste and smell could be so intoxicating. He carefully dipped his tongue into her newly opened vagina and collected the nectar that had gathered there. It was the 'Robin' taste that was distinctly hers alone; mingled with the coppery taste of her recent injury. He tried to soothe it with his tongue, lapping her gently, the way that he imagined a male within the animal kingdom would do for a female that he had just recently 'claimed'.

He knew that taking her virginity had hurt her, because breaking her hymen hadn't been all that easy to do for him, since it caused him some pain as well. But she hadn't made him stop. She had allowed him to finish and for that he had tried to complete the act as quickly as possible. And now it was his pleasure to bring her to climax this way. He worked on her pussy with gently repetitive strokes until the trembling in her body turned into earthquakes. He gripped her thighs and pushed his tongue insistently against her clit until she bucked and wailed. Her hands gripped his head; fingers threading though his hair and gripping him roughly. Her pelvis rolled and rocked and thrust against him. He had no complaints.

Soon her body jerked and she grunted out her climax through tightly clenched teeth. When she was nothing more than spasming nerve endings, he ended the love kiss and rose to join her at the top of the bed. He gathered her in his arms. They were both out of breath and covered in a sheen of sweat. Robin placed her head on his shoulder and snuggled there in the crook of his neck. There was no need to talk. Jason lightly stroked the skin of her shoulder while she practically turned into liquid within his arms.

CHAPTER 28

Jason stared at nothing as he listened to Robin's soft breathing as she slept. His stomach felt strange; empty and full at the same time. He'd made love for the first time, and he'd brought Robin pleasure. He was proud and afraid all at the same time; now that he knew that his love for her was so big that it felt almost too big to be contained.

Then he remembered; I'm not a virgin anymore. He looked at Robin and grinned. Damn, you know it's all good when you bring so much pleasure to your woman that she falls asleep after cumming. He looked at the ceiling and his mind began to move forward. Beats began to enter his head and he could hear them as if his hands were manipulating the computer controls. He stored the beats in his head; for once he wasn't interested in making a new beat, he was more than happy to hold his sleeping girlfriend.

They slept until just after five when Robin sat up and looked around in confusion. She grimaced at the soreness between her legs, and Jason's eyes opened and he gave her a sleepy look. He had covered them with the sheet and she held it up against her breasts and then dropped it because that was sort of stupid under the circumstances.

"Hi, Sweetheart," he smiled sleepily and yawned.

"Hi, Top," she smiled and then looked at his clock. "I gotta get home and get dressed. When are your friends going to get here?" He sat up and placed his hand around her waist.

"Sometime after six. Link has to get his equipment loaded and they all have to get ready. You don't have to rush." He leaned in to kiss her. "We have time if you want to do it again." She flashed him a look that caused him to back up. "I was just kidding. I'm sure you're still sore."

"Okay, get up. I'm going to take the sheets home with me and get them washed; and the towels too." She swept herself off the bed and he moved to sit on the edge in disappointment.

"You don't have to do that. I'll wash them-"

"The last thing I want is for your mom to find stained sheets and towels."

He stood up with the help of his crutches. "You're probably right. I don't know anything about getting out stains. She'll be wondering where the blood came from." He could see his mom questioning him; berating him on whose blood it was if it wasn't his. That would just be unpleasant. Robin removed the bedding and then quickly pulled on her underwear.

He wondered how she felt about nudity. Now that he'd seen her shapely body in all its glory it seemed a sin to cover it with clothes. He'd ask her about it later, when she wasn't so anxious.

"You're not still nervous about the party tonight are you?"

She paused in pulling on her jeans. "A little, I guess."

"I'll be there, and so will my friends. You shouldn't feel anxious or nervous."

"I know. I'll be okay."

He nodded his head. She would have fun and then wouldn't have to be afraid of college parties after. It was a simple cure for her party anxiety. He understood; he'd been afraid the first time he'd gone to a party. But he was convinced that he would cure her of each of her phobias by having her face them straight on; just like the singing. She had been afraid at first, but now she hummed and sang in front of him all of the time.

He instantly dismissed any concerns that he should have. "Sweetheart, I need to go to the bathroom, want to help me?"

"Sure honey, go ahead and get started and I'll be right in." She was buttoning her sweater and he scowled at her lack of nudity, and then went into the bathroom naked. After she helped him clean himself, Jason ran a bath and Robin put fresh sheets on the bed. She peeked at him in the bathtub as she left the bedroom and it's now freshly made bed. She noted that there wasn't even enough water in it to cover his legs.

"Is that enough water?"

"Yeah. It's just enough so that I can't drown in it if I black out."

"Oh yeah." He couldn't even submerge his head. He used a pitcher that he filled with water to wash his hair. "Do you need help, babe?"

He could tell that she was anxious to get back to her own place and to do whatever ex-virgins did. "No. I'm fine. When are you going to be back?"

"I'm going to try to get back by seven, but it might be seven-thirty."

"Okay babe." She leaned down and gave him a quick peck. He held her in place and gave her a longer, lingering kiss. He looked at her closely. "I'm sorry that I hurt you so bad. But it got better, right?"

"Yes," she gave him a half smile. "It got better after; a lot better." She kissed him again and stood, hurrying to the door. She stopped. "I love you."

"I love you too," he responded. It was only the second time that they'd said it, and it made her feel warm and tingly. On the drive home, she nearly wrecked when she spaced out thinking about her loss of virginity. She and Jason had made love and she loved someone that loved her back. She felt a goofy smile spread across her face.

Back at her apartment, Robin took the bedding to the laundry that was in the basement of her building and then she ran a bath filled with soothing, peppermint oil. She took some ibuprofen and soaked in her tub with a mug of hot tea. It helped with the soreness that still throbbed between her thighs, as well as the fact that she needed the stress reliever. She was used to seeing Jason's friends during lunch break. But she wasn't necessarily expected to interact with them.

Now she'd be expected to be social and that was not something she had much practice with.

She agonized on the way she looked in her black skinny jeans, wondering whether or not a girl with as much ass as she had should be caught dead in low riders. The shirt hugged her. Her stomach was flat even though she thought of herself as 'thick,' but it was all about curves. The neckline plunged to showcase the tops of her chocolaty breasts and she wondered if she should add a t-shirt beneath it. In the end, she decided to throw caution to the wind.

She put on make-up; not much, just liner on her upper lids and a bit of eye shadow. It made her narrow grey/green eyes pop. Then she applied a blush of lipstick. She had ankle boots with a nice heel; she normally went for flats, but they looked so good with the jeans. After accessorizing, she looked into the mirror and liked what she saw; which made her instantly want to change into a pair of old jeans and a t-shirt.

She sighed. This being painfully shy was just not going to do it. It wasn't working. Shy people brought more attention to themselves than not. She knew this, but it was still hard to start witty, engaging conversations with people that she didn't know.

Jason got dressed quickly in black jeans and a black T-shirt with a headshot of Jack Skellington from 'A Nightmare before Christmas' on the front. He pulled on black Timberlands and stared at his long hair in the bathroom mirror. His lip poked out and he pulled a knit cap over the mess of curls. He had a seizure, but had time to lower himself onto the floor and when he woke up, he had somehow ended up with his head in the hallway while the rest of his body was in the bathroom.

This was the part that wasn't all that easy; getting up from the floor and onto his feet. He had to actually move himself into the living room with his hands, scooting until he reached the wheelchair and then he pulled himself up into it. He wheeled back into the bathroom and got his crutches and used them to continue walking.

Link called while he was messing around with some beats that he had in his head; beats not for the gig tonight, but ones that made him think of the woman that had slept so soundly in his arms after they'd made love for the first time. It wasn't something that would go on YouTube or be played in public; it was a song for just the two of them. He already had a name for it; *Sweetheart in Hamilton County*.

"What's up? You on your way?"

"We're heading out the door." He ran down a list of vinyl that he was bringing and asked if there was anything else he should include.

"No, it sounds good. I'm just going to have my beats on computer."

"Okay, dude, see you in a few."

Jason met them at the door a few minutes later. And the three friends just stared at him standing there tall. Amberly burst out laughing and clapped her hands.

"I told you! He's just standing up there at the door like he's been doing it for years." They all laughed and crowded into the house. Amberly gave him a big hug, careful not to cause him to fall. "So you've been keeping up with the walking!"

"Why haven't you done it at school?" Patty asked.

"I'm not strong enough yet. I just do it around here, and my girlfriend helps me."

Everybody got quiet.

"Your girlfriend?" Link asked. "Is it, your invisible girlfriend?"

"Yeah." Patty added. "Does she look like your right palm?"

"Who...?" Amberly asked, a frown on her face.

"Robin."

"Your aide?!" Amberly barked. "But you don't like your aides!"

"Normally I don't. But, she's special."

"Well," Amberly's face was pinched. "Isn't she kind of old?"

Jason chuckled. "She's 21. That's how old you are."

"Hmmph," was her response.

"Also, she's Sweetheart."

"Sweetheart?" Link asked. He had already wheeled to the computer and was fumbling with the controls.

"You mean the girl that was singing on that new mix of yours?" Amberly asked. "*She's* Sweetheart?"

"Yeah."

"Too bad we're broke up." Patty said as she turned on the rarely used big screen television set. "We'd have our fifth member." She put in a DVD and the opening credits for 'Beat Street' came on. Everyone stopped what they were doing. 'Beat Street' was everyone's favorite movie; they knew all of the lines, all of the music and all of the dance movies. Even the two members of Wheels of Steel that had cerebral palsy could do all of the arm movements from the break dances of the movie.

"You know what we should do!" Link said excitedly. "We should start off with that opening! The one when he's chanting 'It's working!'"

"Oh my God, that would be so *sick*!" Patty exclaimed. The opening they were referring to was of the two DJ's in the movie who were playing a house party in which they used some of the most classic rap beats of the 80's.

Jason was all grins. "Oh son! You're right! We gotta do it." The two hurried to the studio. "Are we going to use *Looking for the Perfect Beat*?" Jason asked.

"We've got to! Afrika Bambaataa! Nothing's better than that."

"They ain't going to have any idea what we're doing."

"Doesn't matter! We know what we're doing and that opening is classic! We gotta do it."

"Yeah," Jason agreed enthusiastically. "So I do the beat and you do the scratch?"

"Yep, that's it, Son. Ready?" Jason winked. Link didn't have a mic, but he yelled out the words of the movie until he practically screamed; *"Now here's a funky beat..."* And that's when Jason did his magic, making a funky beat. *"And here's a scratch beat..."* Link began scratching something new but completely funky and then they put it together. Link began mixing in *Looking for the Perfect Beat* BY Afrika Bambataa and then they started free styling. Patty was jumping up and down and break dancing; which she was pretty good at. Amberly had her cell phone out and was recording their antics. Jason thought they should be selling tickets to this performance, never mind the Omicron party later.

Robin was getting out of her car and could hear the beat thumping from Jason's apartment all the way to the parking lot; as could other people that were walking about. Several younger guys were even out dancing. She couldn't believe it. One guy stopped her as she headed to Jason's door.

"Hey! You know that guy that lives there?" She nodded

"Oh dude, he should open his door so that we can listen to their jam session!" Several other people agreed.

"Well, he's playing at the Omicron house tonight. I'm sure they won't care if you go since their charging." She gave them the information and they promised to show up.

Robin knocked on the door. Patty answered, smiling. "Hey!" She greeted Robin happily. "You don't have a key yet?!" She turned back into the room. "Hey, slacker! Get your girlfriend a key!"

341

Jason took off his headphones and wheeled over to Robin; he stared at her opened mouth, but it was Link that spoke.

"Day-um..." Robin stood there inside of the door shyly. Jason reached for his crutches absently. He pulled himself up to a standing position. She looked awesome in all black. He remembered what they had done earlier as he glanced at her exposed cleavage.

"Damn is right," he said. He gave her a kiss and she returned it timidly. "You look great, Sweetheart."

"Hi, Sweetheart!" Link yelled.

"Yeah," Patty chimed in from where she had sat down on the couch. "Seems you have the only nickname that's not insulting."

Amberly turned off her video and placed her cell phone into her purse. "I officially want to change nicknames. I don't feel that Tramp Stamp accurately portrays me."

"Too late." Link piped up. "Wheels of Steel are officially no more."

Robin gave Jason a curious look. Wheels of Steel were no more. What? He just shrugged. "We decided to 'unofficially' disband. But it's a secret."

"We're not going to make any new music as a group. We're just going to do our own thing." Link added.

"Oh ok, I hate to hear that. You guys were really good."

Amberly eyed her. "Did you like the videos?"

"Yes I thought they were great!" Robin replied. She was still standing in the middle of the room as if she needed an invitation to enter, so she quickly sat down in the armchair.

"Patty and I did the videos."

"They were really good. Oh, some guys were outside wanting to hear y'all jam. So I told them about the party tonight-"

"It's only for college students," Amberly said. "So I hope they don't show up; because without a college ID, they'll be turned away at the door."

Oh shit, those guys will probably be pissed, too. And she didn't have a college ID. She hoped they wouldn't give her any problems entering.

"Come on, let's finish jamming." Jason wheeled back to the computer.

"Oh, Sweetheart!" Patty said. "You should have heard the shit they just laid down! Do you know the movie 'Beat Street'?"

Robin shook her head.

"Oh, wow Jason, you're going to have to school your girl." Link said playfully. "Check out the TV. 'Beat Street' is *the* most important event to occur in hip hop culture. A film shot from the perspective of the people that revolutionized- no that *created* hip hop. Without this movie, white kids like me would still be playing John Denver!"

"So you're saying that 'Beat Street' started a nation of Wiggers?" Amberly asked.

"No. But it took it from Brooklyn and the Bronx and brought it to people in the Midwest; to the farmland."

"Boy!" Patty said dismissively. "You ain't ever been on a farm in your life!" Robin looked at the movie that was playing on television. It looked like an 80's B movie, but there was some good beats in it.

Jason started a beat going and like a well-oiled machine and Link joined in with the scratching. Robin began to relax a little in her chair as she watched him from across the room. Amberly went into the kitchen and returned with bottled water. She handed one to Robin, who thanked her politely and then passed one each to her friends, placing Links and Jason's on the table that the computer sat on. She stared at what Jason was doing.

"Ooo, let me try Top."

He looked up at her. "You want to?"

"Yeah!"

"Okay, come on." Amberly bounced on her tiptoes happily and then sat on Jason's lap. She mimicked what she'd seen him doing, pressing the buttons in the same sequence that he had and she created a very nice beat. Link followed her every move with a responsive scratch sound. Amberly laughed happily.

Robin felt a little tense. She came over to join them and watched Amberly bouncing up and down on her boyfriend's lap. She couldn't lie; she didn't like it. But she'd seen it before and figured it was 'acceptable' in their circle.

Amberly flubbed a little but even so, it still sounded good. Jason guided her to the correct buttons to press and gave her encouraging squeezes when she did well. Patty was mimicking some break dancers from the movie. Wow, she was more than good. Robin wished that she could be as comfortable as they were. Why did things always come so much harder for her?

"Come over here, Sweetheart. I'm going to show you how to scratch."

"Oh, I don't know...I don't think I can-" But there was a part of her that wanted to be like Amberly, to not be afraid, to be comfortable.

"Yeah. It's easy. Come here." She went over to him and stood awkwardly watching him scratch. "Now do this." He did a simple scratch.

"Okay." She reached for the controls. "Sit here." He patted his lap. Her face felt hot, but she did as he asked. Then she reached for the controls again. She had seen Jason making beats before, but hadn't seen him scratching with controls. But she did exactly what Link did and when it sounded over the speakers, she grinned proudly.

Link clapped. "That's it! Good job, Sweetheart!"

He let her freestyle and she and Amberly were playing together. It wouldn't be a hit on YouTube or anything, but it was all hers. She looked over at Jason in excitement. He smiled at her, but as soon as her attention turned back to the studio, he glared at Link. He couldn't stop thinking about Link's dick being separated from Robin by just a few layers of cloth.

His teeth clenched. "Okay, Amberly. Good job." He urged her off his lap. "We need to get practicing." Link glanced at him. "Pshaw, son. We don't need to overkill on the practice. Hey, me and Sweetheart should battle you."

Link placed his hands over hers and together they began scratching. "Keep doing that." Then he moved his hands and began spinning his vinyl. Robin understood what she needed to do to compliment his scratches with hers.

"Damn." Patty said. They didn't sound bad. Amberly watched quietly. Jason just seemed to pout more. Almost angrily he threw out a beat, and the three of them played together for a few minutes. It was good, very good in fact.

By the time Robin had removed herself from Link's lap, Jason was almost red-faced. He couldn't even think straight. All he could see was Robin's nude body from earlier and Link with his overused dick only inches from her. He knew he was wrong for wanting to smash his fist into Link's face, but why were his hands so comfortable on her hips? And if he was fucking Patty, then why wasn't *she* sitting on his lap?

Robin made to walk past, but Jason's hand snaked out quickly and gripped her wrist. "Come here, Sweetheart. Sit with me." She did and put her arm around his shoulder and snuggled with him while Link and Patty went aw and made smooching noises, even though they weren't kissing. Amberly just stood there quietly, a look of misery on her face.

CHAPTER 29

They crowded into the van a while later. Robin wanted to take her own car, but Jason insisted that they all ride together. He reached out and held her hand and felt that it was moist. He peeked at her and small beads of sweat had formed on her forehead. He gave her hand a reassuring squeeze and she smiled.

When they got to Omicron house, Patty helped some of the frat brothers to unload the van, so Robin pitched in too. It helped her to feel good to be doing something when she walked into the crowded house. Dance music was coming loudly from the opened door and people were milling around the yard. Once inside she understood why; it was hot, smoky and crowded. Someone brushed against her and she almost dropped the heavy crate of albums that she was holding. Why she had grabbed this instead of a speaker, she wasn't sure. The guys got busy getting the equipment set up and Patty grabbed her wrist.

"Let's get a drink." She glanced over to Jason, but he was preoccupied with running wires, so she followed Patty to the open bar. Several people were already shouting 'WHEELS OF STEEL', even though none of their music was playing.

"What do you want to drink?" Patty yelled over the loud music. Robin's eyes scanned the bar seeing bottles of liquor, not knowing the difference from one to the other since she wasn't a drinker.

"What are you drinking?"

"Hennessey."

"Oh. I'll just have a beer." Patty passed her a can of beer from a cooler. Robin thanked her and looked around.

"So, this is a college party."

"Your first?"

"Yes."

Robin cracked open the beer and took a small drink. She wasn't a beer drinker, but the cool liquid felt good going down her dry throat. She took a larger swallow.

"Jason's a real good guy." Patty said while bouncing slightly to the techno house beat that was currently playing.

Robin nodded quickly. "He is," she smiled shyly. "He's a real good guy."

"Sometimes he comes off a little rough," Patty said. "But that's only because he's been hurt bad."

Robin frowned. "How do you know Jason?"

"I met him through Amberly. We share classes and since he hung with her and I hung with her, we sorta just hung together. And we all liked music and hip hop, so we gravitated together."

"Cool."

A black guy came up to her. "Want to dance, beautiful?"

She shook her head quickly. "No thanks." She looked down at her beer.

"Aw, come on." He took hold of her wrist and she gave him a surprised look.

"No. Really, I don't want to dance."

The guy flashed her a bright smile. "Why don't you give me your number-?"

"Fucker. Leave." Patty said calmly. The guy, who plainly had too much to drink, gave her a dismissive look.

"Not talking to you dyke." Robin just turned and walked away. She heard some noise behind her; something like a smack or a crack and then something heavy hitting the floor. But she just kept walking until she was back in the room where Jason and Link were setting up the equipment. She held her beer in both hands tightly, almost strangling the can. Jason glanced up and met her eyes, giving her a wink. Her heartbeat stopped racing and she smiled back.

Patty joined her a few moments later with a fresh drink. Robin gave her an apologetic smile. "Sorry, I'm not good in crowds."

"No worry."

Amberly came over, she was holding a bottled water. She gave Robin an appraising look. "I like your jeans."

"Thanks. I like yours too."

"Do you want to dance?"

Robin swallowed and looked around. "Okay." She didn't want to, but if she said no, Amberly might think she was just trying to be stuck up. They danced; Robin doing nothing much more than a two-step while periodically moving her shoulders. She sipped her beer just to have something to do, but soon it was empty. Amberly was dancing, swinging her long hair and looking comfortable, even if she didn't quite look like she was dancing, more like she was spasming. Patty actually looked good dancing, but she wasn't doing anything as wild as break dancing; just grooving to the beat.

Suddenly the sound of scratching could be heard and the music stopped. Link said; "Testing...Testing. One two, one two, on the mic is Link and my main man Top. We're going to do our own thing up here. Y'all cool with that?!" The crowd roared. "Y'all ready for a little Ol' Skool?!" Again there was madness. Robin felt her heart drum in anticipation. Link sure was good at getting the crowd going.

"*It's working! It's working...Party people if you're ready to rock let me hear you scream!*" And they did just that. The crowd knew that the routine Jason and Link went through was from the movie 'Beat Street' because they began chanting 'Beat Street, Beat Street' over and over. A bunch of white kids knew more about this hip hop movie than she did. She was definitely going to check it out.

Robin watched Jason, mesmerized as he seemed to transform when he was performing. He was completely lost in his actions. She became lost in it as well as her body began to react to the music. Patty placed a fresh beer in her hands and she gave the girl a grateful smile. The beer helped to loosen her up and soon she was moving in ways that she never knew she could.

Jason's eyes would meet hers and he'd give her a wink and she felt like she was flying on cloud nine. She raised the beer can to her lips, but it was empty. How did that happen? Did she drink it all? She danced her way out of the room and into the next, where the open bar was located. She looked around wondering why she had ever been so nervous. No one cared about her and they were all just trying to have fun.

She picked up the bottle of Hennessey, wondering what it tasted like.

Jason thought that being a DJ was the way to go. It felt awesome being up here with his best friend and hearing the crowd out there cheering for them; dancing and feeling what they were doing. And then seeing Robin out there with Amberly and Patty, dancing and enjoying herself was the icing on the cake. And by the way, he was getting paid for this.

He glanced up and searched for Robin. He saw Patty and Amberly, but not her. She was probably in the bathroom. Jason and Link moved from Old Skool to techno; which was Link's thing, but he was feeling it as well. He glanced up again, and still didn't see her. He felt a bit uneasy. He tried to catch Amberly or Patty's eyes, but both were grooving too hard. He cursed under his breath and continued to play.

A few minutes later, when he still hadn't seen her, Jason leaned in to Link. "Let a song play out." Link nodded his okay. He put on a long Dubstep that would end in a hard drum solo. It would give him about twenty minutes. He wheeled from behind the table and several people immediately converged on him.

"Top, that was hot!"

"Top, you gotta upload that to YouTube!"

"Top you're the greatest!"

He tried to politely acknowledge them, but it was soon apparent that his wheelchair wasn't getting through the thick crowd of people. He felt panicked and anxious. How could he find Robin if he couldn't move ten feet in front of himself?

"Patty! Amberly!" They looked over at him and came to him with all smiles. "Where's Robin?"

Patty blinked. "Dancing," she looked around. "She was dancing."

"I haven't seen her for over half an hour," he said urgently.

"She's a big girl, Jason." Amberly said; a stony look in her eyes.

"Well, she's not used to crowds. Look, can you check to see if she's in the bathroom?"

Amberly sighed, but did as he asked.

"I'll check to see if she's in the other room. She had a couple of beers." Patty said while hurrying away.

"Top!" A drunken girl slithered up to him and sat in his lap. She wrapped her arms around his neck and her drink went down the back of his shirt; she'd evidently forgotten that she was holding one.

"Shit." He gently nudged her away and she pouted, calling him something unintelligible. He tried to look through the throng of people, but couldn't see two feet in front of him. They were dancing wildly in front and in back of him. He was basically trapped.

His teeth clenched in a panic. Why hadn't he told her the rules of a college party; stay with your friends, don't take any drinks from anyone you didn't know, don't leave your drink unattended, and for God's sake—don't go off with someone you don't know.

CHAPTER 30

Amberly returned an impossibly long time later. "Jason, I checked all of the restrooms, she wasn't in any of them." Link whistled shrilly and Jason swung around to him. He gestured for him to get back on stage. The Dubstep was at the end of the drumbeat solo. Jason felt numb. He sat there indecisively.

Jason made a rolling signal with his fists and Link gave him a surprised look. Essentially he was saying; go on without me. He turned away, not able to think about Link right now when Robin was lost, gone, disappeared, kidnapped — he had no idea.

Patty returned with a look of concern on her face. She knelt down beside Jason so that he could hear her. "She's not in the other room. I'm going to ask around." Jason suddenly felt afraid and helpless as he watched his friend push through the crowd of people. He should have brought his crutches, but what good would that have been? One unintentional shove and he'd be sprawled on the floor. He wasn't the most patient person but all he could do was sit there and wait.

Patty's eyes scanned the thrashing people for one black girl; it wasn't like there were all that many black girls at an Omicron party.

"Hey?!" She yelled to the person that was dancing next to her. "Have you seen a black girl? Short hair; wearing all black?"

"No. I ain't seen nobody." The half-drunk person slurred.

Patty scowled and moved to another person repeating the question.

"Yeah," the guy responded. "I saw her. She's outside. She was fighting with someone."

Oh shit. Patty took a step towards the entrance and then stopped. She hurried back to where Jason was. He gave her an expectant look.

"Stand up!" She commanded. He used the hand rest of his chair to push up and Patty grabbed him by his waist and hoisted him to his feet.

"Where-?" He began.

"Outside!" She bent and swept him over her shoulder in a fireman's hold. Patty was almost as tall as Jason, but much stockier. She did this with little effort and shoved her way through the crowd. Amberly caught a glimpse of them and hurried to catch up, tripping and half falling over the feet of the rude partiers who didn't have enough sense to move out of the way of someone with an obvious walking issue.

"Hey, wait up!" She yelled. But they didn't hear her. Why was Patty carrying Top over her shoulder?

When Patty got to the entrance, she stopped two girls. "Have you seen a black girl, short hair, wearing all black?"

They both nodded. "Yeah, she went off with three guys."

Jason was hanging upside down and the blood was rushing to his head, but it sounded like they had said that Robin had went off with three guys. He felt his very toes begin to curl. Patty hurried out of the house. Chauncy was standing at the door. He was one of the brothers of the fraternity and he was collecting money.

"Chauncy! Where's the black girl that was with us?"

Chauncy gave Patty and Jason curious looks. "Uh, what black girl? And why are you carrying Top around?"

"Chauncy! Black girl! Stay focused!"

"With short hair? The drunk one? I made her and her friends leave."

"What the fuck?!" Jason yelled. He slapped Patty's ass to be put down. She lowered him carefully to the ground, still holding him around the waist so that he didn't topple over. "Where'd she go?"

Chauncy shrugged. "I don't know. She left with those guys."

"And she was drunk?" Patty asked.

"Yeah, falling on her face drunk. Look, she didn't have a student ID so I didn't let her in. Plus she was with those guys and they didn't have student ID *and* they were under 21, so I told them to leave or I'd call the cops on them-"

Jason felt lightheaded and sick. Robin had gone off with three strange guys. "Oh Jesus," he said.

Amberly had finally caught up with them and rubbed his back. "She'll be okay. Maybe she called you-"

Yes. He quickly reached into his pocket for his cell. Yes. There was one text from Robin. It was left about half an hour ago. He tried to read it but it didn't make sense. It said:

JAON % 8&?3 3ell3hem I wi3hyou

"Jason...something...tell them I'm with you," he repeated.

"Call her," Patty said.

He nodded and hit redial.

Chauncy was moving nervously back and forth from one foot to the other. "Look, I didn't know she was with you guys or I would have let her in. But she was drunk and since that problem a few years back, you know we're banned from having house parties unless it's students only-"

Amberly held up her hand to shush him.

Jason looked at them, holding the phone to his ear. "She's not answering..." He got her voice mail. "Robin! Where are you?! Call me...did you leave with someone? Call me as soon as you get this. I'm going to try to ring you again."

Amberly hurried to two guys that were heading up the stairs to the house. They'd already been inside because they wore red stamps on the back of their hands.

"Hey, have you guys seen a black girl with three other guys? She's probably drunk?"

They both pointed down the street. "Yeah, they're trying to get her drunk-ass home, but she won't go."

The second guy chuckled. "Not sure why drunk people won't get in the car with their sober friends-" Amberly's face paled. She hurried back up the steps, tripped, landed on her palms. Jason and Patty were looking at her in concern.

"Sh-sh-she's." She pointed down the street. "Th-th-THEY…are TR-TR-trying to guh-guh GET her in a C-C-CAR!"

Patty grabbed Jason around his waist and dragged him down the stairs like he was a ragdoll. He hung on, the whites of his eyes were red and the green of them had darkened until they looked brown. He was furious; his mouth was a pale slash in his other-wise red face.

Amberly limped behind them, trying to keep up. But her body was so tense that she couldn't manage more than a halting shamble. She hadn't wanted Jason with anybody else, but she didn't want anything bad to happen to that girl, either. This is how college girls got raped every day in America. Why would she just go off with three strange guys?

Patty finally spotted Robin sitting on the curb with three guys standing around her. They were surrounding her and her head was down. What the fuck?

"Get away from her!" Jason began screaming. The guys looked up at them in surprise. The three young men thought that Patty looked like a bull as she charged towards them while holding the crippled dude against her body. That sight was more than enough to cause them to take a step back.

"What are you doing with this girl?" Patty bellowed.

"Nothing." One guy spoke, holding up his hands in submission.

"Robin?" Jason said. She was leaned over with her arms crossed around her middle. "Patty take me over to her!" Patty glared at the three punks as she dragged Jason over to the curb.

"What did you do to her?" They fell over themselves, trying to deny any culpability.

"Nothing! She was drunk!"

Jason slipped from her grip, sinking hard to the ground where he placed a hand on the back of her neck. She was rocking back and forth.

"She said her stomach hurt. We were just going to get her home. But hey, dude, if you're her friends, then we'll leave her with you. This is too much fucking drama." They guy talking turned and headed for his car. His friends followed.

"All this just to hear some fucking music..." The other spoke. Jason ignored them. He was rubbing the back of Robin's neck.

"You!" Patty said to the first guy. "Look, we're sorry...and thank you." He waved without looking back and they crowded into their car and drove off.

"Is she okay?" Amberly asked. Her words were very slurred, she didn't know how Jason managed to understand her, but he did. He was the only one that could when her speech got very bad.

"I don't know." She wouldn't look at him.

Amberly rubbed her arms anxiously. Why would Jason want to be with a trouble maker like her? Why would she get so drunk that she couldn't even lift her head up and end up just sitting on the curb of the street like a bum? Amberly's face took on a dark cast. Jason would see that this girl was not for him; a drunk and a drama queen. He deserved so much better.

Jason continued to rub Robin's neck. "Robin, baby, does your stomach hurt?" She nodded slowly. "Do you need to throw up?" After a minute, she nodded again. Amberly rolled her eyes and looked up and down the street for whoever might be watching.

Patty crouched down beside her. "Robin, do you think anyone might have put something in your drink?" Robin didn't answer. Jason and Patty's eyes met. She looked at the black girl again. "Robin, can you stand up?" No answer.

Patty had a scared look on her face; the first that Jason had ever seen. "I can't carry you both..." The three friends looked at each other helplessly. Then Robin slowly pulled herself up, however she didn't straighten. Once she was on her feet, she placed her hands on her knees, still in a crouch. Spit started streaming from her mouth, and then finally she puked.

"Ew!" Amberly exclaimed while turning away. "It smells like Hennessey and pizza." Patty clutched

Robin's arm to prevent her from falling into her own mess, when she began weaving on her feet. She glanced at the vomit and then her eyes locked on to it. She looked at Robin slowly.

"Can you stand up?" Robin nodded. She felt a little better now. Her stomach still burned and her head still hurt but she managed to straighten.

"I'll help her." Amberly said. "Just get Top." She placed her arm around the stooped girl. Amberly just hoped that Top would break up with her after this disgusting display.

Patty reached down and pulled Jason up to his feet with ease. She tossed him over her shoulder and led the way back to the house. Chauncy looked at Robin and Amberly and tried to stop them from following.

"Hey, she can't come in. She's drunk and she not a student-"

"Go to hell Chauncy!" Amberly said angrily. "She could have been raped! You let a drunk girl go off with three guys! You're a creep!" Amberly pushed her way into the house after Patty, ignoring Chauncy's weak protests. She walked the drunken girl to one of the lower level bathrooms, which was fortunately unoccupied. Then she turned on the water at the sink. Robin immediately began splashing her face and rinsing her mouth. She lurched over to the toilet and vomited again.

Amberly was shuddering and trying not to gag at the sounds and smells in the little bathroom. "Oh my God, that's so gross. Hey, are you going to be okay?"

Robin sat on the floor, panting; her back against the wall. Her stomach hurt, it burned so bad.

"I want to go home," she whimpered. She covered her face and started crying. She felt so bad; so sick and so stupid.

"Don't cry." Amberly said miserably. She twisted her fingers. "You shouldn't drink so much if you can't hold your liquor." Robin wiped her eyes and nodded in agreement. "I'll get Patty." She hurried out of the bathroom, grateful that Patty was better at these things than she was. Patty always got drunk.

Patty had deposited Jason back into his chair. She looked up at Link, who was watching them in confusion. "Top, you go on up there and finish out. I'll watch Robin. I won't leave her." Jason looked at Link up there holding it down for the both of them and felt instantly guilty. He nodded though he wanted to be with Robin—yet he still felt frustrated and afraid and didn't know where to direct it. So yeah, he wheeled himself back up to the equipment and followed Link's lead. For the first time in his life, he had no joy in mixing music.

Patty met Amberly in the next room. "Where is she?" Amberly pointed to the bathroom. Patty headed in that direction and Amberly called after her. "She needs an intervention. She just ruined this party for us!" Patty ignored her and knocked on the closed restroom door.

"Robin." She didn't hear a reply so just entered. Robin had her head resting on her bent knees and was sitting on the floor. Patty turned off the water and then reached over to flush the toilet. She hesitated staring into the bowl. She flushed it and sat down next to Robin on the floor.

"Hey? You're vomiting blood." Robin looked up weakly and gave her a confused look. She shook her head in denial.

"Yes. There's blood in your vomit. Not a lot, but enough. So...why?"

"I don't know. I don't normally vomit-" and with that said, she quickly scrambled to the toilet and vomited again. This time she stared into the bowl. It was unmistakably blood.

"Your stomach hurts?" Patty asked.

"I have irritable bowel." She tried to find a reason for the blood.

Patty reached over and flushed the toilet then she got a towel and wet it, dabbing Robin's sweating face. "Robin, you need to go to a doctor."

Robin took the towel from her and dabbed her own face and neck. "I'm okay. I just had too much to drink. I'm no drinker, and I guess I over did it." She gave Patty a direct look. "Is Jason mad? He's probably so angry at me."

"Don't worry about Jason. He's back up playing with Link."

She looked relieved. "You're not going to tell him about the blood? Please don't, okay? That isn't something that normally happens."

"I'm no busy body, Robin. If he don't ask, then I won't tell."

Someone knocked on the door. "Hey, there's a line out here. Can you hurry up?!"

"Use a different one!" Patty bellowed. She stared back at Robin. She was a pretty girl; dark skinned, short hair and eyes that were like Asian eyes, except not slanted and with jewel coloring. She was shapely; no thin stick girl. She could see why Jason was crushing on her.

"You like Jason, maybe even love him?" Robin met her eyes and nodded. "If this is a game for you, please find someone else to play. Jason acts tough, but he's not; it's just his hard outer shell that protects his cushy innards."

"I don't want to hurt him. I'm just happy he lets me love him. In the beginning, he pushed me away a lot and I didn't know what he really felt, I thought he hated me actually. But I guess, I passed whatever test and he let me in." Robin didn't know why she was talking so openly to this girl that she had barely exchanged ten words with since they had first met. Maybe she was still drunk. The world still had that hazy, not-quite-real feel to it.

Patty nodded. "Once he lets you in, he won't let you go so easy." She looked away. "I just wish Link was more like that."

"You and Link are-?"

"We're fucking. But whether we are ever going to be more, well that depends on him."

"Oh. You don't think he feels the same way about you that you feel for him?"

Patty took a deep breath. "I don't really know what I feel about him." She gave Robin an earnest look. "I always see him with these cute girls with tight bodies and big boobs. Even after his accident, he attracts those girls that laugh all of the time and bounce on their toes. Fuck, I'm just me." She ran her hands through her short hair and gave Robin a sharp look. Robin didn't look away. She waited patiently for Patty to finish. After a moment, Patty's expression softened.

"My real name is Belinda, not Patty. And I'm not gay, or bi. And I know I look hard like a guy. But if you look hard like a guy, people won't fucking pick on you. If you're willing to back it up, you don't have to go through life defending yourself—people just know to leave you the fuck alone." She cussed a lot, Robin noted. She ran her hands through her hair again and stood. "Look, I need to go outside and have a smoke."

"I'll go with you. I think I'm done puking." Patty nodded and Robin took a moment to splash her face and rinse her mouth again. The two young women went outside and sat on the porch stairs. Chauncy looked at them as if Patty would beat him down, but she ignored him and so did Robin. After a moment he retreated into the house to act as security from there.

Patty lit a cigarette and rested her arms across her knees. "I want Link to see me the person and not just some glammed out *chick*. I'm no *chick*!" Robin was sitting next to her. Her stomach still hurt, but she was used to this type of pain. She wasn't going to barf again and her body wouldn't allow her to have a bowel movement in that foul toilet, so for now she was in a physical state of limbo. She watched Patty/Belinda and nodded. Their two fellows were still playing music and the crowd was still going crazy.

"Are you going to tell Link how you feel?"

"No."

"Do you love him?"

"Maybe. He was the first guy I ever did it with. Maybe that makes you love someone. I certainly wasn't planning for this to happen. I just wanted to know what all the hype was about. But, God his dick was so good!" Robin blushed at her frankness.

"W-was it good even the first time?"

"Yes. It was awesome."

"Didn't it hurt?"

"No. Girl, I got rid of that pesky hymen years ago when I first got my period. Broke the damned thing myself. I wasn't going to let some guy have all that power over me. I've been getting my body ready for fucking, using my vibrator. No, I made sure my first time wouldn't hurt, and that I'd be good at it." Patty smirked. "I think I was successful, because I sure got Link sniffing after me. He says my pussy is like magic."

Wow, she could talk so honestly about it. Robin took a deep breath and plunged forward. "It really hurt the first time we did it. I don't really know if I want to even do it again."

"You and Top already did it?" Robin covered her face in embarrassment. Patty placed her hand on the girl's wrist. "It's okay. It's no shame in that. But it's going to get better." Robin peeked at her and then lowered her hands. Patty was nodding. "It gets much, much, better. I'm still new at it. I only lost my virginity a few weeks ago, but we do it all of the time and every time is better." She grinned. "We even do it in the van between classes." Robin laughed.

Patty's expression went grim. "Girls are always trying to get next to him. I guess I'm just waiting for him to slip up. And when he does, I'm done. It's over."

"But what if he thinks it's just casual, since you never told him your true feelings?"

Patty shrugged. "Doesn't matter. I don't want to fuck another guy, and if he wants to fuck another girl, then I know how he feels about me and we're done."

Robin sighed. Patty was tough and unyielding, but she could already tell that it was because something from her past had hurt her. If Link was another in a list of people that hurt this girl, then there was no telling how she would turn out. Robin hoped that the two would have enough sense not to destroy what they had before it even had a chance to grow.

They talked for a while longer before hearing Link announce the end of the show. They dragged themselves off the stairs and made their way back into the house. Two girls were sitting in Link's lap as he laughed and thanked them. Robin glanced at Patty, who did a good job of ignoring him. Jason was wheeling past people that tried to talk to him. His face was closed and most took it as a sign not to bother him. His attention was completely on Robin and as he wheeled to her she met him half way.

"Robin, how are you feeling? Does your stomach still hurt?" She had to ask him to repeat himself. He was very slurred and jerky.

"I'm feeling better," she lied. Her stomach felt like there were rocks in it. He stared at her. "Come here, baby." He gripped her hand and sat her in his lap. His hands clutched her face firmly, their foreheads touching.

"You scared me so bad. I couldn't find you-"

"I'm sorry Jason. I tried to get back but they wouldn't let me in-"

"I was so scared. When I saw you on the curb I couldn't get to you, I couldn't lift you, I couldn't carry you." He was trembling. "I was-I was-I was...helpless." He stuttered. He had never felt so helpless in his life. She hugged him.

"I'm sorry. Oh Jason, I'm so sorry-"

He roughly gripped her upper arms. "Why did you go off with those guys?!"

"I..." she stared at him stunned at his sudden anger. She had just gone into the other room for another beer and had decided to try the Hennessey. It was strong, it felt like fire, so she had mixed it with coke and then it had tasted good. So she had another, because the music sounded so good and the people were having so much fun. And when she drank everything got better. Then she saw the guys from Jason's apartment.

She remembered that they had been outside dancing and enjoying Jason and his friend's jam session. So she went to the door to greet them. But the big mean man at the front of the door wouldn't let them in. So she had tried to explain that they were with her, that she had invited them to come. And they had all pointed to her, saying that they were with her.

But the big mean guy at the door said that it was only for people with student IDs and twenty-one or over because of the open bar. When her friends heard about the open bar, they really wanted to get in. They were getting loud and she had gone out to promise that her boyfriend would get them in. He was the DJ tonight.

But for some reason, even though she was no longer drinking, she seemed to be having more difficulties with talking and walking straight. She tried to walk straight and was walking to the side instead. And when she fell, one of the guys caught her. The big mean guy threw up his hands and a different guy; Chauncy, came out to see what was wrong.

"Don't let them in!" He yelled and then he disappeared into the house. Robin headed in to get Amberly or Patty so that they could ok her friends to enter, but the new guy wouldn't let her back in. She kept explaining that she had already been inside, but she didn't have a stamp so he wouldn't let her in. She had tried to say how ridiculous this all was and if he could just go inside and ask the DJ-

But then the bouncer guy had gotten very belligerent and nasty and had started calling her names; like drunk and slut, and wouldn't let her go in to get Amberly or even Patty. Even the guys didn't care about getting in now, but trying to convince the bouncer that she was supposed to be back in there. She texted Jason to come tell this guy to let her in, but she knew he wouldn't get the message since he was performing. The bouncer told them to leave or he would call the cops. And that's when her stomach started to hurt.

They all retreated and she didn't know where to go. She just followed them. They told her that they'd take her home and then she could call her boyfriend later, but she couldn't leave Jason. He'd be worried if she did. Then her belly started burning and that hard feeling that she sometimes got began to settle in. She sat on the curb hoping to throw up, while her new friends tried to get her into their car. And that's when she heard yelling. She wasn't sure what was happening, but the pain in her belly was so bad; the worst it had ever been. There had been too much drinking, how did people drink like this?

Then Jason's soothing hand was on her neck and she could think again. That's what had happened. She wanted to tell him, but the words wouldn't come.

"Say something! Why did you go off with those guys?!" He waited, staring at her with red-rimmed eyes.

"I d- I don't know."

He was quiet. "That's not good enough. That's not good enough."

She nodded in agreement. Sweat was beading on her forehead. "Because...I was drunk." She could see that he wanted to strangle her, or maybe punch her in the eye. He nudged her off his lap.

"I need to help take down the equipment." He wheeled back up to join Link behind the table where they had worked for the last three hours. Patty was helping to load things into the van. Amberly was just standing at a distance, watching her. Had she seen their fight? Amberly turned her head away as if she had never looked at Robin at all. Robin stood there, feeling like crap.

The ride home was quiet, which made Robin feel bad again. Link wanted to talk about the music and how they'd played, but Jason was silent. He turned on some music and they drove without talking. Finally, Link turned down the music.

"Why did you leave the party? You were outside sitting on the curb?"

"Link," Patty warned.

"Well, I'm just curious. I mean, why shouldn't I ask? Jason had to stop playing to go look for her." Jason didn't say anything.

Robin gathered up her courage to speak. "I saw the guys from the apartment, the ones that wanted to hear your jam session. And they couldn't get in...so, I guess I was trying to help them get in."

Jason looked at her. "But why were you fighting with the guy at the door?"

She rubbed her belly. Patty was watching her closely.

"Hey! Leave her alone guys." Patty snapped. "Obviously she wasn't going off with them. She wouldn't get in their car!"

"Well, she shouldn't have been down the street with them," Amberly chimed in. "I'm just happy that nothing bad happened."

Robin wanted nothing more than to go home and to go to bed, and maybe cry for how bad this had all turned out. She stared down at her hands and when they pulled into the parking lot, she reached into her purse for her car keys.

"Robin," Link began. "You can't drive. You're still drunk."

"I'm okay," she said.

"Give me your keys," he said. She gave him a surprised look. Why was he in her business? He suddenly turned in his seat and grabbed her wrist. He yanked the keys roughly from her hands. He tossed them to Patty.

"She'll drive you home. Or you'll stay the night with Top."

Jason was staring out his window. "My mom will be here in the morning. She can't stay." Patty opened the van door and Robin stumbled out of it. She hurried to her car and waited for Patty. Patty climbed out of the van, glaring at Jason.

"Nice."

He didn't speak. She went to the Volvo and unlocked the doors. Robin quickly entered the passenger seat and buckled up, slinking down in her seat and staring at her feet. Hot tears were already building in her eyes and she hoped that Patty would drive them away before they fell.

TO BE CONTINUED

WHEELS OF STEEL VOL. 2
~PREVIEW~

"Okay, look you two!" Patty yelled. Robin jumped. "Get it out in the open right now. Nobody leaves this van until you two start talking!" She heard the distinct click as the locks engaged. Robin and Jason sat there quietly and avoided looking at each other.

Link cleared his throat. "I'll start. Robin, I didn't mean to seem pushy about the keys. I just don't want to ever have to lose anymore friends to drinking and driving." Robin met his eyes.

"I understand. And I'm sorry about making anybody worry." Her eyes flitted to the window. No one said anything and then Jason grumbled.

"Robin?" After a moment she looked at him. "I know that I yelled at you and I'm sorry. I shouldn't have done that. " She nodded. Patty looked from one to the other of them and then rolled her eyes.

"Patty, stay out of it," Link warned.

"Well, they're being stupid. Jason is still mad." Robin peeked at him and saw by the tilt of his chin that, indeed, her words were correct. He was mad at her; specifically at her and not just at the fact that he hadn't known where she had gone. She gave him a confused look.

"Robin," he said in a tight voice that reminded her of when they had first gotten together. "Why did you let yourself get so drunk that you were puking on the ground and sitting in the street? I mean, if you know that you get drunk like that-"

"But, I didn't know!" She exclaimed. "I've taken a sip of my dad's beer before, but besides a glass of champagne on New Year's Eve or a sip of my mother's wine, I've never drank before!"

Patty raised her hand in confession. "I gave her a couple beers." But she hadn't known that Robin wouldn't know how to hold her liquor.

Robin stared at Jason. "It seemed like the beer made everything nicer. So I tried the Hennessey and that made it even nicer. So I had another." Jason frowned and Link's mouth dropped. "I mixed it with Coca Cola and it tasted pretty good. But then I started getting drunk really fast."

"Damn, Robin." Jason said.

"What?" She asked a little irritated. Patty smiled inwardly and looked at Link. Link shrugged slightly not sure why she wanted them to argue.

"I mean, I know you got this nervous condition but getting drunk and going off with some guys is not the answer!"

"Nervous condition? I don't have *some* nervous condition. I just get nervous easily, that doesn't mean I have a condition! I didn't know I was going to get drunk and I didn't *go off* with those guys! I was just trying to help them get into the party-"

"But you didn't even know them."

"But," Robin sighed and felt her throat tighten and her eyes sting. "When I was drinking, it felt like I did know them. It felt as if I was doing something good for friends." She was breathing in deeply. "And then that guy at the door said he was going to call the cops so we left. I tried to call you Jason-!"

"But if I'm on the freaking stage, how can I answer my phone?!"

"I don't know!" She sat there for a moment. "I didn't go with them. We just walked away from the house together. And then they wanted to take me home and I said no. I didn't go." She looked at him. "Do you see what happened?"

"All I know is that I don't want you to drink anymore."

"Well, I don't want to drink anymore." She responded angrily.

"Fine."

"Fine."

Patty didn't seem happy with the way things had ended. "Robin, what does he mean that you have a 'nervous condition'?"

"Patty, stay out of this," Link mumbled.

Robin took a deep breath and hoped that she would stop feeling like she was about to cry. "I guess it's just hard for me when I'm around people I don't know."

"Were you nervous Friday?" Patty asked with concern. Robin nodded. "Is that why you were vomiting blood?"

Robin's head swung in her direction and she gave her an accusing look. "You promised!"

The muscles in Jason's face seemed to slacken. "Robin? Baby, you're vomiting blood?"

"I'm okay now." She tried to stand up but the van was too low. She reached for the door handle but it wouldn't open. Then she remembered Patty wasn't going to unlock it until they cleared the air. "Will you let me out, please?"

"You're okay now? No more stomach pain?" Patty asked.

"No more stomach pain." Robin said firmly.

Patty reached out calmly and poked her in the stomach. Robin yelped and doubled over in pain.

"Oh my God," Jason said. He pulled her down to his lap. "Robin, baby, you have to go to the hospital!"

She tried to get up but Jason wouldn't let her go and instead gripped her more tightly. "No! I'm okay. It goes away on its own! It only happens when I'm nervous."

"How often do you have this pain?" he asked.

"I don't know." She was panting and couldn't catch her breath. Her stomach was churning and she gripped her middle. "I just need some air. Can you open the door, please Patty?" Jason nodded his consent and Patty released the locks, reached over and then slid the door open.

When the door was open, Robin instantly relaxed and the sweat stopped forming on her brow. She began to regulate her breathing. Jason was rocking her in his arms and kissing her face. "Sweetheart, I'm so sorry. I'm not mad at you. I'm just mad! I'm mad because I can't fucking-" He groaned and she felt hot tears splash her arm. She looked up to see tears dripping down his cheeks. "I just want to be like everybody else.

"

PEPPER PACE BOOKS

STRANDED!
Juicy
Love Intertwined Vol. 1
Love Intertwined Vol. 2
Urban Vampire; The Turning
Urban Vampire; Creature of the Night
Urban Vampire; The Return of Alexis
Wheels of Steel Book 1
Wheels of Steel Book 2
Wheels of Steel Book 3
Angel Over My Shoulder
CRASH
Miscegenist Sabishii
They Say Love Is Blind
Beast
A Seal Upon Your Heart
Everything is Everything Book 1
Everything is Everything Book 2
Adaptation
About Coco's Room

SHORT STORIES
~~***~~

Someone to Love
The Way Home
MILF

Wheels of Steel book 1

Blair and the Emoboy
Emoboy the Submissive Dom
My Special Friend
Baby Girl and the Mean Boss
A Wrong Turn Towards Love
The Delicate Sadness
1-900-BrownSugar

COLLABORATIONS
~~***~~

Seduction: An Interracial Romance Anthology
Vol. 1
Scandalous Heroes Box se

ABOUT THE AUTHOR

Pepper Pace creates a unique brand of Interracial/multicultural erotic romance. While her stories span the gamut from humorous to heartfelt, the common theme is crossing racial boundaries.

The author is comfortable in dealing with situations that are, at times, considered taboo. Readers find themselves questioning their own sense of right and wrong, attraction and desire. The author believes that an erotic romance should first begin with romance and only then does she offers a look behind the closed doors to the passion.

Pepper Pace lives in Cincinnati, Ohio where many of her stories take place. She writes in the genres of science fiction, youth, horror, urban lit and poetry. She is a member of several online role-playing groups and hosts several blogs. In addition to writing, the author is also an artist, an introverted recluse, a self proclaimed empath and a foodie. Pepper Pace can be contacted at her blog, Writing Feedback:

http://pepperpacefeedback.blogspot.com/

PepperPace.tumblr.com

pepperpace.author@yahoo.com

Wheels of Steel book 1

AWARDS

Pepper Pace is a best selling author on Amazon and AllRomance e-books as well as Literotica.com. She is the winner of the 11th Annual Literotica Awards for 2009 for Best Reluctance story, as well as best Novels/Novella. She is also recipient of Literotica's August 2009 People's Choice Award, and was awarded second place in the January 2010 People's Choice Award. In the 12th Annual Literotica Awards for 2010, Pepper Pace won number one writer in the category of Novels/Novella as well as best interracial story. Pepper has also made notable accomplishments at Amazon. In 2013 she twice made the list of top 100 Erotic Authors and has reached the top 10 best sellers in multiple genres as well as placing in the semi-finals in the 2013 Amazon Breakthrough Author's contest.

Wheels of Steel book 1

www.ingramcontent.com/pod-product-compliance
Lightning Source LLC
Chambersburg PA
CBHW060145260626
47160CB00001B/130